THE GUEST

LORRAINE MACE

ACCENT

First published in 2023 by Headline Accent
An imprint of HEADLINE PUBLISHING GROUP

2

Cataloguing in Publication Data is available from the British Library

ISBN 978 1 4722 8391 7

Typeset in 11.25/15.25 pt Bembo Std by Jouve (UK), Milton Keynes

Printed and bound in Great Britain by Clays Ltd, Elcograf S.p.A.

Headline's policy is to use papers that are natural, renewable and recyclable
products and made from wood grown in well-managed forests and other
controlled sources. The logging and manufacturing processes are expected
to conform to the environmental regulations of the country of origin.

HEADLINE PUBLISHING GROUP
An Hachette UK Company
Carmelite House
50 Victoria Embankment
London EC4Y 0DZ

www.headline.co.uk
www.hachette.co.uk

Dedicated to Antonio Denham 1932–2015
Always such a proud and supportive father

Prologue

July 2022

The weight of Sarah's body had her pinned to the floor. Lynda tried to push her off but it was impossible while at the same time keeping a hand on Sarah's neck to staunch the blood. An odd thought suddenly manifested in her head: she'd never realised how heavy a dead body could be. But Sarah wasn't dead? No, she wasn't dead. What more could she do? If only she could reach her phone to call for an ambulance, but it was on the desk on the far side of the room.

Think! Think! Using her elbows as levers, she slithered and slid, inch by inch, across the floor, dragging Sarah with her. Each second seemed to take an hour, but she finally reached the desk. She tried to reach up for the phone, but it was impossible unless she pushed Sarah off her. How long would it take for Sarah to die if she took her hand off the wound?

The strap of her bag was hanging over the edge of the desk. Keeping her hand pressed on the slash in Sarah's neck, Lynda reached out with her other hand and pulled the strap. Her bag came tumbling down, spilling the contents across the blood-covered floor. Grabbing the scarf she'd bought on the way to the charity to give to Georgina as a birthday gift next week, she thrust it against the wound in Sarah's throat.

She hated Sarah, but she hadn't really wanted it to come to this. Or did she? Yesterday she would have been glad to know Sarah had died in agony. Lynda had handled it all wrong. She hadn't meant for things to go this far. Her gaze fell on the knife lying in a pool of blood. Her fingerprints were on the handle. All she'd planned to do was to confront Sarah and get at the truth. Make her admit what she'd done.

'Don't die,' she whispered. 'Please, please don't die. I'm so sorry. I'm sorry for everything. I didn't really want you dead.'

Was Sarah still breathing? The flow of blood felt more sluggish now. Did that mean she was close to death?

'Help me!' she yelled again. 'Somebody, help me!'

She could hear sirens. Were they coming this way? Yes, they were getting closer and closer. Someone must have called the emergency services. Thank God!

'Hold on, Sarah. Hold on.'

The siren's howling crept closer until it seemed to stop right outside. Why wasn't anyone coming in?

'Help! Help! She's dying!' she screamed.

The charity door burst open and suddenly the room seemed to be full of uniformed bodies. Sarah was gently lifted off and Lynda was able to move again. She tried to get to her feet, slipped in the blood and fell down again. An officer reached out and pulled her up. She turned from him to see what was happening to Sarah, but there were too many people in the way. She moved forward, taking small steps on the slippery floor.

'Can you save her? I never meant for this to happen. Please, can you save her?'

She felt a hand on her arm and was pulled round to see a police officer facing her. It was the same one who'd helped her to her feet. He looked too young to be a policeman.

'You need to come away, miss, and let the paramedics do their job.'

Lynda nodded and allowed him to lead her towards the main door of the charity office. The floor seemed to be covered in blood. How had it spread so far? Can someone lose so much blood and still live? She turned back to see a paramedic leaning over Sarah.

'Is she going to be OK?' she asked. 'I tried to save her. Honestly, I did. I didn't mean for this to happen.'

The paramedic glanced up, but avoided her gaze. Instead, he looked at the policeman still holding on to her arm and shook his head.

'I'm sorry,' he said. 'She's gone. There's nothing more we can do.'

Chapter One

December 2021

Lynda looked at the Christmas tree, intending to count to ten, but she only got as far as five before exploding.

'Jason! You've moved the baubles around.'

He came out from the kitchen, his face wearing that nervous look she had come to hate. Even though she knew she was being unreasonable, she couldn't stop herself from screeching at him.

'You've moved stuff on the tree.'

'Honey, I swear I haven't touched it. The tree is exactly as you left it last night.'

'No, it isn't. Don't try and make me look stupid,' she said. 'That bauble's lower than it was. It's hanging much too close to the lights and that's not where I placed it and you know it.'

'No, I don't know it. The weight of the ornaments has probably pulled down the branch a bit and it just looks different. That's all. Come through to the kitchen. I'm making pancakes.'

Lynda wanted nothing more than to go with him, but something held her back. 'You go ahead and enjoy your breakfast. I need to fix the tree.'

As she said the words, she could hear the accusation in her voice. *I need to fix the tree* you *messed up!*

'The tree doesn't need fixing,' he said. 'It looks perfect just as it is. Come on, Lynda, lighten up. It's just a bloody tree.'

'Is that all it is for you? Just a tree? It's our first Christmas living together and I'm trying to make it perfect, but all you can say is that it's just a tree.'

He walked towards her with his arms held out. 'Lynda, we don't need the perfect Christmas, the perfect tree, or the perfect anything for that matter. We have each other. Isn't that enough?'

She nodded and walked forward for a hug. 'You're right. I know I get a bit OCD, but I just want to make our first Christmas together really special.'

She felt his arms tighten as he kissed the top of her head. 'I know, but you have to stop trying so hard, Lynda.' He sighed. 'I sometimes feel as though everything I do is irritating you, or making you angry. I don't know how much longer . . .'

'How much longer what?' she said, pulling away and looking up at him.

'Let's sit down,' he said. 'We need to talk.'

She followed him to the sofa and sat next to him. He reached out and took hold of her hand. The hurt look on his face broke her heart. She knew she'd put it there with her constant need to have everything just so, but he used to be able to understand that she couldn't help herself. When they lived apart, he said he found her OCD tendencies quirky and loved her even more when she went through one of her rituals, like having to put her mug in exactly the right spot on the work surface when making a cup of tea. The order was critical as well – sweetener, tea bag, milk and only then the hot water, which had to be poured the second it came up to the boil. Now that they were living together, though, he didn't seem to feel like that any more when she insisted things had to happen in a certain way. She knew she was too quick to find fault with the way he did things.

'This isn't easy to come out with,' he said, 'but I'm wondering if we should have a bit of time apart after Christmas.'

'You don't want to be with me any more?' she asked, a lump in her throat making the words come out in a voice that didn't sound like her own.

'I want to be with you, but I think you need to get help, and it might be better for both of us if we lived apart while that happens.'

'What sort of help? And why would we need to live apart?'

'You want the truth? It's because I can't go on like this,' he whispered. 'I'm struggling to deal with your constant rituals, your non-stop straightening of things that aren't even remotely crooked, and the accusations that I've moved things when I haven't. The ornaments on the Christmas tree are exactly where you left them, but I could see by the way you looked at me that you're convinced I moved them just to mess with your mind. I love you, Lynda, but I can't go on like this.'

'I don't always accuse you. It's not fair to say that. Besides, sometimes you do put stuff where it doesn't belong. You know I need everything to be in its place. I don't like change.'

'I understand that,' Jason said, 'but I live here too and even if I have shifted something slightly it's not a crime. You make it sound as if I were deliberately trying to make your life a misery. You need to get professional help. I just think maybe giving you a bit of space will make it easier for you.'

'Have you found someone else?' she asked, trying to work out when he would have the time to cheat on her. Apart from going to work, they spent all their time together.

'No, of course I haven't found anyone else. You're the only one for me, but from the day I moved in here, you seem to be even more fixated on your rituals. I thought we could live together and I could help you, but I think I'm making you worse. I know it was hard for you after . . .'

'After what?' she demanded, but knew what he was going to say before a word had left his lips.

'It's been nearly a year since . . .'

'Don't you say it! Don't you dare bring my family into this!'

'Lynda, I know you're hurting and I would do anything to take away the pain if I could, but ever since the car crash, you've changed. I feel like I'm not allowed to breathe in case I blow something out of alignment. You never used to be this . . .'

'This what? Why don't you ever finish a sentence?'

'Because you twist whatever I say to make it sound like I'm having a go at you!'

She took a deep breath. 'OK, I promise not to flare up. I never used to be so . . . what? Come on, you can say it.'

Jason reached for her hand. 'Neurotic. You never used to be so neurotic.'

She snatched her hand away. 'I am not neurotic! How dare you say that?'

'The way you've just reacted proves my point. Lynda, I am so tired of the way we are. Please, please won't you get some help? Let's get Christmas out of the way and then I'll help you find the right therapist. If he or she thinks staying together is in your best interest then that's what we'll do, but I'm finding it hard not to react when you accuse me of stuff I haven't done.'

'Fuck you!' she said, standing up and moving to the far side of the room. 'If I'm so hard to live with, why don't you leave now? Why wait until after Christmas? Who the hell are you to say whether or not I need therapy?'

Jason heaved himself to his feet. Lynda could see the concern on his face, but instead of softening the way she felt, it added fuel to her burning sense of injustice. Why couldn't he understand what she was going through?

'Don't be like this,' he said, reaching for her. 'I love you.'

'Really? You've got a funny way of showing it. Tell you what, Jason, pack your bags and get out now. I'll be so much happier on my own than with you moaning about every little thing I do.'

Jason shook his head. 'I'm not going to leave you alone over Christmas.'

'I'm not a charity case,' she said. 'I can manage perfectly well on my own. I don't need you here. Actually, I don't want you here. Go on, get your belongings and get out. Enjoy your big family Christmas without me there to ruin everything. I didn't want to spend the day with your stupid boring family anyway.'

It was a cheap shot and she knew it. 'I'm sorry,' she said. 'I didn't mean that.'

'Yes, you did,' he said, his face like stone. 'You've made it very clear that you don't like my family. I don't know why, because they've never been anything but nice to you. Don't worry, you won't have to spend a second with them. I'm going. I'll be back at the weekend for my stuff. I can't live with you like this. If you just got some help, I'd be here for you, but you won't even admit you need it. I can't keep fighting like this.'

Ashamed of what she'd said about his family, she hung her head, but as she did so her gaze fell on the running shoes he'd left lying around, just as he always did. She had a special rack next to the front door to keep their trainers nice and tidy, but would Jason use it? Oh no, he'd come into the lounge, take his running shoes off and leave them next to the chair until he needed them again. She picked one up.

'This is one of the reasons we fight, Jason. You leave your stuff lying around all over the place. Running shoes belong in the hallway, not in the middle of the lounge.'

He ducked as the shoe sailed across the room, just missing his head. The shoe landed against the wall, bounced off and slid onto the coffee table, knocking off the mug Jason had left there from the night before. She picked up the other shoe, ready to launch it, but he held up his hand. She had never seen him look so sad.

'No, Lynda, that's not why we fight, but until you realise the real reason we do, you are never going to get better. I'll find somewhere to stay for a few days. I'll be back for my stuff. You don't need to put up with me any longer.'

He left the lounge and she heard him in the bedroom, opening and closing doors and cupboards. More than anything, she wanted to run in there and beg him to stay, but her pride kept her fixed to the spot. If he couldn't cope with her as she was, why should she change just to suit what he wanted? Even as the thought entered her head, she knew it wasn't the truth. He didn't want her to change. He wanted her to get the help she needed, but that would mean owning up to something she'd spent nearly two decades trying to forget.

The sound of the slamming door told her he really had gone. She slid to the floor and sobbed. She'd finally driven away the person she loved most in the world. Would Jason ever forgive her? How could he when he didn't even know how evil she'd been back then? As miserable as she felt, she knew it was far less than she deserved.

Chapter Two

March 2022

Lynda woke up feeling, yet again, as if she'd been awake most of the night, but she knew that probably wasn't the case. She couldn't remember her dreams, but they couldn't have been good judging by the way she'd tied herself up in the duvet.

Three months had passed since Jason had left, but the bed still seemed too big for just one person, despite the fact she'd slept in it alone quite happily before he'd moved in.

But Jason was not likely to be coming back, even though they saw each other quite often for drinks. He, at least, seemed to have been able to make the shift from lover to friend. She shook herself. Thoughts of her time with Jason would get her nowhere.

She got up and rummaged in the cupboard for her running gear, knocking her lightweight hoodie on the floor. She reached down to pick it up, remembering how thrilled she'd been when Jason had given it to her to celebrate completing her first marathon. He'd had it specially made for her by one of his designer friends. It was unique and a sign of how much he loved her back then. She shook her head. A five-kilometre jog would sort her out. Running always gave her the chance to put her thoughts in order. As she pulled on her shoes and tied the laces, she felt her spirits rise. Carefully closing her front door, so as not to disturb her neighbours, Lynda ran down to the ground floor and headed out to begin the best part of her day.

By the time Lynda had reached Bath Row her mind was finally calm again. Turning into St Peter's Lane, she thought about the last few years and the number of races she'd run to raise money for various charities. Keeping her breath as steady as she could, she ran carefully over the cobbles of King's Mill Lane and then into Austin Street.

Had she done enough to make up for the hurt she'd caused in the past? No, definitely not.

As she reached Rutland Terrace she came to a decision. She would look for a therapist. She had to deal with her past or she'd never find peace. She finished the rest of the run feeling better than when she'd set out.

She upped her pace to finish with a sprint and arrived at the front door of the Victorian terrace. Pressing the button on her watch to end the recording, she leaned over, gasping for breath. This was the only way to start the day.

As she straightened up, she heard a soft mewling coming from the bushes on the other side of the road. It sounded like an animal in distress. She crossed over, listening for the exact location of the sounds. As she approached, a black cat started to crawl away.

'Oh, you poor thing,' she said, taking in how skinny and bedraggled it was.

The cat stopped and looked back at her, mewling piteously.

'Are you hungry? You look hungry.'

Lynda could see the animal was malnourished and she made a decision. Reaching forward, she scooped the cat into her arms.

'Come on, you. I'll give you some milk and then take you to the vet. Let's see if someone has reported you missing.'

She carried the creature upstairs and put her down in the kitchen. As she poured milk into a saucer the cat rubbed itself against her ankle.

'I'm going to have to shut you in here while I shower,' she said, putting the saucer down. 'I'll be right back.'

The cat began to lap at the milk as Lynda edged her way to the door. She closed it firmly behind her and ran to the bathroom. She had no cat litter and not even a newspaper to put down, so she needed to hurry before she ended up with a kitchen in need of deep cleaning.

Lynda put the cat into the wicker basket that usually housed her spare toiletries. It was the only thing she had with a lid that would also allow air to flow through it. It was a tight squeeze, but surprisingly the cat didn't put up a fight. Carrying it down to her car she realised just how undernourished the cat must be as the basket felt very light in her arms.

She opened the passenger door and put the basket on the floor by the passenger seat. Driving carefully so as not to upset the basket too much, she followed her satnav directions to the nearest vet. The receptionist was helpful, but explained that as she hadn't made an appointment, she might have a long wait ahead of her. Lynda settled herself down on one of the seats, cradling the basket.

The receptionist had said that no one had reported the cat as missing, which didn't really surprise Lynda, considering the state it was in. After ten minutes, during which she texted her boss to explain why she was going to be late for work, the door to the surgery opened and the vet beckoned her in.

'Good morning, I'm Dr Meadows. What do we have here?'

Lynda explained how and where she'd found the cat.

'She must have belonged to someone at one time as she's been spayed, but she doesn't have a chip,' Dr Meadows said as he checked the cat over. 'It's possible she lived with an elderly person who has passed away, or has gone into residential care and couldn't take the cat with them. Do you want to take her to the local cat charity?' he asked. 'They might be able to find a home for her if no one comes forward to claim her.'

Almost as if she understood, the cat moved across the metal table towards Lynda's hand and meowed softly. The cat was almost pleading to be with her, but no way could she have a cat in the flat. Or could she? Weren't cats supposed to be clean animals? Maybe she could give it try. She could always take the cat to an animal shelter if it didn't work out.

'No,' she said, wondering if she'd regret it later. 'I'm going to take her home with me. If her owner makes contact, can you give them my number?'

Dr Meadows nodded. 'We'll also put up a notice in the waiting area to say a black cat has been found and to enquire at reception. You should let the various animal charities know you have the cat, just in case the owner contacts one of them.'

'I will,' she said. 'Can you check her over and give her whatever shots she needs? I'm going to the pet shop to pick up various things. I'll need some advice on feeding her as well.'

The vet smiled. 'No problem at all. Ask my receptionist for the leaflet on caring for a cat. We'll keep her here until you have everything you need. What are you going to call her?'

'I don't know. I'll think about it while I'm shopping for her stuff.'

Lynda left the vet feeling more hopeful about the future. With the cat in the flat she wouldn't feel so lonely. It was a lucky meeting for both of them. Lucky – that's what she'd call her new friend. She found herself hoping that she'd be able to cope with any mess and that no one came forward to claim her.

Chapter Three

May 2022

'Good morning, Lynda. My name is Angelica Dorrant and I'll be interviewing you today. I hope my assistant explained the way this will pan out.'

Lynda smiled and nodded. 'She did, but I sort of guessed how it would go. I watch your programme from time to time.'

As Angelica sat down, Lynda forced herself to relax. Watching others being interviewed hadn't prepared her for the anxiety she was feeling. Waves of nausea washed over her. Why, oh why, had she agreed to be the face of the marathon? Just because she'd run a few, that didn't make her newsworthy, but Greg had insisted she was the best one to get lots of people to sign up for the race. 'Get out there and smile,' he'd said. 'Tell everyone about the work we do and how much we need others to get involved. Go on, Lynda, you can do it!'

She sure didn't feel as if she could, but there was no way out, so she'd just have to get on with it.

Angelica smiled. 'We have a few minutes before we go on air. Do you have any questions?'

Lynda had plenty of questions running through her brain,

but couldn't find the words to verbalise any of them. She shook her head. Her mouth was so dry it would be a miracle if she managed to answer a single question. She watched the countdown clock above Angelica's head, mesmerised as the seconds raced towards zero.

'Good evening and welcome to Lincolnshire News. My name is Angelica Dorrant and tonight I am delighted to introduce Lynda Blackthorn. Lynda has joined us as the spokesperson for one of our important local charities: Stamp it Out. Lynda, could you tell our viewers a little about the charity and the work you and the other volunteers do?'

Lynda could feel the sweat running down her back and prayed it wouldn't be visible. She swallowed hard.

'St . . . St . . . Stamp it Out,' she stammered before taking a deep breath. 'Sorry, I'm a little bit nervous,' she said and smiled. 'This is my first time being interviewed on television. Stamp it Out is a small local charity operating on several levels. We are dedicated to stamping out bullying through our helplines and self-awareness courses. These courses are targeted at changing the behaviour of bullies and counselling their victims. We also visit schools, when invited, to talk to pupils and teachers.'

'How is this paid for? Is the charity dependent on public donations for funding, or are you receiving government support, either local or national?' Angelica said.

'We don't receive any government funding and rely entirely on donations,' Lynda answered. 'We also run fundraising events such as bring-and-buy days, book sales and tea parties, but this year we are aiming to organise a marathon and two shorter races to bring in some much-needed income.'

'That sounds ambitious.'

Lynda nodded. 'It is, which is why I'm here tonight. We are hoping to encourage not only race entrants, but volunteers to help out with all the behind-the-scenes activities this will entail. We will have three categories: a 5km fun run, a half-marathon and a full marathon.'

'Good heavens, all on the same day?'

Lynda shook her head. 'No, over a three-day spread. The fun run on a Friday, the half-marathon on the Saturday and the full marathon on the Sunday. As you can imagine, this is going to take quite a bit of organising.'

'So what are you looking for in the way of help?' Angelica asked.

'First and foremost, we need someone to set up a website so that runners can enter their details online and pay the entrance fees for the various categories, and maybe purchase some merchandise if they feel so inclined.' Lynda paused. 'We don't have anyone in the charity at the moment who can do this.' She looked directly into the camera, finally relaxing now that she was discussing the race needs. 'Come on, you techie people. Please help us out with your skills.'

Angelica nodded. 'I'm sure our viewers will respond to that plea. What other assistance will you need?'

'Race stewards – those who will make sure the runners keep to the correct routes. Oh, and people to man the water tables. Volunteers to clean up the streets after each event. Lots of helpers really, no special skills required. Oh, I nearly forgot. If there is an accountant out there prepared to look after the financial side of things, we would be very grateful.'

'We will, of course, put up details at the end of this segment showing how and where those wishing to give their time and skills can contact the charity, but as we have a few minutes left, let's talk about you and how you came to get involved with the charity. What made you passionate about helping those who have been bullied or are being bullied?'

Lynda felt her spine stiffen at the question. She hadn't bargained for this. The idea was simply to come on air, talk about the charity and the races and then get out of there. She swallowed. How to answer?

'I saw the impact bullying had on someone I was a school with and wanted to try to help others who might be going through something similar.'

'Have you been with the charity long?' Angelica asked.

'No, less than a year,' Lynda said, praying there wouldn't be time for more questions, but Angelica was clearly ready to ask another.

'Forgive me,' she said, 'but I think your schooldays must be further in the past than a year.'

Trying to maintain her smile, Lynda felt as if her face had stretched into a gargoyle's image.

'No, I left school many years ago.'

'So what made you decide to join the charity? What was the catalyst that made you decide to act?'

'There was a lot of media coverage of bullying, as well as cyber-bullying. It made me remember my school friend and what she'd had to endure. I felt compelled to try to do something about it.' She had to head off any more questions. 'As we have a few moments to spare, can I also point out that we are always looking for people to man our helplines, particularly over evenings and weekends? Full training is given in how to deal with the calls.'

Angelica smiled.

'As you know, we always end these interviews on a personal note by asking our guests to share a moment in their lives that was special. I'm sure our viewers have enjoyed listening to you being so passionate about the charity and the three races, but can you give us a glimpse of Lynda the person?'

Lynda had watched enough of Angelica's interviews to know the question would be coming, so she'd prepared for it.

'Yes, it was finding a bedraggled cat and giving her a home a couple of months ago. She is my constant companion and I love her dearly. She even comes out with me in the mornings when I go for my run. She stays with me for a couple of streets and then goes off to do her own thing. Usually by the time I get home she's waiting on the doorstep, but sometimes she disappears for a day or two and then reappears with a gift for me in the form of a dead bird or mouse. I don't love her as much on those days!'

Angelica laughed. 'I can imagine. I don't think I'd be too pleased with that kind of gift. Well, viewers, that is all we have time for tonight. If any of you feel able to offer their help in any way with regard to the races being planned, or if you feel you could be part of the telephone counselling team, all the details are now on the screen. This is a very worthwhile charity and I hope many of you will come forward. It just leaves me to thank my guest, Lynda Blackthorn of the charity Stamp it Out, and to say goodnight.'

The studio on-air light went out and Lynda was finally able to breathe a sigh of relief. It's just as well no one would ever know the real reason for her charity work. She needed to atone. Mark had committed suicide because of her.

Chapter Four

On Saturday Lynda went out for a run and Lucky followed her down the stairs and went off to do whatever it was she did. Usually the cat would be waiting for her when she got back, but this time there was no sign of her.

'Lucky! Lucky!' she called, searching the bushes where she'd first found her.

After about ten minutes, she realised she'd be late for her stint at the charity call centre if she didn't get a move on. She decided to go upstairs and shower before coming back down to search for Lucky. As she turned to go back inside, the front door opened and her young friend from the ground floor apartment looked out.

'I thought I could hear you calling Lucky,' Georgina said.

Lynda laughed. 'She seems to know when I'm pushed for time and makes a point of coming back later, usually just in time for her breakfast. The problem is I have to be at the charity call centre in under an hour, so I really need to get upstairs and shower.'

Georgina smiled. 'I'm not going anywhere this morning. I can look out for her if you like.'

'Would you? That'd be great. If she's not back by the time I'm ready to leave, would it be OK if I gave you my spare key so that you can let her in upstairs?'

'Sure. No problem at all.'

Lynda thanked her and raced upstairs.

Half an hour later she rang Georgina's bell.

'Here's the key,' she said when Georgina opened the door. 'I've put out food and drink for her in the kitchen next to her basket. There's a litter tray as well, but she rarely uses it. Could you just let her in and then lock the door?'

'Of course,' Georgina said. 'Call in when you get home to get your key back.'

'Thanks so much,' Lynda said, rushing to the front door of the apartments. 'Sorry I can't stop. I'm close to being late already.'

She ran to her car and drove into Stamford centre, relieved the local yobs weren't hanging around opposite the charity office. Dealing with them would have delayed her as they seemed to believe surrounding her and making sexist comments was as much fun for her as it was for them. She glanced at her watch and saw she only had a couple of minutes to spare as she opened the door.

Expecting to see only Greg, the charity manager, she was surprised to find him chatting to two women. He glanced up as she came in, looking relieved to see her.

'Ah, and here's Lynda, the very person we need,' he said. 'I've just been explaining what a great response we had after your stint on the local news. We've now got more volunteers

23

than we'd hoped, but these two ladies have the specialist skills you mentioned. Can you explain to them what you're after?'

'Wow, that's great,' Lynda said, 'but don't you need me to man the phones?'

'Don't worry about that,' Greg said. 'I can do that, but what I can't do is sort out what needs to be done for the race you're organising. Perhaps the three of you could go into our meeting room and chat.'

'Good idea,' Lynda said. 'Come this way, please.'

Once inside the room, Lynda introduced herself, asked them to sit down, and took stock of the two women. One looked very much younger than the other. The older woman, who appeared to be about Lynda's age, reminded Lynda of someone, but she couldn't quite put her finger on who it was.

'Could you give me your name and an indication of your area of expertise?' she said to the younger woman.

'Yes,' she said. 'I'm Cassandra Grace, but everyone calls me Cassie. My background is in IT and I saw you needed someone to set up a website for the race. I could do that for you. The website would cover everything that's needed, from gathering the entrants' details, to giving bib numbers and taking the entry fees. I could also set up the e-commerce part of things, if you want to sell merchandise.'

'Cassie, that would be amazing. I am not in the least techie-minded, so wouldn't know where to start.'

'Will you be running in the race?' Cassie asked.

'Yes, I hope to, as we now have enough volunteers to act as stewards and so on, but if necessary, I would drop out and help wherever we might need an extra body. What would you need from us to get the website started?'

Cassie smiled. 'I'll make a list of the info I'll need from you to start with, such as maximum number of entrants, age restrictions, medical requirements and any other categories you feel are essential. Eventually I'll need to test out the system with someone's details, but that can wait or I can use my own.'

'Not a problem,' Lynda said, grabbing a sheet of paper from the desk. 'You can use mine.'

She scribbled her name, address and phone number on the page and passed it to Cassie.

'You live in Marlborough Road?' Cassie said. 'It's such a small world. My aunt used to live there. Number nineteen? Isn't that one of those old Victorian terraced houses that were converted into flats? My aunt owned number six, but sold it to a developer years ago.'

Lynda nodded. 'Yes, I think all the old houses in the street are now apartments. It's a lovely part of town.'

She turned to the other woman who smiled at her.

'You don't recognise me, do you, Lynda?'

Lynda shook her head. 'I thought you looked familiar, but I can't place where I know you from.'

The woman grinned. 'My name's Amanda Fowler now, used to be Amanda Soames, and I am from your murky past. I hated you once, but got over it years ago. You stole my boyfriend when we were at university.'

Lynda felt as if a freight train had ploughed into her stomach. Oh God, yet another thing to add to the pile of past actions she had to atone for.

'Don't look so stricken,' the woman laughed. 'That was over a decade ago. I promise you, I forgave him, and you, long ago. I'm happily married to someone I would never have even looked at if you and John hadn't broken my heart. I was consoled by Lennie, his roommate, and never looked back.'

Lynda forced herself to smile. 'John! I remember I fell for him hook, line and sinker in my first term. He was older and gorgeous. Would it help if I told you I didn't know he had a girlfriend until I was completely under his spell? When one of your friends tracked me down to tell me how John had treated you, I didn't believe her. I asked John and he claimed you were stalking him and that he'd never been in a relationship with you. It was only after he did pretty much the same thing to me that I realised your friend had told the truth and John had lied.'

Lynda suddenly remembered Cassie. 'Oh my God, I'm so sorry. This is so embarrassing. Here we are talking about our youthful broken hearts instead of the charity's needs.'

Cassie laughed. 'Don't worry about it. We all have things in our past we'd rather didn't come to light in front of strangers.'

Lynda smiled and turned back to Amanda. 'Did you come because you recognised me on television?'

Amanda shook her head. 'I did recognise you as you've barely changed over the years, but that's not why I'm here. I'm a chartered accountant and you said in the interview you need someone to look after the financial side of the race. I can do that for the charity.'

'Well, this is great. It looks like we have our accounts and website sorted out; I will need Greg's final OK but I don't see that being an issue.'

Lynda glanced up expecting to see smiles on both faces, but Amanda looked more worried than pleased.

'Have I said something wrong?' she asked.

Amanda laughed. 'Not at all. Sorry, I was just wondering if I would need to come here on a regular basis, or if this is something I can work on from home.'

Lynda nodded. 'Good point. Again, this is something we would need to discuss with Greg. And you, Cassie, do you have any questions?'

She shook her head. 'No questions, but I would definitely prefer to work from home initially. I could bring my laptop here on Saturdays to get any additional information needed or to give you an update, but I would feel more comfortable working on it on my own time until I've got the basic site set up.'

There was a brief tap on the door and then it opened. Greg stuck his head round.

'Great,' said Lynda. 'Here's the man we need to finalise everything we've discussed.'

'In a moment,' he said. 'There's someone to see you. Not a volunteer. She says she saw your interview. Apparently she knew you long ago.'

Amanda grinned. 'Maybe it's another one whose boyfriend couldn't resist you,' she said.

Lynda shook her head. 'I didn't make a habit of it, you know.'

'I'm sorry. That was my feeble attempt at humour. I didn't mean anything by it.'

'Did she give her name, Greg?' Lynda asked, trying not to feel annoyed by Amanda's comment.

He shook his head. 'Nope, she said she wanted to surprise you. Seemed quite excited at the idea of catching up with you after all these years.'

'OK, ladies, I'll leave you in Greg's capable hands for now. I'll be back shortly,' she said and passed into the main office.

A woman was standing with her back to Lynda, facing the kitchen area.

'Hi,' Lynda said. 'Greg says we were friends long ago.'

As the woman turned to face her, Lynda felt the blood drain from her face.

This was another person she'd harmed in the past, but in a far worse way than stealing a boyfriend.

Chapter Five

'Sarah?' Lynda said, instinctively touching her cheek when she saw the woman's blemish-free face.

Sarah mirrored her action, touching the left side of her own face. 'It's still there, but I now know how to cover it with make-up. It would have made my life so much less painful if I'd known how to do it when we were in school.'

'How . . . how are you?' Lynda said, carefully closing the door behind her to ensure no one in the other room would be able to hear whatever Sarah had come to say.

'I'm good,' Sarah said, 'which is more than I can say about you right now. You look terrified.' She laughed. 'Not at all like you were the other night on local TV. I couldn't believe it was you talking about combatting bullying.'

'Sarah, about what happened . . .' She stopped, unable to put her thoughts into words.

'Don't worry, I haven't come to upset you. I just wanted to catch up,' Sarah said. 'Look, why don't we go and have a chat somewhere? I was hoping we could be friends again. We were close once.'

Hearing the door open behind her, Lynda knew she had to stop Sarah from saying anything more. 'I can't leave right now as I have to stay to man the phones for the next couple of hours,' she said.

'What about when you knock off? Let's meet for coffee. Come on, you owe me that at the very least.'

Lynda nodded. 'You're right. I do.'

Before she could think of where to suggest they meet, her phone rang. She put her hand up to signal she had to take the call and swiped the screen.

'Hi, Georgina. Is she back?'

'Yes, I've put her upstairs in your flat. She's fine. I just thought you'd like to know. Are we still on for a drink this evening?'

'Can I let you know later? I may not be able to make it,' she said, looking at Sarah. She ended the call. 'That was my neighbour. She was just letting me know my cat had come home. I was worried about her.'

Realising she was babbling, Lynda smiled. 'Not that you'd be interested in Lucky, but I'm glad she's home.' She heard a noise behind her and looked back. Not only Greg, but Cassie and Amanda were in the room, clearly waiting to speak to her.

'Look,' she said to Sarah, 'let's meet in Peterborough. Do you know the Queensgate Centre?' Sarah nodded. 'There's a great café in there called Ringo's,' Lynda said. 'It's one of my favourite places. Let's meet there at five, shall we? We can catch up then.'

Sarah smiled. 'I'd like that. See you later.'

She waved and left. Lynda turned, trying to recall exactly what had been said and wondering how much the others had heard. The last thing she needed was any of them wondering about her schooldays.

'Can we finalise the way our two volunteers will slot into the way we do things here?' Greg said, sounding irritated. 'We're lucky there haven't been any calls, but we're sure to get some coming in this afternoon, so let's get on.'

After a brief discussion, it was agreed that Cassie and Amanda would both come in on Saturday mornings to liaise with Lynda, Greg and each other. As the two women left, Lynda felt Greg's eyes on her. She turned to smile at him.

'I think both of them will do a good job for us, don't you?' she said.

Greg nodded. 'What was that all about with your visitor? Is everything OK? I don't like to see you looking stressed.'

Lynda smiled. 'I'm not stressed at all,' she said. 'I was just surprised to see Sarah, that's all. Fourteen years is a long time.'

Greg shrugged. 'Fair enough, you don't have to tell me if you don't want to, but just know I'm here if you need a sympathetic ear. I was badly bullied myself at school, as you know, and even now I wouldn't want to come face to face with any of the boys from those days.'

'Really, Greg, I'm fine,' she said, remembering that the last time Lynda had seen her, Sarah'd been holding a bloodsplattered rock. She'd had to use it to defend herself because Lynda had let her down.

Lynda closed her car door and pressed the button for the central locking to kick in. As she walked across the Queensgate car park, she wondered why she had decided to do this and not just told Sarah they had nothing to discuss. But that wasn't true. They had lots to talk about and none of it reflected well on her. All the shame she'd spent the past fourteen years trying to atone for was back with a vengeance. None of the work she did for the anti-bullying charity, none of the money she'd raised for other charities running marathons and half-marathons could wipe out what she'd allowed to happen, standing by as Sarah was mercilessly mocked.

As she walked in to the familiar sound of a Beatles classic playing softly in the background, she scanned the booths for Sarah. Almost immediately, Sarah jumped up and held out her arms as if she'd intended to reach out for a hug, but dropped them to her side when Lynda took a step back.

'Sorry, I'm not a very huggy person,' Lynda said.

Sarah shrugged. 'You never were. I forgot about that. I'm forever grabbing people and squeezing, completely overlooking the fact that not everyone is as touchy-feely as me. Maria is always on at me about it. She says I invade everyone's personal space.'

Lynda pointed to the booth. 'Shall we sit and order some coffee?'

'Sure. I've only just got here, so haven't had chance to look at the choices yet.'

'I always go for a cappuccino and a slice of carrot cake,' Lynda said.

'Are they good?'

Lynda felt as if whatever she said was going to be judged by how she had behaved fourteen years earlier.

'I love them,' she said. 'Look, Sarah, about what happened before your parents took you out of the school—'

Before she could say more, a waitress dressed in the sixties uniform of black and white geometric mini dress arrived to take their order.

'I'll have the same as her,' Sarah said after Lynda had told the waitress she'd have her usual.

'So,' Sarah said, 'shall we go back in time, or talk about what's been going on in your life? I was stunned to see you on television, as I told you.'

Before she could answer, Sarah laughed. 'Just look at us back together again. Just like we were before Mark came along. I can't believe it's been fourteen years since we last got together.'

'I know. But I suppose it was inevitable we'd lose touch after you moved to a different school.'

'After I was expelled, you mean?'

Lynda didn't know how to respond. She felt sick just thinking about what Sarah had done after she'd finally snapped.

Sarah shook her head. 'Still the same old Lynda, always trying to find the right words so that you don't upset anyone.' She reached across the table and touched Lynda's hand. 'What happened to you after I left?'

'It was OK,' Lynda said. 'I got some A levels and went to Uni.'

Sarah laughed. 'You did? Really? What did you study? You weren't exactly the studying type back then. You were too busy falling in love and planning to run off with Mark the traveller.'

Lynda thought about all that had happened in the year she'd last seen Sarah. So much to feel guilty about, and the bullying Sarah had endured wasn't even the worst of it. Did Sarah know about Mark's suicide? Lynda was saved from having to think about what she'd done to him by the arrival of the waitress.

'Here you are, ladies,' she said, putting the tray down on

33

the table and moving the coffees and cakes in front of them. 'Give me a shout if you want anything else.'

When the waitress moved away, Lynda watched Sarah's face as she lifted the cup and took a sip.

'Mmm, good coffee.' Sarah grinned. 'Do you ever think about how you went overboard for the "love of your life" back then?'

Lynda could hear the double quotes in Sarah's voice but she shrugged and picked up her cup. 'Sometimes,' she said. What happened to Mark had always hovered on the edge of her consciousness, but she had no intention of sharing that with Sarah or anyone else. The guilt cut too deep.

'Look, Sarah, I'm glad we've met up again,' Lynda said. 'I've long wanted to apologise for not being there for you when you needed me.'

Sarah touched the side of her face where a faint trace of her birthmark could be seen if you knew where to look. 'Because of this, you mean?'

Lynda nodded. 'I was too scared to stand up to the bullies.'

Sarah shrugged. 'No, you weren't. You protected me just fine until Mark came into your life. Then I was expelled and the next few years weren't good, but I got through them.'

'I've always felt guilty about what Hazel and her gang put you through. When I left school, I tried to turn my life around. You know, be a better person.'

Sarah laughed. 'You sound as if you've become some sort of evangelical.'

Lynda shrugged. 'Not that, no, but I do try to do my bit to support anti-bullying charities.'

'Apart from running marathons, what do you do? Hang

around shopping malls with a collection box?' Sarah asked, grinning.

Lynda shook her head. 'No, but I volunteer for a helpline on Saturdays. I don't think I'll ever forgive myself for what happened to you or . . .' She stopped herself from saying out loud what Sarah had needed to do to stop the bullying.

Sarah sat forward, staring at Lynda so intently she instinctively sat back.

'I did some online research after I saw you on that news station asking for volunteers to help with your latest project. I found a report from a couple of years ago where you were smiling at the camera while some big shot handed you an award for raising money to combat bullying. Quite the local heroine at the time, weren't you?'

Lynda felt the familiar flush of shame whenever that award was mentioned. She hadn't deserved it, but there hadn't been any way to refuse it without making a fuss. She'd thought turning up and saying thank you would have been the end of it, but it must have been a slow news cycle because all the local papers had covered it and run articles about her. She shuddered. After that she'd tried to avoid getting in the news, but had needed to handle the publicity for the marathon after Greg had refused to do it. He'd made it quite clear that no way was he going in front of a camera.

'I got more coverage than I deserved,' Lynda said.

'It was an interesting article,' Sarah said. 'You spoke about our schooldays. They weren't quite as I remembered them, but then I suppose we all gloss over the painful parts of our lives.'

'It was because of that award ceremony that I got involved

with the local charity.' There was no need to tell Sarah it had really been her therapist's idea.

'What sort of advice do you give on your helpline? Punch the bullies in the face?'

Lynda laughed. 'No, quite the opposite. We advise them to try to find a friend they can trust to talk to about their feelings.'

Sarah smiled. 'That's one of the reasons I came to see you. I remembered how close we were before you went crazy over that boy. You see, I could do with a friend right now.'

Guilt at everything Sarah had endured burned through Lynda's brain. She heard herself promising to be the friend Sarah needed and wondered if this was the redemption she'd been searching for.

'This is on me,' Lynda said.

'Thanks. Tell you what, if we're going to be friends again, why don't we exchange phone numbers so we can keep in touch?' Sarah pulled out her phone and looked up at Lynda. 'What's your number? Let me call you now. That way you'll have mine as well.'

Lynda gave her number. When her own phone buzzed she took it out of her bag and accepted the call.

'There,' Sarah said. 'Now we can be proper mates again.'

'I'd like that,' Lynda said, thankful to be given a chance to make up for not being a good enough friend in the past.

Lynda had no sooner put her phone away than Sarah's rang. Lynda was surprised to see a wary look on Sarah's face. She grimaced before picking the phone up.

'Hi, Maria, I'm going to be a bit late home today.'

Lynda could hear whoever Maria was raising her voice, but

couldn't make out the words. Even so, it was clear she was mad at Sarah for something.

'I signed on at the job agency this morning and the girl said she'd give me a call if anything came up, but that there wasn't anything at the moment,' Sarah said.

Lynda couldn't quite hear, but whatever had been said obviously upset Sarah because her whole demeanour seemed to change. She looked defeated.

'What are you going on about?' She looked across at Lynda and shrugged. 'I told you I was going to call in on that woman I saw being interviewed on local TV. The job agency is in Stamford, just along the road from the place where she volunteers.'

Maria's voice must have gone up a notch because this time Lynda heard her loud and clear.

'Who is she? Is she yet another one of your affairs I'm supposed to turn a blind eye to?'

Sarah mouthed an apology and then spoke into her phone.

'Firstly, Lynda is someone I was at school with. Secondly, I haven't seen her for fourteen years, and thirdly, it was a spur of the moment decision to meet for coffee, not a date.'

Maria's voice hissed. 'So you say.'

'Maria, I love you. I'm on my way home now.'

Sarah ended the call and dropped the phone in her bag.

'I'm really sorry about that. Maria can be a bit possessive. I'd better be going, but I hope we're going to keep in touch.'

'I don't want to cause an issue with your girlfriend,' Lynda said.

'Don't worry, you won't. Maria gets upset easily, but I know just how to calm her down.'

Chapter Six

On Sunday morning Lynda set out for her run with her
mind reeling. Seeing Sarah had brought to the fore so
many things she'd spent years trying to forget. She'd have to
try to sort out all the jumbled thoughts in her head during her
Friday therapy session.

She was meeting Sarah again next Saturday, so it was essential to talk her feelings through before then. Maybe Penelope
could help put everything into perspective.

She nodded and upped her pace. There was nothing like a
good run to make her feel better. By the time she reached her
street she was drenched in sweat and breathing heavily, but felt
a hundred times better than when she'd set out.

Lynda straightened up and went up the stone steps to the front
door. She opened it as quietly as she could as it was still so
early, but she needn't have worried because Georgina was
standing in her doorway.

'I was hoping to catch you when you came back,' she said,

smiling at Lynda's efforts to regulate her breathing. 'You look shattered. I can't understand why you put yourself through that every morning.'

'It makes me feel alive,' Lynda said.

Georgina laughed. 'If I tried it, I think I'd be feeling more like death.'

'You might change your mind once you get to my age.'

'You make it sound like you're as old as my granny,' Georgina said.

'I feel like that some days. I'd best be heading upstairs to shower,' Lynda said. 'Did you want me for something?'

Georgina laughed. 'Yes, I'd totally forgotten why I was waiting for you. You had a delivery yesterday while you were out. I was going to bring it up last night, but Steven rang and we got into yet another row because I wouldn't tell him where I'm living. By the time we'd finished arguing I'd completely forgotten all about going up to see you. Hang on a moment and I'll get it,' she said, disappearing back inside her flat.

A minute later she reappeared with a miniature shrub in her hands. As she handed it to Lynda, a lovely fragrance wafted up.

'Wow! Are you sure this was meant for me?'

'I presume so. The envelope has your name on it.'

'Did the delivery person say anything? I've no idea who would send me a plant.'

'It was on the doorstep when I came back from meeting one of my clients in Stamford,' Georgina said. 'I was going to give it to you when you came home, but as I said, Steven rang and we ended up yelling at each other.'

'Are you OK?' Lynda asked. 'He didn't threaten you again?'

Georgina shrugged. 'No more than usual.'

'I thought you weren't going to answer him when he called?'

'After everything he said last night, I won't be answering the next one.'

'Good!' Lynda said. 'You don't need men like that in your life.'

'Aren't you going to open the envelope and look at the card? I'm intrigued, even if you aren't.'

Lynda smiled and nodded, realising Georgina didn't want to discuss whatever Steven had said. It must have been bad. She put the plant on the floor and lifted up the small envelope. As she looked at the card she felt as if all the air had left her lungs.

Someone had drawn a train on a railway track, but that wasn't what had caused her heart to almost stop. It was the stick figure placed across the track in front of the train that took her breath away.

Chapter Seven

'Are you OK?' Georgina asked, reaching out to touch Lynda's arm.

'Yes, I'm fine . . . fine . . . just . . .'

'You don't look fine. Come inside for a few minutes. Excuse the cliché, but you look as if you've seen a ghost.'

Lynda glanced up from the card, trying to focus on what Georgina was saying. She knew she had to move, but her brain couldn't quite make her legs work. She felt a gentle tug on her arm.

'Come on. I think you might be in shock. Let me make you a cup of tea. It won't take me a minute.'

Lynda followed Georgina into her flat and closed the door before realising she'd left the plant outside right where someone could trip over it. She opened the door and went back out to pick it up. Should she just go straight upstairs and throw it in the bin? Before she could make up her mind, Georgina called out from her kitchen.

'I thought you were right behind me. Aren't you coming in? I've put the kettle on.'

Lynda looked down at the plant in her hands. 'I'm going to throw this away. I don't want it,' she said, going back inside the flat and shutting the door. 'Sorry, I'm behaving like an idiot.'

'Come through to the kitchen. We can sit in there. I'm here to listen if you want to tell me what's upset you, but don't think you have to. I don't want to pry.'

Lynda followed her into the kitchen. The bright lemon walls immediately made her feel better. She put the plant on the floor and sat on one of the stools at the breakfast bar.

'I don't really know what's going on,' she said.

Georgina put a mug in front of her. 'Drink this. It will make you feel better.'

Lynda tried to smile. 'Will it?'

Georgina laughed. 'I have no idea, but isn't that what people say when someone's had a shock?'

She felt she owed Georgina some sort of explanation, but didn't want to show her the card. 'Someone wants to upset me. Whoever sent this, referenced a terrible time in my past.'

Lynda watched the expression on Georgina's face change from mild interest to indignation on her friend's behalf.

'Oh, that's mean,' she said. 'Who would do something like that?'

Lynda knew the drawing was about Mark's suicide, but why now, after all these years? Realising Georgina was still waiting for an answer, she forced a laugh.

'I don't know,' she said. 'Clearly someone wants to scare me.'

'Could it be your ex-boyfriend?'

'Jason? No! Why would you think it was him?'

Georgina put out a hand as if warding off an attack. 'Sorry, I didn't mean to upset you. It's just that, you know, from what you've told me, the way you split up wasn't good for either of you.'

It couldn't be Jason. He didn't even know about Mark. Besides, there was no way he would sneak around leaving random plants with disturbing images. Plus, they had been getting on so much better recently.

She thought about how quiet the flat was without him. She missed him so much, but knew it could never work out between them as long as she still had what he called *her issues*. At least Lucky didn't judge her.

Georgina pointed at the plant. 'If they wanted to remind you of a painful time in your life, they definitely chose the right plant.'

'How do you mean?'

Georgina reached down and picked up the pot to put it on the breakfast bar. 'It's rosemary. In plant terms it stands for remembrance.'

A cold shiver ran down Lynda's back. 'How do you know?'

Georgina laughed. 'Have you forgotten that one of my many jobs in the past was working at a nursery? In the herb department we had to be able to talk to customers about what the plants are used for and also daft stuff like knowing that basil is for love, sage is for wisdom and rosemary signifies remembrance.'

Lynda shivered as she realised there was more to this than just a card in bad taste. Someone had gone to the trouble of picking the right herb to upset her. She stood up. 'I have to go. I'm sorry for leaving the tea.'

'That's no problem. As long as you're OK,' Georgina said, picking up the pot and holding it out. 'Aren't you going to take your plant?'

'No, I don't want it,' Lynda said. 'Can you bin it for me?'

'But there's nothing wrong with it. You could use it when you're cooking.'

Lynda shook her head.

Georgina held it to her nose and sniffed. 'I love the smell of rosemary. Would you mind if I kept it?'

'Be my guest,' Lynda said, suddenly wishing she'd never agreed to come in for the cup of tea. If she hadn't, she wouldn't have known about the plant's hidden meaning.

Georgina put the plant down on the breakfast bar. 'Are you sure you're OK? You're looking at me as if I'd turned into your worst nightmare.'

Lynda closed her eyes. When she opened them again, her friend's face was creased with concern.

She shook her head. 'You're not the nightmare; it's the plant and the card. It feels like a threat.'

Georgina picked up the pot. 'OK, into the bin it goes.'

She turned back to Lynda, blue eyes sparkling, and Lynda thought how well the new blond streaks in her shoulder-length hair suited her. In spite of the seven-year age gap, they'd become good friends since nearly two years earlier when they'd literally bumped into each other in Ringo's and Lynda had showered Georgina with hot coffee. The friendship had deepened since Georgina had moved into the apartment downstairs after escaping from Steven. The moment the flat had become vacant Lynda had let Georgina know so that she'd have a safe place to move into.

44

Her friend was a good listener, too, giving out sensible advice more in keeping with a forty-year-old than someone who'd only just turned twenty-three.

'Your new look suits you,' Lynda said.

'Thank you,' Georgina said, 'but I'm more concerned with you. You look stressed out. Don't let that stupid plant get to you.'

'Sorry, Georgina, it's not just the plant. I've got other stuff going on at the moment that's unsettling me.'

'Can I help?'

Lynda shrugged. 'Not really. It's someone from my school-days. I'm meeting her on Saturday morning, but seeing her again has made me remember things I'd rather forget.'

Georgina stood up. 'Fair enough, but I'm here if you need me. Forget about the plant. It's probably someone's idea of a sick joke.'

Lynda looked at the card again and shuddered. Being the cause of Mark's suicide wasn't something she was ever likely to forget.

Chapter Eight

Friday evenings were often the best and the worst of times for Lynda. As she climbed the stairs to Penelope's office she wondered where she should start with this week's therapy session. So much had happened in the week since she'd last been here, and none of it felt good.

She sat in the small anteroom outside the therapist's office waiting for her to open the door and beckon her in. Lynda loved the anonymity of the way Penelope used one door for clients coming in and a second door leading directly out to the hallway for those going out. In the months she'd been coming here, Lynda had never seen another of Penelope's clients. Or did she mean patients? That was a better name for what she was, and after the week she'd had, she probably fit the bill even more than when she had first started her therapy.

Lynda picked up a magazine and tried to interest herself in home décor. She'd read half a page without taking anything in when the door to the inner sanctum opened.

'Good to see you, Lynda. Come in,' Penelope said, standing to one side to allow Lynda to pass her.

'You have a new picture,' Lynda said, pointing to a land-scape painting on the wall behind Penelope's desk.

'It was a thank you gift,' Penelope said.

Lynda liked the fact that she hadn't given any indication of who had given her the painting. She felt her secrets and fears were safe in this room. As she settled herself into her usual armchair, she looked around.

'I like it here,' she said. 'This room has a peaceful feel to it.'

Her gaze came back to Penelope's face. She must be at least fifty, Lynda thought, but she had a quiet elegance.

'Have you changed your hair colour?' Lynda asked.

Penelope smiled and shook her head. 'You have commented on the room and now have asked about my appearance, both of which are diversionary tactics. Shall we talk about what has happened since you were last here to make you so nervous?'

She always knew when something bad had happened, Lynda thought. That's what made her so good. She sighed.

'I don't really know where to start,' she said. 'I suppose the plant is the worst thing. Well, the card was really the bad part, but it came with the plant, so maybe I should start with that.'

'OK, Lynda, deep breath. Tell me what happened.'

'It's probably easier if I show you the card,' she said, rummaging in her bag. No matter how many things she moved during the search, she couldn't find it. 'Damn, I've left it at home.'

'What did it say?'

Lynda explained how the plant had been found on the doorstep by Georgina.

'The card had a drawing of someone lying down in front of

an oncoming train. A friend of mine from my teenage years committed suicide that way.'

'The reminder must have been deeply upsetting,' she said.

'It was,' Lynda said and burst into tears. 'I can't bear the thought that someone would be mean enough to remind me of it.'

'That is a normal reaction. Have you thought about who might have left the plant?'

Lynda reached forward and took a tissue from the box on the table and wiped her eyes.

'I have no idea, but these days it almost feels as if my past has come back to haunt me. An old school friend has been in touch. In fact, I'm meeting her tomorrow morning for coffee.'

Penelope nodded. 'That seems quite coincidental. Do you feel she might have been responsible for sending the plant?'

'I don't know. I can't think why she would. She has a completely valid reason to hate me, but it seems she just wants to be friends.'

'Would you like to tell me about her?'

Lynda wanted to say no, but there was no point in coming for therapy if she wasn't going to be honest. Well, honest about most things.

'We were really close friends at one time, but then we had a massive argument and I stopped protecting her. I let her down badly.'

'In what way did she need your protection?'

'When she first came to the school she was bullied. She has a livid birthmark on one side of her face, almost in the shape of a question mark. It used to be really noticeable, but she's found a way to cover it up with make-up. If I hadn't known where to look last Saturday, I don't think I'd have noticed it was there.'

'You've seen her? Sorry, I assumed that tomorrow was to be your first meeting after many years apart.'

Lynda explained about the interview on local television and what had followed after Sarah visited the charity.

'She wants to be friends again, but I feel so guilty for what happened when we were teenagers, it's hard to be in her company.'

Penelope made a note on her pad. 'Were you one of the bullies?'

Lynda shook her head. 'No, but I might just as well have been. We were close friends for a while. I used to stop the bullies from picking on her as much as I could, but then I met someone and fell in love. Sarah didn't like him. She constantly tried to come between us and we argued about what she was doing. The bullies realised Sarah and I were no longer close friends and made her life a misery. She was expelled.'

'Sarah was expelled? Not the bullies?'

'No, she attacked Hazel, the ringleader, with a rock. She simply couldn't take any more. I know I was her only friend until she came between me and Mark. I never saw her again after she was expelled, but then she walked into the charity after she'd seen me on the local news.'

'You appear to have unfinished business with her. I believe talking about your shared past could help you draw a line under what happened. However, if it unsettles you then I'd advise against it for now. Perhaps you should put it off for another time.'

Lynda nodded. 'I want to, but I think it would be wrong,' she said, wiping away more tears with the sodden tissue. 'I owe her.'

'For not protecting her?'

'It goes deeper than that. Sarah decided to confront Hazel. She arranged a time and place and asked me to come along for moral support. I think she knew Hazel, like most bullies, wouldn't attack unless the odds were firmly in her favour. I promised Sarah I would be there, but then . . . then, something happened and I was late arriving. When I got there Sarah had a rock in her hand and Hazel was on the ground, her face covered in blood.'

'Sarah had attacked Hazel with the rock?'

Lynda nodded. 'She said Hazel and her friends had surrounded her, calling her names and pushing her from one to the other. She stumbled and Hazel kicked her while she was on the ground. She said she grabbed a rock and jumped up, lashing out at Hazel in self-defence.'

'What happened when you arrived?'

'One of Hazel's friends lived nearby and she had run home to get her parents. They took charge, got Hazel to hospital and then reported the event to the police and the school. Sarah was expelled.'

'Did she not explain she had started out as a victim and was trying to protect herself?'

Lynda nodded. 'Yes, but all Hazel's friends told the same story, which was that Sarah had attacked Hazel with the rock for no reason other than being jealous of Hazel's good looks. The story they concocted was that Sarah wanted Hazel to be as disfigured as she was. In a way they were right; Hazel was left with a terrible scar down one side of her face, but I don't think that was Sarah's intention. I believed her when she said she had just wanted to meet up with Hazel to put a stop to the bullying. I should have been there for her that day. I've never been able to make it up to her – after she was expelled, we lost touch.'

Penelope smiled. 'As you know from our previous sessions, in addition to grief counselling, one of my other areas of professional interest is helping people deal with the aftermath of childhood bullying, for both the victims and those who carried out the acts.'

Lynda nodded. It had been one of the reasons she'd chosen Penelope in the first place. When she'd been searching for a grief counsellor to help her deal with the loss of her family and had been given Penelope's name, she'd run an online search to find out more about her before making the first appointment. She'd found several articles written by Penelope and a few written about her. One of those covering her personal and professional background had mentioned that her son had committed suicide, which was why she'd decided to specialise in grief counselling. Lynda often wondered if Penelope's son had been the target of bullies, but knew she could never ask.

'Would you like to talk about your current feelings towards Sarah?'

How did she feel about her?

'She's come back into my life at a time when too much is going on. I'm struggling with my new promotion, wondering if I'm out of my depth; I still miss Jason like crazy. I'm just not sure I'm able to deal right now with the guilt I feel about Sarah, after suppressing it for so long.'

'Lynda, let's take these issues one at a time. Firstly, you can ignore Sarah if you wish. You don't have to meet her tomorrow if you don't feel up to it. You can simply send a message putting her off for another day. However, why not meet her for coffee as arranged? You cannot do more than apologise for your actions in the past and it might enable you to deal with the guilt you feel.'

Lynda sighed. 'You're right. That makes sense.'

'However, my second point is slightly less positive. Clearly the drawing on the card was intended to upset you. Would you like to talk about your feelings regarding your friend's suicide?'

Lynda thought back to the last words she'd said to Mark before his death. The guilt she felt about Sarah was a drop in the ocean compared to the tsunami that overwhelmed her because of Mark.

She shook her head. 'Not today. I will at some point, but not today.'

'OK, shall we talk about our last session? How are you getting along with the coping routines?'

'Fine. I'm doing OK,' Lynda said, but knew that until she stopped hiding the real reason she was so messed up, she'd never get better.

Chapter Nine

Lynda came back from her run on Saturday morning feeling better than she had over the past few days. Therapy with Penelope always calmed her. Today she'd meet Sarah, have coffee, and apologise fully for letting her down all those years ago, exactly as Penelope had advised.

As she showered, she thought about all she knew about the Sarah of today that she'd found out from her social media images. Lynda rarely posted photos of herself, but it seemed Sarah was one of those who took every opportunity to take selfies, either on her own or with whoever she was with at the time. Lots of the images showed Sarah with the same friend, Maria Guest. Lynda knew from overhearing part of the phone call that Sarah and Maria were an item. Many of the photos reminded her of the poses she and Jason used to strike back in the days before they stopped taking photos. Sarah's birthmark wasn't visible in any of her photos. She'd learned some good make-up techniques since their schooldays.

Thoughts of Sarah brought back other memories she'd rather ignore. Yes, she should have protected her friend from the bullying she'd received. *But what about Mark?* her treacherous brain reminded her. *Don't forget what you did to him. He was the reason you weren't there for Sarah.*

She mustn't think about those days. They were far in the past. She had to concentrate on what was happening now. Maybe if she could get her life sorted, she and Jason could get back together.

As she thought about what had caused their relationship to fall apart, she felt the tears well up. If only Jason had been able to understand. She'd been mildly obsessive since childhood. He'd known that and even found her habits adorable at one time, like when she counted potatoes as she put them in a bag at the supermarket. He hadn't complained back then that she couldn't bear to see a crooked picture frame and had the compulsion to straighten it, even if it wasn't hers to move. His parents and his sister hadn't even minded when she did it in their homes.

His family! His family was still alive. Still available to share birthdays and Christmas dinners. Unlike her parents and brother. She'd never see *them* again. She slid down the wet tiles and sobbed as the water cascaded over her shaking body. Would she ever get used to them no longer being there for her? Forcing herself up, she switched off the water and reached for a towel.

As she went through the ritual of drying first her left arm, then her right, before moving on to her left leg, she thought about how empty the flat felt after he'd left.

She'd made sure she was out when he came to get his things, only coming home a couple of hours after she'd known he'd been and gone. The note he'd left in the kitchen had made her wonder if he had a point. Her obsessive behaviour had worsened since the accident which had killed her parents and only brother almost a year and a half ago. It had taken weeks for her to accept he'd been right. Now that she'd been in therapy for a few months, there had been many times when they'd talked on the phone and she'd been on the point of telling him she was trying to get her life back on track, but she wasn't ready yet to share that experience with him.

If he wanted them to get back together then he needed to accept her with all her faults. She wasn't going to use the fact she was going to therapy as a lure to beg him for another chance. She sat on her bed and Lucky jumped up. The cat snuggled into her lap and she stroked its back.

'What would I have done without you?' Lynda asked over the sound of rapidly rising purrs. 'Finding you has kept me sane.' She laughed. 'Well, as sane as I'm ever going to be.'

Did Jason like cats? She realised that getting a pet of any kind had never come up during the time they'd lived together. Although she'd told him about Lucky's arrival in her life, he'd not commented one way or the other. If Jason wanted them to get back together, he'd have to realise Lucky was a permanent fixture now. Oh God, she missed him so much. All the things she loved about him far outweighed his untidiness. Why had she driven him away?

Realising she'd been in a trance for half an hour while going down a memory lane she would rather not have travelled, Lynda put Lucky on the floor and walked over to the wardrobe. What should she wear? What should she wear to have coffee with someone who reminded her too much of the person she used to be?

Settling for black jeans and a striped shirt, she dressed quickly and sat down to put on some make-up. Her therapist had given her lots of tricks to get over her compulsions, but for Lynda this still had to be done in a fixed regime. She knew it was weird putting on lipstick before anything else, but whenever she tried to change the order, she ended up feeling so anxious she had to remove whatever she'd put on and start again.

Chapter Ten

Lynda looked at her watch for what felt like the fiftieth time. If the traffic jam didn't clear soon she was going to be late. Maybe she should call Sarah and let her know she had been held up. Just as she reached for her bag on the passenger seat, the car in front moved. Maybe she would make it on time after all.

She arrived at the Queensgate centre with seconds to spare, only to find herself in a long queue of cars waiting to get in. Taking the first available space, she parked and ran to Ringo's to find Sarah seated in the same booth as before, studying her watch and looking far from pleased.

'I'm so sorry I'm late,' Lynda said. 'There was an accident just outside Wittering and it took ages for the traffic to clear.'

Lynda settled herself and signalled to the waitress. She waited until the woman had taken their orders and then smiled at Sarah, but there was no answering smile.

'I thought you weren't coming. I kept looking for a text to say you'd changed your mind.'

Lynda shook her head. 'I'm sorry, I should've texted you

to say I was running late. I kept thinking I'd still make it on time, but then there was a queue to get into the car park here and I ended up being a bit late. I'm really sorry.'

'Not to worry. You're here now and that's all that matters.'

Pleased that the awkward moment appeared to have passed, Lynda relaxed.

'Did you want to meet up again for any particular reason?' she asked.

Sarah shrugged. 'Not really. I thought we could have a proper catch up. So much must have happened in both our lives and we used to be such close friends, but we know nothing about each other now. Well, I know some of what you do, but you know nothing about my life.'

'That's true,' Lynda said. 'What do you do?'

'I'm currently out of work,' Sarah said, 'but I'm looking for a job.'

'What kind of job?'

'To be honest, I would settle for anything at the moment.'

'Have you been to the local agencies here in Peterborough? That's how I got my current position.'

Sarah looked as if she was about to answer when the waitress came over with their coffee and cakes.

'Here you go, ladies. Enjoy!'

As soon as the waitress left, Lynda reached across the table and touched Sarah's hand. Making small talk had never seemed so pointless.

'Sarah, I'm sorrier than you will ever know for letting you down that day. I am really so very, very sorry. Can you forgive me?'

'Of course I can. I know you would have been there if it

58

hadn't been for Mark. All I want is for us to be friends again,' she said, returning Lynda's grip on her hand. 'It's in the past. Let's get to know each other all over again. Wouldn't that be great?'

Lynda nodded, her eyes full of tears.

'Thank you,' she said. 'You've taken away years of guilt.'

Chapter Eleven

Lynda pulled up outside the charity, shocked to find she'd already arrived. She must have driven from Peterborough to Stamford on autopilot because the last thing she remembered was saying goodbye to Sarah and walking to the car park. All her thoughts had been on why she had let Sarah down that day and what she'd done to drive Mark to kill himself.

'Hey, sexy arse, give us a wiggle.'

Lynda locked her car door, ignoring the yobs. She crossed the road to the sound of laughter and jeers, determined not to feel intimidated.

She opened the charity door and waved hello to Greg, who was on the phone, then headed straight to the kitchen. She dumped her bag on the counter, filled the kettle and switched it on, then turned it off again. The last thing she wanted was more coffee.

Feeling a touch on her shoulder, she jumped and knocked her bag off the counter. As the contents spilled across the floor, she whirled round to find Greg smiling at her.

'Sorry,' he said. 'I didn't mean to scare you. Are you OK? You seem a bit on edge. Is it those bloody yobs outside? I've spoken to the police again, but they say they can't do anything more than give them a warning at this stage.'

'I'm fine,' Lynda said, reaching down to pick up her purse and phone, slipping them back into the bag. 'They are a nuisance, but I'm getting used to them. I didn't hear you come into the kitchen. I was miles away.'

Greg knelt down and picked up a lipstick which had rolled to a stop at his feet.

'Here,' he said, holding it out to her.

'Thanks.' She smiled and dropped it into her bag. 'Want a coffee?' she asked, holding out his cup.

'Yes, please. Look,' he said, 'don't take offence, but you don't look fine.'

'I've had an odd morning,' she said.

'Want to talk about it?'

She shook her head. 'Not really.'

'Fair enough,' Greg said, 'but you know I'm here if you change your mind.'

Lynda smiled. 'Thank you.'

'By the way,' he said, 'Cassie and Amanda will both be coming in this afternoon to talk to you about the race. They'll be here just after lunch.'

'Oh? I thought they both wanted to work at home.'

'They do, but apparently they've been liaising with each other and now need your input on something, and it's easier to do it here.'

Greg looked as if he was about to say something more, but both phones started ringing in the call room.

'We'd best get to it,' he said.

Two hours later, Lynda took off her headphones, finally feeling more relaxed. She looked over at Greg who had also just finished a call.

'Fancy a sandwich or a pie?' she said. 'I could go and see what they have in the bakery.'

Greg nodded. 'I'm starving, but I have an errand to run, so I'll go. What shall I get for you?'

'A pasty,' she said, getting up. 'I'll fetch my purse.'

'Don't worry about it now. Pay me when I get back. Pass me your mug.'

She handed it to him and watched as he took both mugs back into the kitchen. Lynda thought about how kind he'd been to her since she'd agreed to join his charity as a phone volunteer. He was a good-looking man, gorgeous brown eyes and floppy hair that gave him a young Hugh Grant look. Any woman in her right mind would fancy him, but for some reason she just couldn't see him that way. Maybe it was the beard. She'd never really gone for men with facial hair. Or maybe it was because he reminded her far too much of Mark. She knew Greg wanted more than friendship, but couldn't imagine herself in a romantic set-up with him.

He came back from the kitchen. 'You're looking very pensive. Are you sure you don't want to talk about whatever it is that's upset you since I saw you last week?'

Lynda shook her head. 'No, I'm fine, honestly.'

He nodded and walked to the door as she put her headphones

back on and got ready to listen to a person who desperately needed to talk to someone who understood.

Three calls later and she was able to take the headphones off for a rest. Listening to others made her realise how lucky she was to have been given this chance to at least try to atone for the wrong she'd done all those years ago.

Feeling her mood slipping again, she was glad when the phone rang and she could concentrate on something other than her own past.

'Hi, my name is Lynda. How can I help you?'

'. . . ow . . . you . . .' came out in a hissed whisper.

'Sorry, I can't hear you,' Lynda said. 'I want to help.'

'No, you don't.' The voice was fractionally louder this time, so she could just about make out the words.

'Yes, I do want to help you. My name is Lynda and I'm here to listen.'

'Bitch'

Lynda's stomach lurched. She tried to speak, but no words came out. Then the line went dead.

Chapter Twelve

Lynda thought she'd recovered by the time Greg came back clutching a bag from the bakery, but there must have been something on her face because he immediately came over.

'What is it? What's happened?'

She shook her head. 'Nothing. I'm a bit tired. That's all.'

He shrugged. 'You don't have to tell me if you don't want to, but please don't make me feel as if I'm intruding. I'm concerned about you.'

As Greg turned to go towards the kitchen, Lynda felt tears welling up.

'I'm sorry, Greg. Really, I am. I had a horrible call and it's upset me.'

Through blurred vision she saw Greg drop the bag on the kitchen counter and rush back.

'One of our regulars or a newbie?'

'What?' she said. 'Oh, no, not someone looking for help. Quite the opposite. It was a crank caller, I think.'

Suddenly, it felt as if Greg was too close, crowding her

personal space. She stood up so quickly her office chair spun back and hit the wall.

'Hey,' Greg said. 'You're really spooked. Come on, tell me what's going on. Even if it was just a crank call, it's clearly got to you.'

'I met Sarah for coffee this morning and it's brought back memories I've been trying to suppress for years.'

'Is Sarah your friend from last week?'

She nodded.

'I didn't think you looked happy to see her.'

'It wasn't that so much. More that it was a shock as we'd lost touch years ago. And then there was the plant that turned up on my doorstep.'

Realising she wasn't making sense, Lynda told Greg about the rosemary plant and went to the kitchen to get the card from her handbag. She took it back to the office and showed it to him.

'That's unpleasant,' he said. 'Any idea who sent it?'

Lynda shook her head. 'I've searched my mind over and over. I can't think of anyone.'

'And the phone call? Was it nasty?' he said.

She nodded. 'Pretty much.'

'Have you upset anyone?'

Greg's words felt a little too close to how Lynda felt. Not that she had upset anyone recently, but she had done a lot of damage in the past.

Lynda crossed her arms and then uncrossed them when she realised she'd given a non-verbal signal for Greg to back off.

'Not as far as I know,' she said.

'You don't sound very sure.'

'I am!' Lynda said.

Greg smiled as if he was humouring her. 'Fair enough if you don't want to tell me. We all have our secrets. OK, let's see if we can trace the call.'

'I already tried. The number was withheld.'

Greg sat down and wheeled his chair over to her workstation. 'You want to rescue your chair from the wall?' he said, grinning.

The smile was clearly meant to take the sting out of his words, making Lynda feel an even bigger idiot for overreacting. She walked over and dragged her chair back into place.

'Right, then,' said Greg. 'Let's see if we can get to the bottom of this. Was the caller male or female?'

Lynda shrugged. 'I honestly couldn't tell. The voice was muffled, as if there was something over the speaker. If I had to guess, I think it was a man, but I'm really not sure.'

'Let's say it was a man,' Greg said, 'any idea of his age?'

Lynda could feel the tears threatening again. 'Not a clue. Look, Greg, I know you're being kind and want to help, but I don't want to talk about this any more.'

'Look, why don't I call Cassie and Amanda to put them off until next week. We can pack up and I can buy you a drink somewhere. We can talk about anything you like and not talk about anything you don't like. What do you say?'

The eager look on his face made Lynda feel like she would be kicking a puppy if she said no, but she guessed if she gave in it would give Greg the wrong impression. Every time he asked her out for a drink or a bite to eat it was clear he was hoping for more than just being friends.

She shook her head. 'Thanks for the offer, but I doubt I'd be the best of company. Thanks for the pasty. What do I owe you?'

Greg laughed. 'Don't be daft. You can treat me to one next time.'

Yet again she got the feeling that she'd hurt Greg in a way she'd never intended. He was such a sweet person who she knew had taken years to get over being bullied when he was younger.

Every moment she spent with him reminded her of what Sarah must have gone through. That was why, even though he'd asked a few times in roundabout ways, she'd never told him the real reason why she'd joined the charity. As far as he knew, the anti-bullying movement was simply something she had come to feel passionate about after its profile had been raised by several news reports.

Right on the stroke of one the door opened. Cassie and Amanda came in. Lynda wondered if they'd arranged to travel together and realised she hadn't asked where either of them lived.

'Hi, ladies, come through to the other room,' she said, taking off her headphones and leaving them on the desk. 'Greg says you both need my input on the race.'

She led the way and waited until they'd both sat down before asking if they wanted something to drink.

'Not for me, thanks,' Cassie answered, opening her laptop.

Amanda also shook her head. 'We went to Starbucks before coming here.'

Lynda closed the door. 'OK, what do you need from me?'

'For me,' Amanda said, 'I need some financial details, such

as how much each entry fee will be and whether there will be other charges, such as for medals, tee-shirts and such like.'

'Same for me,' Cassie said. 'I can't really get stuck into setting up the website without knowing exactly what you want on there.'

An hour later and Lynda's head was reeling.

'You know, I've run in many races, but hadn't realised quite how much background work must have gone into making them a success.'

'That's always the way,' Cassie said. 'People take things for granted just because they haven't actually seen the work that others have done.'

Her voice was sharp, as if she was irritated. Lynda was about to ask her if she was having a go at her when Amanda's phone rang. As Amanda glanced at the screen Lynda saw the blood drain from her face. She looked as if she might pass out.

'Are you OK?' Lynda asked.

Amanda stood up and grabbed her papers. She stuffed them into her bag. 'Yes, I'm fine. I need to take this call. I'll be outside,' she said, looking at Cassie.

She opened the door and rushed from the room.

Lynda was trying to think of something to say when Cassie closed her laptop and slid it into its case.

'That'll be Lennie, her husband,' she said. 'I'd better go as I'll need to drive her home. He wasn't at all happy about her coming out today, so I think she'll want to get home as soon as possible. If we need anything else, is it OK if we call you direct, or do we need to go via Greg?'

'Call me direct. You already have my number. Would you make sure Amanda has it as well, please?'

'Of course. Look, don't say anything to Amanda about her running out like this, will you?'

'I won't say a word. There's nothing for me to say, but . . .'

'But what?'

'I thought she was happy in her marriage. That's what she said last week, but she certainly didn't look thrilled to receive that call.'

Cassie laughed. 'We don't tell the truth to everyone all the time, do we? I think she doesn't want anyone to know how things really are. I'll call you if I need anything more for the website.'

After Cassie left, Lynda tidied up the table and went back into the main office.

Greg took off his headset and smiled. 'All sorted? I saw Amanda rush out. She looked as if the hounds of hell were after her. I hope nothing was wrong.'

Lynda shrugged. 'She had a phone call that upset her. Nothing to do with the charity or the race. Look, Greg, would you mind if I left early today? My mind is all over the place, so I'm not sure I'd be the best person for troubled souls to talk to.'

'Of course you can go. Look, are you sure you wouldn't like to go for a drink later?'

'I honestly wouldn't be good company. Best if I just go home and get an early night. I'll see you next Saturday.'

She was glad to get outside and couldn't wait to drive home. It had been a shitty day so far. As she rummaged in her bag for keys that she couldn't seem to find, she wondered what else could go wrong. She put the bag on the car's bonnet so that she could have a better look inside. Nope, no keys. Realising she must have left them inside, she went back in.

Opening the door, she was rewarded with a hopeful look on Greg's face.

'Did you change your mind?'

'Sorry, Greg, no. I can't find my keys. I must have left them in the kitchen.'

He jumped up and almost ran into the kitchen ahead of her.

'They might have skidded under the fridge when you dropped your bag earlier,' he said.

She followed Greg in to find him on his knees on the floor.

'Yes,' he called out, holding her keys aloft.

Lynda went to take them as Greg hauled himself upright, but he held on to them. The moment he was on his feet, he took a step forward; he seemed to be towering over her. She stepped back. Feeling intimidated, she put out a hand to ward him off.

'Hey, no need for that,' he said. 'You looked as if you thought I was about to attack you.'

'I'm sorry, Greg. I have no idea why I did that.'

'You looked so scared. Surely you know I'd never hurt you. How could you think I would?'

Lynda looked up and tried to smile. 'I don't! I'm sorry. I really don't know what's going on in my head at the moment.' She took the keys he now held out. 'I'll see you next week.'

'Yeah, of course. Look, if you want to talk, as friends, no strings, you have my number. OK?'

She nodded. 'OK.'

Feeling as though she would burst into tears if she stayed a moment longer in the kitchen, she rushed back out to her car. As she climbed in, she tried to work out why she'd reacted as she had and realised it was because, deep down, she didn't fully trust Greg. All she knew about his life outside the charity was that he worked for a removal company. He'd never opened up about his past, saying it was hard for him because he no longer wanted to see himself as a victim, but sometimes she got the feeling there was more to it than that.

What would he think of her if he knew where she'd been and what she'd done instead of keeping her word to Sarah? That was something she would have to deal with in her therapy sessions. But not yet. She wasn't ready to face that truth. She'd never even told Jason.

Maybe it would always be her secret shame, but what did Greg mean about everyone having secrets? Was it Greg who'd made the phone call while he was out of the office? No, of course not. Why would he? She was being stupid.

Chapter Thirteen

As she entered the house Georgina was opening her front door.

'Good timing,' Georgina said. 'Want to come in? I'm about to treat myself to a glass of cold white wine. You look as if you could do with one.'

Lynda managed a smile. 'I thought the answer to life's ills was a cup of tea.'

'It usually is, but sometimes wine does a better job.'

Lynda thought about going upstairs to her empty apartment where only Lucky would be there for her and the walls sometimes felt as if they were closing in. Right now she needed the warmth of Georgina's kitchen and someone to talk to.

'A glass of cold white sounds perfect,' she said.

She followed her friend into the kitchen and sat at the breakfast bar while Georgina opened the bottle she'd taken from the fridge.

'Here you are,' she said, putting a glass next to Lynda. 'It's only a supermarket special, but it's cold. You look like you need a bit of TLC, and white wine always does it for me.'

Lynda was touched. 'Thank you.'

Georgina raised her glass. 'Here's to us!'

Lynda lifted her own glass in salute before taking a sip. She felt overwhelmed by her friend's kindness and a tear slid down her face.

'Hey, what's up?'

Lynda poured out her tale of woe over the phone call and the way she'd reacted to Greg.

'And you couldn't tell if the voice was male or female?'

Lynda shook her head. 'I couldn't make out anything really. It was creepy. There was so much venom in the voice, it scared me.'

'I've been thinking about the plant,' Georgina said. 'Do you think you should report it to the police? If it had been left for me, I don't think I'd be able to sleep at night, worrying about who might be out there. Even if the only thing the person wanted to do was upset you, that still shows whoever it might be is a bit disturbed.'

'What could the police do? There's no specific threat in sending someone a plant and we get lots of crank calls through to the charity number.'

'Well,' said Georgina, 'if you change your mind, I'll go to the station with you whenever you like.'

Lynda wondered if she should report what had happened to the police, but the thought of doing so was more than she could cope with right at that moment. She'd decide later.

She glugged back the last of the wine and stood up.

'I'm sorry, Georgina, it's been a difficult day. Thank you for the wine. I need a good long soak in the bath and an early night.'

'Sure you wouldn't like another glass? There's plenty in the bottle.'

Lynda shook her head. 'Save it for later. I meant to ask if you'd heard anything more from Steven but keep forgetting. Some friend I am!'

Georgina stood. 'I've made it clear he has to stay away. If he turns up here you'll hear me yelling for help.'

Lynda picked up her bag. 'And I'll come running down! It would be the first and last time I came face to face with Steven. I feel as if I know him inside out, even though we've never met, but I promise, I won't let him anywhere near you.'

Georgina shrugged. 'I doubt he'd be stupid enough to show his face.'

As they walked to Georgina's front door, Lynda thought about Jason and how much he'd meant to her, still did. She'd never be able to say she didn't want him around. She missed him every day.

Lynda opened her own front door and dropped the keys into the bowl on the hall table, instinctively straightening the mirror above it. Lucky sauntered out of the kitchen meowing hello, or demanding food. Maybe both.

She went into the kitchen, opened the cupboard and took out the cat food, thinking about what she'd really like to do that evening. The answer, to lie in Jason's arms, was impossible, but maybe they could spend some time together. She'd call Jason and suggest . . . what? What should she suggest? Coming over? No, too many memories, both good and bad. Meeting for a drink? A walk in the park? By the time she'd fed Lucky, she'd decided to leave it for another day.

Opening the cupboard over the kettle she frowned and

reached up to straighten one of the mugs that wasn't quite in line with the others. She took down the mug she always used. One of Jason's last gifts before she drove him away. Placing it exactly in the centre of the work surface, she began her coffee ritual. First a level teaspoon of instant coffee, then milk up to the line that didn't exist. Once the kettle boiled, she poured in the hot water until it was a centimetre and a half from the top. She didn't need to measure the distance. She knew when to stop. Three stirs clockwise and three stirs anti-clockwise.

As she left the kitchen to take her coffee through to the lounge, she paused to straighten the hall mirror again. She felt compelled to do it every single time she passed. Clearly she wasn't yet in control of her urges, so maybe it was better not to call Jason at all.

As she sat down, her mobile rang. She put the coffee on the side table and reached into her bag for the phone. It stopped before she could reach it. She looked at the recent calls received, but it didn't show a number. As she was about to put the phone down, it rang again. Again, no number showing.

'Hi, Lynda speaking.'

'Bitch,' a voice hissed. Lynda almost dropped the phone. It was the same muffled tone as the one in the charity call room.

'Who are you? How did you get my number?'

The sound of someone laughing was followed by the dialling tone.

Chapter Fourteen

Lynda woke on Sunday morning fighting against the restraints on her arms and legs. She finally managed to get an arm free and realised she was tightly wrapped up in a cocoon of sheets and duvet. She was drenched with sweat and felt sick as her heart beat a thumping tattoo against her ribs. The remnants of last night's dream lingered on the edge of consciousness. She vaguely remembered trying to escape from people screaming that she was sorry she'd hurt them in the past.

She forced herself free of the covers and half sat up, trying to clear her head.

Greg hadn't been far behind Mark in the mob trying to lynch her during the nightmare. What was her subconscious trying to tell her about him? She didn't fancy him, but that wasn't a crime. It was probably just because he'd asked her out yet again and she'd refused. And then there'd been Sarah, birthmark blazing a questioning red trail down one side of her face, telling her what a coward she'd been!

Shaking her head, she got up to put on her running gear.

What she needed to shake off the last thoughts of her nightmare was a good run.

'Come on, Lucky, it's run time.'

Lucky yawned, stretched and finally leapt off the bed.

Lynda laughed. 'You act as if you're doing me a favour.'

The cat looked at her as if it was agreeing and Lynda was certain Lucky understood every word she said to her.

After her run, as Lynda turned into her street, she kept a lookout for Lucky, but there was no sign of her. She found herself hoping that Georgina wouldn't be waiting in the hallway. She didn't feel up to talking to anyone until she'd sorted out her thoughts.

Feeling like a burglar in her own home, she crept up the stone steps and opened the door as quietly as she could and then gently closed it behind her. She silently moved to the stairs and went up, only letting out a sigh of relief when she reached her own front door. Relieved to have made it home, she paused to straighten the hall mirror before heading to the shower.

A couple of times during the day she went down to see if Lucky was waiting on the doorstep, but there was no sign of her. Clearly this was one of her serious hunting days. *Please don't let her bring back another dead bird or mouse*, Lynda prayed.

By mid-afternoon, all the tension of the day before and her nightmare had dissipated. Her stomach was rumbling and she was just wondering what to make for lunch when her mobile rang. Picking it up, she saw Sarah's name on the display.

'Lynda . . . I need someone to talk to.' Sarah gave a big sob, as if she was trying to stop herself from crying. 'You said yesterday that you do the counselling stuff at that charity place. Please help me. I'm desperate. I don't have anyone else to turn to.'

Lynda listened helplessly as Sarah burst into tears.

'Of course, I'll do my best. Take a deep breath and try not to cry. What's happened?'

The sobbing continued for a while until Lynda heard Sarah give her nose a good blow.

'Sorry,' Sarah said. 'I didn't mean to dump on you when we've only just found each other again, but I didn't know who else to call.'

'That's not a problem,' Lynda said. 'Do you feel like talking?'

'Yes, but not on the phone. Can we meet somewhere?'

Lynda saw her relaxing Sunday disappearing into the mist, but knew she couldn't turn her back on Sarah when she was so distressed.

'Of course. Where is good for you?'

'I'm at the Stamford retail park. How about McDonalds?'

'OK. Give me twenty minutes and I'll be there.'

Sarah gave a watery sniff. 'Thank you.'

Lynda parked and walked towards the entrance wondering what on earth had happened.

Sarah was already waiting, sitting in the booth closest to the door. She had a coffee in front of her, but no food. Lynda wondered if she could get away with ordering a meal to eat while Sarah poured out her troubles, but quickly realised that wouldn't be a good idea. Sarah looked like a ghost of the woman she'd seen the morning before. Although she had covered her birthmark, she hadn't used any other make-up. Her eyes were red rimmed and her hair looked as if it hadn't seen a brush since yesterday.

'I'm just going to get myself a coffee and then I'm ready to listen. OK?'

Sarah nodded, so Lynda went to join the queue, trying to ignore her gnawing hunger, but the smell of fries and burgers made it so much harder. As soon as the server placed the cup in front of her, she picked it up and headed back to the booth. Sarah didn't appear to have moved an inch. She was staring into space as if waiting for something or someone to appear.

Lynda slid into the booth and sat opposite Sarah. She took the lid off her paper cup and took a sip. She waited a few minutes for Sarah to speak, but it soon became clear that she wasn't going to volunteer anything.

'How can I help?' Lynda asked.

Sarah shook her head and her eyes filled with tears. 'I don't think you can,' she said. 'I don't think anyone can. I shouldn't have bothered you.'

'It might help just to talk. Get things off your chest.'

'It's Maria,' Sarah said. 'She thinks I've cheated on her.'

'Did you?' Lynda asked.

Sarah's head shot up. 'No! I told her I haven't, but she came up with all sorts of what she called proof. She wouldn't listen to anything I had to say.'

Remembering her fight with Jason where she'd also yelled things she didn't mean, Lynda found herself more in sympathy with Sarah than she'd imagined she ever could be.

'So what happened?'

Sarah sighed. 'Truth be told, we haven't been getting on

very well since I was laid off a couple of months ago. She's been covering all the bills while I've been job hunting. One of the things she yelled at me was that I'd been taking her for granted and using her money to shag other women while she works her fingers to the bone.'

'Why would she think that?'

'Look, this is embarrassing, but Maria has been giving me an allowance. She said I must be using her money to treat others, but even though I swore I hadn't done any such thing, she said she didn't believe me and called me a liar.'

'I'm so sorry, Sarah,' Lynda said. 'I wish there was some way I could help you, but I don't see how I can.'

'I know. I've no idea why I called you, but seeing you yesterday reminded me of how close we once were. I suppose I thought of you as my oldest friend. To be perfectly honest, since I've been with Maria, I've lost touch with all my other friends. What can I say to make Maria see I'm telling the truth?'

'Oh, Sarah, I'm so sorry. I've no idea how you can make her see sense.'

'That's OK. Just being able to talk this through with you has helped.'

Lynda didn't feel as if she'd helped, but reached over the table and touched Sarah's hand. 'What are you going to do now?'

Sarah shrugged. 'Go home and try to make up, I suppose. The way things were left it's going to take a lot of grovelling on my part, but I suppose that's what I'll have to do. Thanks for coming,' she said, putting her other hand on top of Lynda's and squeezing it. 'I knew I could rely on you.'

She stood up and picked up her empty cup. 'I bet they all love you at that charity. You're really good at listening.'

Lynda watched her as she went to the bins and slotted the cup in before she walked to the door. Her shoulders were down and Lynda thought she'd never seen anyone look so beaten. She stayed for a few minutes to finish her own coffee and then stood up, picking up the now empty cup. Her appetite had disappeared, so she dropped the cup into the bin and left.

By the time she reached home her hunger had returned and she was regretting not ordering something at McDonalds while she had the chance. Straightening the mirror, she wandered into the kitchen to peer into the fridge and pantry, looking for inspiration. Deciding on a cream and mushroom pasta bake, she set to work.

Poor Sarah. She'd looked devastated. She must really love Maria to be so broken up over their fight. Lynda realised that was exactly how she felt about Jason. She still loved him and knew he'd been right to complain about her constant OCD rituals and the way she'd accused him of moving things when he hadn't even touched them. All the things she did couldn't have been easy to live with. As she sprinkled grated cheese over the pasta and put it in the oven to brown, she promised herself she would bite the bullet and call Jason after she'd eaten. She settled down in the lounge with her book to relax while waiting for the half hour to pass.

She'd just returned to the kitchen and taken the pasta bake from the oven when her phone rang. She put the dish on the worktop and picked up the phone, heart rate rising yet again at Sarah's name showing in the display. She swiped to answer and heard the sound of sobbing before she could even say hello.

'Sarah, what is it? Did things not work out with Maria?'

It felt to Lynda as if minutes passed before Sarah was able to control herself and answer.

'She . . . she's . . . she's . . . thrown me . . . out.'

'Oh no,' Lynda said. 'What are you going to do?'

'I don't . . . know. I've got . . . no . . . money and nowhere to stay.'

Lynda could hear the unspoken question.

'Where are you now?'

Thankfully, Sarah seemed to have found a way to control her tears as the sobbing stopped. 'I'm in my car, surrounded by all my worldly possessions, which isn't much. Look, Lynda, I hate to ask, but could I stay at your place tonight? I'll sort something out tomorrow, but right now I have no one else to turn to.'

'Yes, of course. Have you got a pen? I'll give you my address.'

'Thank you,' Sarah said. 'I promise it will only be for a day or two.'

The line went dead before Lynda could say anything else. She put the phone down and looked at the pasta bake she'd been so looking forward to eating. Maybe she should put it to one side and heat it later when Sarah arrived.

She headed to the spare room to put sheets on the bed. As she put the pillows back her phone rang again. Probably Sarah to say she got lost, Lynda thought, but realised it wasn't her when the display showed an unknown number. Hands shaking, she swiped to deny the call and put the phone in her pocket.

She felt the vibration before the ringtone even started. The display showed the same unknown number. Furious, she swiped up.

'Leave me alone!' she yelled.

'Fine,' Jason said. 'I'll do that!'

'No, wait!' Lynda said. 'Jason, I didn't recognise your number. Sorry.'

He laughed. 'Do you now yell at everyone whose number you don't recognise?'

'No, of course not. I've been getting some crank calls. How come you've changed your number?'

'Long story. I could come over and tell you about it if you're free tonight.'

She thought she could hear hope in his voice. He sounded as if he really wanted to be with her. God, how she wanted him to come over and hold her. He'd find a way to put all the weird stuff into perspective.

'I'd really like to see you,' she said.

'Great, I could be there in less than half an hour,' Jason said.

The intercom sounded and Lynda remembered she was about to get a visitor.

'Look, it's a bit complicated tonight,' she said. 'Can we meet up next week?'

The silence told her all she needed to know about how he felt about being put off.

'Jason, the thing is –'

But he didn't let her finish. 'No explanation needed,' he said, the hurt obvious in his voice. 'Let me know when you have time for me?' The intercom sounded again.

'Jason, wait, I can explain,' she said, but the phone went dead and Lynda went to the hall to let in her guest.

Chapter Fifteen

Lynda came out of her bedroom and looked around, feeling as if her home had been invaded. Mondays were always bad, but this one was the worst ever. Sarah had needed four trips down to her car to bring in all her belongings, and bits of her life were now strewn all over the apartment.

'I owe her this,' Lynda whispered as she put on her running gear. 'It's just until she finds a place of her own.'

Convinced she'd been listening to Sarah tossing and turning all night, she felt as if she hadn't slept at all, even though her rational mind knew that was unlikely.

She tied her shoelaces, put on her sports watch and left the bedroom. She'd almost made it to the front door when Sarah's voice stopped her in her tracks.

'Wow! You're up early. What's wrong? Couldn't you sleep?'

Forcing a smile, she turned to face Sarah.

'I run most mornings before work, so I'm usually up early. Make yourself some breakfast. I'll see you when I get back.'

'OK, thanks. I don't normally eat until later, but some coffee sounds good.'

Lynda nodded and opened the front door. Never chatty in the morning, she couldn't wait to get outside where she didn't have to talk and could just enjoy her run.

By the time she had covered the first two kilometres, her breathing had settled and her peace of mind was back. That was when she heard a car coming up slowly behind her. She looked round at the sound and saw a dark blue car slowing down to keep pace with her.

She couldn't see the driver clearly as his face was partially hidden by the peak of a sports cap. There was no one around who might come to her rescue if the driver was some nut job, so she took the next turning on the left and then the first on the right. She carried on running, taking random turnings and it was clear she was being deliberately followed. Eventually she lost the car. By the time she found her way back to her regular route it was nowhere to be seen.

Heart pounding, she arrived home wondering what else could go wrong in her life. She'd upset Jason, was struggling to get used to Sarah being in the apartment, had been followed by someone in a car – and that was without even taking into account the nasty phone calls, and the card attached to the plant.

She entered the downstairs hall just as Georgina opened her door.

'Lynda, I was listening out for you. I think there's someone in your flat,' she whispered.

Lynda sighed. 'There is. Can I come in for a moment? I don't want to talk out here.'

'Sure thing,' Georgina said, holding her door wide.

Lynda followed her into the kitchen. 'I'm sorry,' she said, 'I'm a bit sweaty from my run. I had an overnight guest, but I'm surprised you heard her from here. The walls aren't that thin.'

Georgina smiled. 'I didn't hear her while she was upstairs. It was when she came back in from outside this morning. At first I thought it was you so didn't take any notice, but when she went in and out a few times and let the door slam, I decided to take a peek and saw a woman. Her arms were full of stuff, so that's why she couldn't close the door quietly.'

'Was she taking her things out?'

Georgina shook her head. 'I don't think so. I got the impression she was bringing her belongings in.'

'Oh great! That's all I need,' Lynda said. 'The flat feels cluttered and overcrowded already. What a morning! First the weird driver and now Sarah's bringing even more of her things in.'

'Sarah? *The* Sarah from the weekend? Your old school friend?'

Lynda nodded. 'The one and only. It's a long story. I'll tell you about it later. Right now I need to find out what's been going on while I was out.'

Georgina nodded. 'And the weird driver?'

'I'll tell you about that, too, but not right now.'

'I haven't seen Lucky since yesterday morning. Is she OK?' Georgina asked.

'She's gone off on one of her marathon hunting sprees, but I'm hoping she'll turn up today.'

'Don't worry. I'll see her safely upstairs if she comes back while you're at work.'

'Actually, would you be able to hang on to her until I get

home? I don't want her to take off again because there's a stranger in the flat.'

'Of course,' Georgina said. 'Fancy going for a drink later? You can fill me in on all the weird happenings in your life.'

There was nothing Lynda would have liked more, but she wasn't sure tonight would be a good time.

'Can I take a rain check until I see what the situation is upstairs?'

'Of course. No probs.'

Lynda went upstairs and opened her front door. She tripped and almost fell over a suitcase. Bags and what looked like debris littered the hallway.

'What the . . .? Sarah! What's all this stuff?' she called out.

Sarah came out from the spare room. 'Sorry, I thought I'd be able to get it all put away before you came back from your run, but it took me longer than I'd thought it would.'

'But you said you'd brought up all your stuff from the car last night.'

'Oh no, that was just what was inside the car and might have tempted someone to break in if it had been left on show. This is all from the boot. I didn't bother with it last night because I thought it would be safe as it couldn't be seen, but this morning I changed my mind. Better safe than sorry.' Sarah scratched her arm. 'By the way, does that large cushion in the kitchen belong to a cat?'

'You know it does. I told you about Lucky. Why do you ask?'

Sarah pulled up her sleeve and pointed to her arm. Lynda couldn't see anything odd about it, although it was a bit red.

'See that rash?' Sarah said. 'I'm allergic to cats.'

'Oh dear,' Lynda said, inwardly rejoicing and then immediately hating herself for feeling that way. 'Lucky went off hunting yesterday, but I'm hoping she'll turn up today.'

To hide her guilt at wanting to get rid of Sarah, Lynda leaned over the suitcase and put up her hand to straighten the hall mirror. As she did so, she caught sight of her watch. If she didn't shower and leave soon she'd be late for work. Sorting the mess out with Sarah would have to wait until she got home.

'Look, I'm sorry, but I am a bit anal about mess. You need to get this stuff moved.'

Sarah smiled. 'Of course, I understand. I'll put it all in my room.'

Lynda heard the words *my room* but the meaning only hit home when she was in the shower. It wasn't Sarah's room! It was her spare room and she wanted it back the way it should be – empty and tidy. She also wanted her cat to come home. As the water cascaded, she tried to reconcile her need for solitude with her desire to make up for her sins of the past. She knew she was being selfish and unfair, but she wished Sarah hadn't come back into her life. No! Not that. She wished Sarah had not needed somewhere to stay. They could have got to know each other slowly over a few weeks. This was too soon and too intimate.

By the time Lynda arrived home from work her head was thumping and she felt sick. It hadn't helped that the latest temp receptionist from the agency hadn't a clue what she was supposed to be doing, so she'd spent half the day going downstairs every five minutes to sort out the woman's many mistakes. How hard could it be to direct people to the right offices and put calls through to the correct people?

She was relieved to find her hallway empty of Sarah's belongings, and would have been even happier if the apartment had been quiet, but it wasn't. The television was blaring out some quiz show and she could hear Sarah yelling the answers at the screen.

Lynda reached up to straighten the mirror and caught sight of her face. Bloody hell, she looked as if she'd aged ten years in a day. She walked through to the lounge and stopped dead in the doorway.

'What have you done?' she whispered.

Sarah looked up. 'Oh, hi, I didn't hear you come in.'

'Never mind that, what have you done? You've moved my stuff.'

Lynda rushed over to the sideboard and started putting her ornaments and photos back where they belonged.

'Oh that!' Sarah said. 'I didn't have anything to do today, so decided I'd clean the flat to say thank you for letting me stay. I thought if I vacuumed up all the stray cat hairs my rash might go down. Then, when I'd finished that and the dusting, I couldn't remember exactly where everything went. Sorry, I didn't mean to upset you.'

'Please, don't touch things while you're here. I like everything to be kept in particular places. It . . . it upsets me if they get moved.'

'I'll try not to do it again,' Sarah said, laughing. 'I had no idea it would be a problem. I was trying to do something nice for you.'

Lynda forced herself to smile and turn back to face Sarah.

'Thank you. It was kind of you to clean, but I am a bit anal about where everything goes.'

'Well, if I'm going to stay here for a few days I'd better try to remember the right places for all your stuff.'

Lynda felt as if she'd been punched in the gut. 'A few days? It was just supposed to be for one night.'

'I know, but I checked my bank account today and got a massive shock. I've been relying on Maria subbing me for so long I hadn't realised how far in debt I am. My overdraft is right on the limit. I'm going to need to get a job before I can pay rent on an apartment.'

'But you said it would only be one night.'

'Lynda, please can I stay for just a few days more? Please! I don't really want to call on my family,' Sarah asked. 'I'll get a job tomorrow and move out as soon as I can. Will that be OK?'

Every atom in Lynda's body was screaming no, it wouldn't be OK, but what could she do? She could hardly throw Sarah out on the street with no money and no one else to turn to. She looked up to find Sarah smiling. Maybe it was her imagination, but that smile would have done the Cheshire Cat proud. She needed to get away before she let her imagination run away with itself.

'I have to go downstairs and talk to my neighbour. I'll see you later.'

Without waiting for an answer, she fled down to Georgina's

and rang her bell. Maybe a glass of wine would help her to put everything into perspective.

'Hi,' Georgina said as she opened the door. 'Does this mean we're going out for that drink later?'

'No!' Lynda said. 'I need a drink now. Do you have any of that wine left?'

Georgina opened the door wider and stood back to let Lynda pass by.

'Nope, not a drop left in that bottle, but I do have another chilling in the fridge.'

Chapter Sixteen

By the time she'd poured out her woes to Georgina, Lynda felt able to cope again.

'I have no idea how you do it, but you're able to bring me back down to earth,' Lynda said as she finished her second glass of wine. 'Maybe it's your sunshine kitchen, but I always feel more at peace after I've been in here.'

Georgina smiled. 'Always happy to listen, but I think you need more than a sounding board. What are you going to do about Sarah? She can't continue to live in your apartment if it's making you uncomfortable.'

Lynda sighed. 'I know. She has to leave, but at the same time I'm going to have to allow her time to get a job so that she has some money to pay for an apartment somewhere.'

Georgina shrugged. 'You're a nicer person than I am!'

If only you knew, Lynda thought. She smiled and took a sip of wine.

'Yes,' she said, 'you'd put her out onto the street without a second thought. I can't. I don't want to get into why I can't do that. I feel responsible for her. I wish Lucky would come back.

I think then the answer would be taken out of my hands. Apparently Sarah has a major allergy to cats. She showed me what she said was a rash on her arm, but it looked to me as if it was only red because she'd rubbed it.'

Lynda put her glass on the counter. 'Thanks for the wine and for listening. I'm going back upstairs to explain to Sarah why I was so tetchy this evening.'

Georgina stood up. 'Good luck. If you need more wine, come back down.'

Lynda opened her front door and felt as if she'd entered some-one else's home. There was nothing tangible she could put her finger on. All of Sarah's belongings were out of sight. Even the hall mirror was properly aligned, although she reached up to make sure, but there was something wrong with the atmos-phere. She took a deep breath and walked to the lounge. Sarah was curled up on one of the armchairs reading. She looked up as Lynda came in.

'Feeling better?' Sarah asked.

'About what?' Lynda felt irrationally angry at being ques-tioned. This was her place, not Sarah's, but she was the one sitting comfortably and acting as if she was in control.

Lynda walked over to the sofa and sat down.

'I'm sorry for the way I reacted earlier,' she said. 'I've had the worst day ever. Every single thing I tried to do seemed to go wrong. There was some weird person following me in a car while I was out running this morning, then I had a diffi-cult day at work, partly because our temporary receptionist is useless. I just hope the agency can send someone tomorrow who actually knows how to do the job.' She shrugged. 'Then I arrived home to find you'd moved things around in here and I freaked out. I'm sorry, I shouldn't have done that.'

'You certainly let me have it,' Sarah said. 'I was expecting a thank you and got an earful instead. Apology accepted. If I clean anywhere now, I'll make sure I put everything back in exactly the right spot.'

She picked up her book and opened it, looking hurt.

'Look, let's just let it drop, shall we?' Lynda said. 'It's been a long day. Let's face it; we're only just getting to know each other again after a long time of not being in touch.'

Sarah shrugged. 'I'm only here because you offered. I don't want to make you uncomfortable. Maybe I should go and sleep in my car.'

Lynda's brain was screaming at her to let Sarah go, so that she could get her life back in some sort of order. Leave her to sleep in her car. It wasn't her concern. She hadn't done anything wrong. But she couldn't do it. She owed her a bed for another night at the very least.

'Sarah, let it go. You don't need to go anywhere. I told you. I've had a shit day.'

'I can see you need some space,' Sarah said, getting up. 'I'm going for a walk.'

Lynda sank back down onto the sofa. She heard Sarah moving around in the spare room and then the welcome sound of the front door closing. At least she didn't slam it, Lynda thought. She tried to work up enough energy to go and fix herself something to eat, but it felt like too much effort. She was still sitting in exactly the same position fifteen minutes later when her phone rang. She reached out a hand for it and looked at the display. Greg.

I can't deal with him right now, she thought, but knew that wasn't fair to him. She swiped to answer and tried to make her voice welcoming, but she must have made a mess of it because Greg's voice was full of concern.

'Lynda? Are you OK?'

She felt tears welling up. 'Not really,' she said. 'It's been one of those days. I honestly shouldn't have bothered getting out of bed this morning.'

She tried to control her emotions, but ended up sobbing uncontrollably.

'I'm coming over,' Greg said. 'You shouldn't be on your own.'

'I'm fine,' Lynda said, wiping away the tears with the heel of her hand. 'Did you want something?'

'I'll tell you when I get there.'

'No!' she said, louder and sharper than she'd intended, but the thought of dealing with yet another person this evening was simply too much. 'Sorry, I need to be on my own right now.'

'Fine,' Greg said. Lynda could hear the hurt in his voice.

'Greg, I'm sorry. I'm not in a good place at the moment. What did you call for?'

'It was just to ask if you could open up on Saturday. I have an appointment I can't change so will be in an hour or so late to man the phones. Also, Amanda and Cassie are both coming in to talk to you.'

'Yes, of course I can open up. Did they say what they needed to talk to me about?'

'Nope. I had a call from Cassie to say she needed more input for the website and then Amanda rang about half an hour ago to say she needs to discuss setting up the accounts with both you and Cassie, so I thought it would make sense to get them both in on Saturday. I've told them to come in around lunchtime as I should be back by then.'

'OK, thanks.'

'I'll get there as soon as I possibly can,' Greg said, 'so that you're not on your own trying to man the phones and discuss the race at the same time.'

'Greg!'

'What?'

'I'm sorry for saying no tonight. I really do need to be alone.'

She had no sooner got the words out than the front door opened and Sarah called out.

'Hi, I'm back and I got us some fish and chips.'

'I thought you wanted to be alone?' Greg said.

'I'll explain on Saturday,' she said.

'You don't need to explain anything to me,' he answered and the phone went dead.

Lynda looked at the phone in her hand and realised she'd now upset Greg even more deeply than when she'd turned down his advances at the charity. She'd have to find a way to make it up to him.

The smell of fish and chips wafting through from the kitchen reminded her she hadn't eaten and had already downed two glasses of wine while she was with Georgina.

'You want yours on a plate or out of the paper?' Sarah called out.

'On a plate,' she said, getting up and heading to the kitchen. 'Let's set it up on the breakfast bar. I've a bottle of wine in the fridge crying out for glasses.'

Maybe the evening would end on a better note, but even if it didn't, it would take the edge off her truly horrible day.

Chapter Seventeen

Lynda put down her knife and fork and smiled.

'That was a brilliant idea,' she said. 'I haven't had fish and chips for such a long time. It was always a family favourite when I was younger.'

Lynda jumped when Sarah reached across and squeezed her hand.

'It must have been hard for you when your family died,' Sarah said.

'How did you know about it? Oh, I suppose you saw it in the paper. The local press pestered me for months afterwards.'

Sarah shook her head. 'No, I saw articles about it online. I told you I looked you up after I saw you on the TV. I suppose the press kept coming after you because the accident was only a few months after you'd been given that award.'

She *had* been constantly hounded by reporters, but that was partly her own fault. She shouldn't have argued with the police version of events during the inquest. Not that the coroner had listened to her either. Accidental death by careless driving was his verdict.

She watched, almost from a distance, as Sarah poured the last of the wine into their glasses. She was already feeling more than a bit light-headed and wasn't sure another glass was a good idea, but what the hell. She picked it up and took a good swig. Maybe it would help her to sleep through the night. Maybe it wouldn't. If she was drunk enough she wouldn't care.

'Lynda! Lynda!'

Vaguely aware of her name being called, she opened her eyes, suddenly aware that her cheeks were saturated with tears.

'Oh, God,' Sarah said. 'Did I bring up painful memories? I didn't mean to do that.'

Lynda shook her head. 'I wasn't even supposed to be in the car,' she said. 'Jason was meant to pick me up from work and we were all going to meet up for a meal in Peterborough, but he had to work late, so my dad stopped by to collect me. Jason was waiting at the restaurant for hours before he found out what had happened. The first he knew about it was when the police called the restaurant to get him to come to the hospital where I was having hysterics.'

'I can imagine,' Sarah said.

Lynda shrugged. 'I doubt you can.'

She realised Sarah still had her hand on hers and gently disengaged herself.

'I don't know about you, but I think I need a few more glasses of wine. What do you say?'

She stood up to walk to the fridge on legs that felt less stable than she'd expected them to be. Was she drunk? Maybe. Did she care? Not right now, no. She might regret it tomorrow, but tonight she intended to blot out the world with another bottle of wine. She opened the fridge and took it out. Turning, she raised the bottle in salute.

'Let's drink this one for my family.'

'I'm up for that,' Sarah said. 'Shall we take it through to the lounge?'

Lynda nodded and attacked the bottle with the corkscrew. After a few wrong turns she managed to liberate the cork.

'Bring the glasses,' she said, proud of the fact she hadn't slurred the words . . . well, not much.

She sat down at one end of the sofa and was surprised when Sarah ignored the armchair and sat down next to her.

'You pour,' Lynda said, passing Sarah the bottle. 'I don't think my hands are too steady right now.'

She watched as the liquid flowed from the bottle and then took a full glass from Sarah. She drained half the glass, and then very carefully, she placed it on a coaster on the coffee table.

'You know, Sarah, I'm glad you're here so I'm not on my own tonight. I'm sorry for what I said earlier.'

Lynda felt Sarah move closer to her.

'Thank you for saying that,' Sarah said. 'It means a lot to me. I want you to be OK with me staying here. I've had an idea about a job, but I don't want to say anything right now in case it doesn't pan out.'

She hadn't noticed it before but became aware of Sarah stroking her hand. The way she was caressing it felt good. It was soothing. Tingly too. Nice.

Sarah reached forward to pick up her own glass from the coffee table and Lynda felt a soft movement against her breast. That felt good too. It was a long time since anyone had been this close to her. Not since Jason had stormed out. Lynda wondered if Sarah was making a pass at her. If she was, would she mind? Nope. Not tonight. It was so comforting to sit here next to another human being. She'd missed the closeness.

Lynda reached for her wine and downed it in one. As she put the empty glass back on the coaster, she felt Sarah's arm move along the back of the couch. She shifted and melted into a comfortable warm embrace as Sarah's arm pulled her in closer. Sarah's breast was soft against Lynda's cheek. She felt like she could rest here forever. The hand stroking her neck was gentle and calming. So soft. So tender.

So this is what it was like to be embraced by a woman, Lynda thought, drifting dreamily on a tide of desire for more. She didn't want it to stop. She was floating. So many emotions to deal with. She was definitely turned on and wanted to explore these feelings. Or did she? This felt right and wrong at the same time.

'I've loved you since we were in our teens.'

The words were whispered so quietly, Lynda wasn't sure she'd heard them. She turned her head to look up. As she did so, Sarah leaned down and dropped a kiss on her brow. She felt Sarah's hand move from her neck and onto her breast. Agonisingly aware of the gentle stroking, Lynda almost stopped breathing.

Her body was screaming for Sarah to keep doing what she was doing. To do more. She couldn't speak, but Sarah must have got the message because she continued to stroke and caress Lynda's breast until her nipple felt like an electrical charge was running through it.

Lynda felt Sarah manipulating her body so that their faces

were just inches apart. She had never wanted anything as much as she wanted the sensations to continue. Then she felt Sarah's lips on hers and it suddenly felt so wrong.

'No!' she said, pulling away. 'I'm sorry. No, this isn't for me.'

She felt the wine mixed with the fish and chips churning in her guts. 'I think I'm going to be sick,' she said.

Sarah laughed. 'All you had to do was say no. There's no need to be rude about it.'

'I really do feel sick. Too much wine,' Lynda managed to say before staggering to the kitchen and throwing up in the sink.

Chapter Eighteen

Lynda woke up on Tuesday morning with a big bass drum pounding in her head. Her mouth was so dry she knew it would take gallons of water to deal with the dehydration. She thought about the dream that had recurred over and over during the night, trying to remember more details. She was underwater, struggling to undo her seat belt. Immediately before the crash something had happened, she was sure of it, but the more she tried to remember, the further away the images drifted. She'd slept fitfully, always waking at the same point.

She must have been totally plastered when she went to bed because she was still wearing her jeans and tee-shirt. Oh God, she hadn't even taken off her clothes!

Then it hit her. What a night. She'd led Sarah on and then run off to be sick. Her mind recoiled as memories flooded back. She'd enjoyed every second of the touching, but when it came to going the full distance, she had almost thrown up in Sarah's face. How the hell was Sarah supposed to take that? Oh God, she owed her a massive apology.

Lynda knew the best cure for a hangover was to get out of the clothes she'd slept in, put on her running gear and head out into the fresh air, but just the thought of getting up was too much for her. The room wasn't exactly spinning, but it wasn't entirely still either.

What had she been thinking last night? How could she have allowed things to go so far? Was that why Sarah had wanted to move in? Had she given her reason to think she was open to a deeper relationship? Well, if she hadn't before, after last night there was little doubt that Sarah would believe she was up for it. As she remembered the sensations when Sarah had touched her, Lynda's body responded by reminding her of the feelings those caresses had brought on. No way could she pretend to herself that she hadn't been a willing participant. So, the question was, did she want to explore further?

She remembered how she'd felt when Sarah had kissed her. No, that wasn't what she wanted. If she could, she'd turn back the clock and have Jason forever in her life and in her bed. That was what she really yearned for.

She stumbled out of bed, clinging to the wall as she made her way to the bathroom. She'd have to talk to Sarah. Apologise for giving her the wrong impression. But first she had to find a way to deal with her raging headache and roiling insides. She slid down to her knees and leaned over the toilet bowl. Maybe if she threw up she'd feel better, but although her body heaved, nothing came up.

Lynda dragged herself upright and moved to the washbasin to clean her teeth. Her face in the mirror showed the remnants of last night's make-up under her eyes. She looked like a moribund panda.

Cleaning her teeth made her feel a little better and removing the leftover make-up improved the way she looked. Determined to get to grips with the hangover, she headed to her bedroom to dress for a run. Never had she felt less like it, but deep down she knew she'd feel so much better afterwards. Although not really cold, she was shivering so put on her lightweight hoodie. Wearing it always made her feel closer to Jason. This morning, she needed that connection more than ever.

Her body was still trembling with the shakes when she opened the downstairs front door and headed out. Just don't throw up, she kept telling herself, and by the time she'd reached the three-kilometre mark the nausea had gone. She continued to run, slower than normal, but just to get it done.

As she turned into her street, Lynda called out to Lucky, but she was still nowhere to be seen.

Lynda tiptoed past Georgina's door and up the stairs, glad she didn't come out to speak to her. Until she'd spoken to Sarah, she didn't feel able to face her friend. She was still trying to compose in her mind the words she needed to open the conversation with Sarah when she reached her front door. Nothing she planned sounded quite right. She'd just have to come straight out and tell Sarah it had been a mistake. It wouldn't happen again.

She opened the front door to the welcoming smell of freshly made coffee. As she headed to the kitchen, she tried to calm her mind. Sarah was sitting at the breakfast bar. She looked up and smiled.

'Good morning. There's coffee in the cafetière. Did you enjoy your run?'

Lynda walked over and poured herself a cup. 'I did. Thanks. I needed it to help me deal with my hangover.'

Sarah laughed. 'I'm not surprised. You were totally out of it last night.'

Lynda sat down opposite Sarah. 'Yeah, about last night. I'm sorry I led you on.'

Sarah looked puzzled. 'What are you talking about? You had too much to drink, threw up in the kitchen sink and then went to bed.'

Lynda tried to smile. 'You're missing something out. I . . . I . . . Look, about what we did, or nearly did, last night, it can't happen again. It was nice, don't get me wrong, but it's not what I want from . . . It's . . . Sorry, it's just not for me.'

If anything, Sarah looked more puzzled than before. 'Lynda, what on earth are you going on about? It's not for me to control your drinking.'

'It's not my drinking I'm talking about. I'm talking about what happened between us. You know, you caressing me. Our almost kissing.'

Sarah stood up. 'Are you still drunk? Nothing like that happened.'

'Yes, it did. You cuddled up to me and we . . . we . . .'

'We what? Are you saying I came on to you?'

'Yes, you know you did. I'm not saying it was one-sided but, you know, it happened.'

Sarah laughed. 'You've got an inflated idea of your charms, Lynda. Nothing happened, but you sure have a vivid imagination. Are you trying to tell me you fancy me? Is that it? You want something to happen between us?'

Lynda shook her head. 'No! Don't mess with me. You know you touched me, so don't pretend you didn't.'

'Dream on, Lynda. I didn't touch you and have no desire to touch you. You're delusional. I'm going to go and shower. I need to go out and look for a job. If you're going to imagine things, then I think the sooner I get out of here the better it would be for both of us.'

Lynda watched her walk out of the kitchen. She wanted to call her back, scream at her to tell the truth, but even as she had the thought, she wondered if she *had* imagined the whole incident. Was she that drunk that she had dreamed it up after she'd gone to bed? No, surely not.

Her phone rang and she shuddered. If this was another of those calls, she didn't think she could take it. She picked up the phone and looked at the display. It was showing Jason's new number. She swiped to answer.

'Hi,' she said, 'you OK? This is early for you to be calling.'

'I know, but I thought if I left it until later you might make plans. I wondered if it would be OK to come over on Saturday evening. I'd like to talk to you.'

'What about?'

'Can I tell you on Saturday? It's not something I want to discuss over the phone.'

'This sounds serious.'

He laughed. 'It could be. Well, are you available or have you already made plans for the weekend?'

'My social life is not that hectic. We could go out for a drink,' she said.

'No, it would be better to stay home. What I have to say would need a proper discussion. I don't think we could do that in a bar or restaurant.'

'OK,' she said. 'What time on Saturday? I'll need to make sure Sarah goes out if it's that important.'

'Sarah?' Jason said. 'Who's Sarah?'

Lynda sighed. 'It's a long story. She's someone from my schooldays. I'll tell you when I see you.'

'I thought you'd lost touch with everyone from back then?'

'I did, but one of the girls I went to school with is staying with me for a few days. Just until she finds somewhere else to live.'

'Have you completely lost your mind? You said you'd got in with a bad crowd and deliberately hadn't kept in contact with any of them for that reason. Now you have some dodgy person living in our . . . your home?'

'She's not dodgy. I did say it was a long story. I'll tell you about it on Saturday.'

Lynda ended the call and looked at the time on her phone. Bloody hell, she was going to be late again. She put her cup in the sink and ran some water to rinse it, then added it to last night's dishes in the dishwasher. She slotted in the cleaning pod and switched the machine on. Damn, she had no time for breakfast.

As she went into the hall she saw the mirror wasn't quite in alignment. She straightened it and carried on to the bathroom, but the door was closed.

'Sarah, are you nearly finished?' she called, banging on the door. 'I need to get ready for work.'

The door opened and Sarah came out in a cloud of steam.

'Sorry,' she said, 'I had to wash my hair. I hope I haven't used up all the hot water.'

'Did you move the mirror?'

'What mirror?'

'You know very well what mirror. The one in the hall. The one you keep moving.'

Sarah laughed. 'Why would I do that?'

Lynda couldn't bring herself to answer. She went into the bathroom and shut the door, reminding herself that she owed Sarah, not the other way round. She stripped off and stepped into the shower cubicle. Within seconds of turning on the tap the water was running barely lukewarm. Not the greatest start to the day.

Once she was dressed and had on her make-up, she grabbed her car keys and left. As she passed Georgina's door she wished she had time to call in and chat with her friend. It felt as if so much of her life was falling apart, but talking things over with Georgina might help her to make sense of it all. She'd try to make time to see her that evening when she got home from work.

Looking up, she wondered if it was going to rain again. The damp street was a sure sign there'd been a downpour overnight. She was almost at her car when she spotted something under the windscreen wiper. As she approached, she saw it was a damp-looking envelope. It must have been put there the night before.

She lifted the wiper and picked the envelope off the screen. The font on the front of the envelope looked exactly the same as on the card that came with the plant.

With shaking hands, she opened the envelope and pulled

out another card. The drawing was identical to the earlier one, except that this time someone had printed **MURDERER** in capital letters across the top.

She went to tear it up, but saw there was a message on the back.

Lynda looked around and shivered. The message couldn't have been any clearer.

I'm watching you!

Chapter Nineteen

June 2022

After three days of constantly looking over her shoulder, trying to shake off the feeling of being watched, home was the only place where Lynda felt safe. She couldn't wait to get back to the apartment so she could relax. She just wished she had the place to herself. Every night she drove home rehearsing all the ways she could suggest to Sarah it was time to move out, but knew she wouldn't say any of the things she'd practised.

Still, she told herself as she parked, at least there hadn't been anything left on her car for the last few days. Pulling on the handbrake, she reached for her bag. As she did so, the sound of her phone ringing made her hesitate. She hadn't had any nasty calls for a few days, but the idea of another one was never far from her mind. She pulled the phone from her bag and looked at the screen. Number unknown. She denied the call, dropped the phone back in her bag and got out of the car.

She'd only taken a few steps when it rang again. Reaching into the bag she found her phone and decided to take the call. She couldn't hide away forever. Swiping to answer, she was annoyed to find her hands were shaking.

'Yes?'

'Hi, Lynda, it's Cassie.'

A feeling of such relief flooded through Lynda's body she felt as if she'd pass out.

'Hi, Cassie. What can I do for you?'

'Amanda and I wondered if you were free this evening? We've done quite a lot of work on the website and accounts, but need a bit more input from you. We can meet up whenever suits you.'

Just the thought of getting back into her car and driving anywhere made her feel tired.

'Why don't you come over to my place? You have the address.'

'That would be great,' Cassie said. 'I'll pick Amanda up and be at yours about half seven. That OK with you?'

Lynda's day had been back-to-back meetings and she really didn't want another one, but the charity needed the race weekend to be a success.

'Sure,' she said. 'That will be fine.'

She went into the apartment entrance hall and climbed the stairs to her flat. The last thing she wanted was to work on the race website and account set-up, but it had to be done so she decided to get it out of the way as quickly as she could.

Opening her front door, she looked immediately at the mirror. Was it out of alignment? She wasn't sure but reached out to straighten it anyway. As she did so Sarah came out from the guest room.

'Oh, for fuck's sake. I didn't touch it, you know!'

'I never said you did,' Lynda said. 'It's just one of my rituals.'

'You're obsessed, you know that, don't you?'

Lynda shrugged. 'I suppose I am, but you don't have to put up with me if I bug you.'

Sarah laughed. 'Oh, very subtle. Don't worry, I will be moving on as soon as I can. What do you feel like doing this evening? We can watch a film if you promise not to make a pass at me.'

Lynda ignored what felt like deliberate provocation. 'Actually, I have some charity stuff going on this evening with two of the volunteers, so I will need the place to myself. OK if you keep to your room?'

'How long for?' Sarah asked.

'I don't know. Could be half an hour, could be the whole evening.'

'Why can't I watch television and you have your meeting in the kitchen?'

Lynda took a deep breath. 'Because I don't know yet what the meeting is about. I haven't decided where we're going to hold it.'

'OK,' Sarah said, 'I'll stay out of the way of your visitors. I'm planning to have a nice long shower, if that's OK with you.'

Lynda decided it was time to lay down some house rules. Now or never.

'No, it's not OK. I am going to shower before you. There was no hot water this morning after you'd finished, so from now on, I go first every morning.'

Sarah shrugged. 'Fine by me,' she said. 'Give me a shout when you're done. As I'm not allowed to use the lounge, I'll download a film on my tablet to watch in my room.'

Lynda sighed as Sarah strode back to the spare room and shut the door with a snap. Ever since the night where they'd almost made out, Sarah had changed. There was something unnerving about her. Lynda shook herself and looked at her watch. She needed to get a move on if she was going to be ready before her visitors arrived.

By the time she'd dressed in tracksuit pants and a comfortable tee-shirt she was relaxed enough even to look forward to working on the charity event. Wondering if Cassie and Amanda would be expecting her to feed them, Lynda went through to the kitchen to have a look in the fridge. Apart from some cheese and cold meat, she couldn't see anything to offer them. Oh well, if they were hungry, she could always order some pizza.

Just before half seven the intercom buzzed. Lynda answered it and heard Cassie announce herself. She pressed the button to open the downstairs door.

'Come on up. I'm on the first floor,' she said.

She went to her apartment door and opened it ready to welcome her visitors.

'Thanks for letting us come over,' Amanda said, sounding slightly out of breath as she reached the top of the stairway.

'No problem at all,' Lynda said. 'Come on in. We can sit in comfort in the lounge or in the kitchen if it's easier to use the laptop and write notes.'

'The kitchen sounds perfect,' Cassie said, arriving just behind Amanda. 'This is a lovely old building. It must have been a massive house once upon a time.'

Lynda waited for them to pass her and then closed the door.

'Go into the first room on the right,' she said. 'I don't know when the houses in this road were converted, but I agree they must have been homes for fairly wealthy people in Victorian times. Please, take a stool.'

Cassie and Amanda sat side by side on one side of the breakfast bar. Lynda settled herself opposite.

'Before we start, would either of you like anything to eat or drink?'

'Not for me,' Cassie said.

'Nor me,' Amanda agreed. 'I can't stay too long so would rather get on with why we're here.'

'Of course,' Lynda said. 'What do you need from me?'

After half an hour of discussion, Lynda realised the charity couldn't have found two better people to take charge of the website and accounts for the race event.

'The website is looking amazing,' she said. 'When will it be able to go live?'

'Thank you!' Cassie grinned. 'Glad you like it. I think another week or so and I'll be happy to launch it.'

Amanda stood up. 'Would you mind if I used your bathroom before we leave?'

'Not at all,' Lynda said, standing and walking to the door so that she could point Amanda in the right direction.

As she went back into the kitchen, Cassie was putting her laptop away.

'I am so happy you offered your help. I don't think anyone could have done a better job for us. What made you want to get involved with this particular charity?' Lynda asked. 'You said it was because you saw my interview, but I know lots of charities make calls for help on that show.'

Cassie sighed. 'Your interview hit me on a personal level. Someone I loved committed suicide and I've always wondered what pushed him to take his own life. Maybe my helping out will save someone else from feeling that suicide is the only way out.'

Lynda stood rooted to the spot. She thought of Mark taking his own life. She'd driven him to it. She'd killed him as surely as if she'd stood behind him and pushed him in front of that train.

She couldn't move, couldn't speak, and was only released from her thoughts when Amanda spoke behind her.

'Sorry, Lynda, can I get through? I need to gather up my stuff.'

'Yes, of course, sorry,' Lynda said, moving out of the doorway.

Cassie stood up. 'It might be a good idea for me to spend a penny before I go. Where is it?' she asked.

Amanda pointed down the hall and then came back into the kitchen. Lynda felt like she was walking through treacle. Her legs refused to move properly. She stumbled towards the breakfast bar and sat down.

'Are you OK?' Amanda asked.

Lynda nodded. 'I'm fine. Just an unpleasant memory from the past rocked me for a minute.'

'I always think of you as one of the lucky ones in life.'

Lynda looked up; was that a note of bitterness in Amanda's voice?

'What do you mean?' she asked.

'Nothing! I didn't mean anything. It's just that you seem to have your life all nicely tied up. I'm happy for you.'

Lynda shrugged. 'There are lots of things in my life I'd like to change, decisions I'd make differently if I could go back in time.'

'You're not still harping on about taking John away from me, are you? I've long since put that in the past where it belongs.'

Although the words were positive, there was something in the way Amanda said them that didn't ring true. She definitely sounded bitter.

Shaking her head, Lynda shrugged again. 'I wasn't thinking of what happened with John, but of a time in my life before I even knew I'd be going to university. If I'd made a different choice back then, who knows how life might have turned out.'

'Sounds intriguing. What would you change?'

Cassie came back at that moment, saving Lynda from having to answer.

'I'll just pick up my laptop and we can go. I'm planning to come to the charity on Saturday to run over the changes I'll be making to the website,' Cassie said. 'What about you, Amanda?'

'Not sure yet,' Amanda replied. 'My gorgeous husband has offered to take me out to lunch.'

Remembering what had been divulged on Saturday about Amanda's marriage, Lynda couldn't help but look at Cassie, who frowned and very slightly shook her head, but Cassie needn't have worried. Lynda had no intention of letting Amanda know Cassie had said anything.

Lynda heard movement in the spare bedroom. Knowing Sarah was capable of creating a scene, she was relieved the meeting had already broken up, and ushered the two women towards the front door.

'Thanks again for letting us come over,' Cassie said, turning back towards Lynda. As she did so, she stood still, staring beyond Lynda down the hallway.

Lynda looked back to see what had caught Cassie's attention and saw Sarah standing outside the guest bedroom. She had already removed her make-up and the question mark-shaped birthmark stood out lividly, disfiguring one side of her face.

'What are you all staring at?' Sarah hissed.

'Nothing,' Amanda stammered. 'I mean, sorry. We're just leaving.'

Sarah covered her birthmark with her hand and turned away, but not before Lynda had seen the tears glistening in her eyes.

'I'm so sorry we upset your friend,' Amanda whispered.

'We wouldn't have done that for the world,' Cassie agreed, also keeping her voice low. 'I'm really sorry. It was unforgivable to stare, but that birthmark came as a shock. Isn't she the friend who came to the charity the same day we did?'

Lynda nodded.

'She covers that birthmark up really well,' Amanda said. 'I didn't see it that day.'

'She's learned how to do that over the years. We were at school together,' Lynda said. 'She was badly bullied over her birthmark, so understandably she's very sensitive about it.'

Lynda ushered the two women out, thankful to be able to close the door on what could have been an awkward discussion if they'd asked any questions. After locking the front door, she turned and walked along the hall to the spare bedroom. She tapped on the door and didn't know whether to be relieved or upset when Sarah refused to open it.

'I came to apologise, Sarah. Open up.'

'Leave me alone.'

Lynda stood outside for a few moments and was about to go back to the kitchen when the bedroom door opened. Sarah had covered her birthmark with make-up.

'I'm going out.'

'Would you like me to come with you?' Lynda said.

Sarah looked her up and down. 'You must be joking. You're the last person I need to be with right now, or have you forgotten how you let me down in the past? Now you've done it again. You let those stupid women laugh at me. It's no good pretending you care.'

'They weren't laughing,' Lynda said.

Sarah pushed past her and headed for the door. She turned back as she reached it. 'Yes, they were. They were laughing at me, the same way Hazel and her friends laughed at me. I swear, Lynda, there were times when I wish I hadn't met you, especially after you promised you'd be there for me and then let me down. But I guess—' she paused '—all things considered, we're even now.'

'What do you mean?'

Sarah laughed, but there was no humour in it. 'Wouldn't you like to know?'

As the door slammed, Lynda tried to work out what the

hell Sarah was talking about. Could Sarah really think Lynda had made up for not being there for her? Was that what she meant by being even? Or was she saying that she, Sarah, had done something equally awful as a payback for Lynda leaving her on her own? No matter how hard she wracked her brains, she couldn't fathom how Sarah could consider them even.

Lynda went to bed expecting to be awake for most of the night, but she fell asleep almost as soon as her head hit the pillow. She woke the next morning determined to find out what Sarah had meant.

She tapped on the guest-room door, but there was no answer, so she tapped again, louder this time.

'Sarah, please open the door. I think we should talk.'

'I have nothing to say to you.'

'Look, I'm going out for my run, but when I get back we need to clear the air. Okay?'

There was no answer, but then Lynda hadn't really expected one.

Going back to her own room she dressed to go for a run. She went into the bathroom to get her hoodie, but it wasn't hanging on the back of the door where it usually was. She thought she'd left it there, but she must have put it in the wash. She'd look properly for it when she came back. Today she didn't really need it as it wasn't that cold.

Maybe this morning she'd be able to find Lucky. Although she'd had the cat for only a few months, she was a massive part of her life and she missed Lucky terribly.

Once she was ready, she tapped again on the guest-room door.

'Leave me alone. I've already said I don't want to talk to you,' Sarah said.

'I realise that, but one way or another we are going to clear the air. See you when I get back.'

There was no answer, so Lynda headed out. She ran lightly down the stairs and reached the ground floor. As she arrived at the front door, she spotted an envelope on the mat. She went to pick it up and saw her name printed on the outside. Just *Lynda* – nothing more.

Her stomach turned somersaults as she reached down to grab it. Now what?

She opened the envelope and took out the slip of paper inside. There were no words, just a crudely drawn image of a hangman's noose.

Chapter Twenty

By Friday evening Lynda knew she was more in need of Penelope's calming influence than she had been for several months.

She sat in the waiting room unable to concentrate on anything other than the jumble of thoughts going round and round in her head. She was in such a deep funk that she didn't hear the door to the consulting room open and jumped when Penelope called her name.

'Sorry,' Lynda said as the magazine she'd had open on her lap slid to the floor. She reached down to pick it up and replaced it on the small table.

'Come through,' Penelope said.

Lynda sat herself on the armchair, but struggled to settle and kept fidgeting. Her usual feeling of being in a safe harbour was missing. She'd reached the stage of not knowing how she felt about anything any longer.

'So tell me,' Penelope said, 'do you want to start by going over the things we discussed last week?'

Lynda nodded, wondering if an hour would be enough

time to cover all that had happened since she'd last been here. Her hands shook so badly she had to grip them together in her lap. She tried to speak, but couldn't get any words to come out.

'Lynda, what has happened since I saw you last? You are even more on edge than when you first came to me.'

'I think I'm being watched by someone. No, I know I'm being watched. Whoever it is told me so.'

'Who?'

'I don't know.'

'Then how do you know?'

'They left a message on my car's windscreen saying so.'

'Do you have the card with you?'

Lynda was about to get the card from her bag and hand it to Penelope when she remembered the drawing on the other side. No way was she ready to discuss why the person thought she was a murderer.

'I don't have that card,' she said, 'but I have this one.' She took the hangman drawing from her bag and passed it across to Penelope.

'So now that's a plant and three unpleasant cards, one of which tells you that someone is watching you. Have you reported any of this to the police?' Penelope asked.

'Not yet,' Lynda answered. 'There's been so much going on over the last few days I haven't had chance.'

Penelope looked startled. 'I don't want to tell you what you should or shouldn't be doing, but it seems someone is targeting you and that isn't something that should be ignored.'

Lynda shrugged. 'I know, but I can't help feeling they'll treat me the same as they did after the car crash. They didn't believe me when I said something caused Dad's car to swerve. If only I could remember what happened.'

'The mind often shuts off memories after a trauma. It is entirely possible the events will come back into your mind one day.'

'I think they are starting to,' Lynda said, 'but only in my dreams. I wake up on the verge of knowing something, but not knowing what it is I should know.' She felt tears streaming down her face. 'I can't bear it. I want to remember! I know, I'm not coping very well.' Lynda said, taking a tissue and wiping the tears from her face. 'It's partly due to Sarah moving in with me and partly other stuff.'

'Sarah has moved in with you? How did that happen?'

'It just sort of happened,' Lynda said.

As she recounted the way Sarah had reached out for help, Lynda could hear how ridiculous it sounded. She'd opened up her home and her life because of the guilt she felt from her teenage years. It felt good to offload. The more she explained, the more she felt she'd been manipulated by Sarah.

'And then she made a pass at me, but denied it the next day.'

'She made a pass at you overtly or in a more subtle way?'

Lynda remembered how she'd felt at the time. 'It was full on and obvious she wanted more, but when I tried to talk to her about it the following morning, she insisted it was all a figment of my imagination. Just like the mirror she keeps moving. She says that's my imagination too, but I know it isn't.'

Penelope wrote something down and then looked up. 'Is this not the same as when Jason was living with you? I recall you telling me that you had accused him of constantly moving things, but he swore he hadn't done any such thing?'

'That was different,' Lynda said. 'I was under a lot of stress

124

when Jason was still with me. I felt then, and still do, that something had caused the accident where my family died, but no one believed me, not even Jason.'

'And you resented him for it?'

'Of course I did.'

Lynda watched as Penelope wrote something else in her notebook. Was she making notes about her state of mind?

'There's no comparison with what I was going through back then and what I'm dealing with now.'

'Lynda, I'm not suggesting you are imagining anything, but let's look at the situation and what that means for your stress levels. Someone intentionally upset you by leaving the plant and the cards. You have been receiving unpleasant phone calls. You feel you have been manipulated into taking Sarah into your home. That is a lot for anyone to have to deal with all at the same time.'

'I know, but that doesn't mean I'm imagining things. Sarah is definitely moving that mirror and lying about it. And she could be responsible for that,' she said, pointing to the card Penelope had placed on the small table next to her.

'Where did you find it?' Penelope asked.

'I found it when I went down for a run. It could have been pushed under the outer door of the flats. But it's possible Sarah had put it there the night before.'

'What makes you think so?'

Lynda told her about the argument they'd had.

'She was feeling pretty angry with me. I can't say I blame her either. Cassie and Amanda saw her without any make-up on and she was really distressed over their reaction, but she was already mad at me before that. She went out that evening and then the next morning I found the envelope in the hall.'

'Did you challenge her over it?'

Lynda shook her head. 'If she did it, she'd deny it, just like she denies moving the mirror, but I know she does. If she didn't do it, I don't want her to know anything about it because I think she'd use the knowledge to get at me in some way. She's also taken my hoodie and hidden it.'

'Why do you think she has done that?'

'Do you mean why has she done it, or why do I think she's done it?'

Penelope smiled. 'Both. What makes you think she has taken it?'

'It was hanging on the bathroom door when she went in there to shower the night we had the argument, but was gone when I went to put it on the next morning.'

'And what reason would she have for doing this?'

'I confronted her when I got back from my run, but she denied all knowledge of it. She even accused Cassie and Amanda of taking it.'

'Who are Cassie and Amanda? You keep mentioning them.'

'They are helping with the charity running event and had been over to my place the night before. Sarah used that to deflect from herself. I think she's hidden it somewhere and wants me to stress out because I can't find it. Funnily enough, all her antics are actually helping me. I know what she's doing, so it's easier to cope with stuff being moved or going missing. I think things through while I'm running and try to work out what she might do next.'

Once again, Penelope wrote something down. Lynda felt like reaching out and grabbing her notes to see what she'd written. She dug her nails into her palms to prevent herself from moving.

'Does running relieve your stress?' Penelope asked.

Lynda sighed. 'Not as much as I'd like. I have to get into the shower first or there isn't any hot water. I am convinced Sarah deliberately leaves it on longer than necessary. When Jason was living with me, we never had a problem with the hot water supply. Also, when I've been out for a run, it's been spoiled a couple of times by some idiot driving up close to me. I think he might have been following me.'

Penelope picked up her pen.

'Look, if you're going to add those two items to the list of things you think I'm imagining, then you might as well add the fact that even my cat has deserted me.'

'I'm not making a list of any kind. I hope you would know that. I'm making notes of the things that are causing you distress so that we can work through them. I will certainly add your missing cat to my notes.'

For the first time, Lynda felt like smiling. 'Don't bother with that one. Lucky has gone off before. She'll be back when she's good and ready. Aren't cats supposed to be canny? Maybe she had a sixth-sense premonition and knew about Sarah coming, so she ran off for a while. I wish I could do the same.'

She left Penelope, wondering yet again why she found it so difficult to be completely honest with her. She wasn't coping well with anything, so why pretend she was? Why couldn't she bring herself to show Penelope the train cards and tell her about Mark's suicide? But she knew the answer to that. She'd been called a murderer and that's exactly how she saw herself. She hadn't physically pushed him, but she might as well have done.

Chapter Twenty-One

On Saturday morning Lynda felt like death on legs after yet another disturbed night. What was it that her subconscious was trying so hard to tell her? Her dreams were all about the car crash and what happened afterwards, but never about the few moments before her dad had swerved off the road. The bend was known to be a driving hazard and the police and everyone else felt her dad had to have been driving too fast, or not paying attention, but Lynda was certain something had happened to make him swerve. If only she could remember what it was.

She usually felt better on Saturdays after seeing Penelope the previous evening, but for some reason this week that hadn't happened. At least she had the charity to go to this morning. Helping people who were in a far worse situation than she was would put her problems into perspective.

First, though, she needed to get out for some much-needed exercise. After finding the hangman's noose drawing, she'd been too shaken to want to go out.

She put on her running gear, annoyed that her favourite

hoodie was still missing. She was tempted to give up the run to search for it yet again, but knew she needed to get out on the road for her mental health. She'd confront Sarah again when she got back.

She headed downstairs, wondering if her legs would protest after not running for a few days. Once she was on the road she realised she needn't have worried. Her adrenaline was pumping and she felt good. Every step bounced her into a better place. Surely Sarah would be gone soon.

She was so preoccupied with her thoughts she wasn't aware of the car trailing her until the engine sound penetrated. She looked behind her and saw the same dark blue car as the previous occasions. Speeding up, she darted down a side street and doubled back on the way she'd come. If she went down a couple of pedestrianised roads she'd soon lose the driver.

Lynda managed to shake him off, but was left once again with a feeling of disquiet. Why was this weirdo picking on her? Was he the person who had left the plant and the notes? But if so, why?

As she opened the main door into the apartments, struggling to get her breath back, she knew she needed some space before going up to her own apartment, which no longer felt like home. If only Lucky would come back, that might make Sarah decide to move out.

Hoping that Georgina might have seen her cat and taken her in, she knocked on her friend's door.

'Any sign of Lucky?'

Her heart sank when Georgina shook her head.

'This is the longest she's stayed away,' Lynda said, trying not to sound paranoid. 'I'm getting worried about her. I keep looking while I'm out running, hoping I'll see her and can get her to follow me.'

'I'm sure she'll be back soon,' Georgina said. 'She's disappeared for a few days before and never looked the worse for wear when she came back. How's it going upstairs?'

Lynda shrugged. 'Can I come in?' she whispered.

'That sounds very mysterious,' Georgina said, standing back and beckoning her inside. Lynda passed her and headed for the kitchen. She sat at the breakfast bar and waited for Georgina to sit opposite.

'I'm really sorry,' Lynda said. 'You must think I've been avoiding you.'

Georgina laughed. 'It's only a couple of days, but I did wonder. I guessed your visitor was taking up your time.'

Suddenly, even though she thought she'd dealt with her emotions the evening before with Penelope, Lynda felt the need to offload. She told Georgina of Sarah's pass at her and then her refusal to admit anything had happened.

'I feel so trapped,' she said. 'It's like being in quicksand and unable to escape. I'm convinced she keeps moving my hall mirror just to screw with my mind. What's more, my hoodie is missing. I think she's taken it.'

'What about the weird phone calls? Are you still getting them?'

Lynda shrugged. 'Only occasionally when I'm at work. I was getting them in the evening as well, but now it's only during the day.'

Georgina opened her mouth, then shut it again.

'You look as if you were going to say something. What is it?'

She shook her head. 'It's probably nothing.'

'Try me.'

Georgina put her head on one side as if she was thinking about what to say.

'I just find it a bit odd that before Sarah moved in you were getting calls in the evenings as well as during the day, but now you only get them during work hours.'

'What are you saying?' Lynda asked.

'Probably nothing, but if it was Sarah making the calls she'd need to do it when the two of you weren't together. That's all.'

'But why would Sarah do that? She's got what she wanted.'

'Which is?' Georgina asked. 'What did she really want from you?'

'Somewhere to live,' Lynda said. 'I think her getting in touch was all part of a scam to get me to take her in because she was having problems with Maria and knew she was going to need somewhere to live.'

Georgina shrugged. 'The phone calls might have nothing to do with Sarah, but it does strike me as weird that you've never received one when she's been in the same room.'

Lynda was still thinking about Georgina's words when she pulled up outside the charity a couple of hours later. Was it possible that Sarah was the one making the calls? What would she gain from it? More to the point, what would anyone gain from it? Were they doing it just to frighten her?

Thinking of that brought back to mind the confrontation

she'd had with Sarah over the missing hoodie. Lynda had turned the apartment upside down looking for it this morning and had even insisted on going through everything in Sarah's room, but there'd been no sign of it. Sarah had stood to one side smirking, as if she knew exactly where it was.

She was still thinking about it when she heard the lock turning. Looking up, she saw Greg come in, but almost didn't recognise him. He was wearing heavy-framed glasses.

'I didn't realise you wore glasses,' Lynda said.

Greg turned to close the door. When he turned back again Lynda thought he looked annoyed, but maybe it was just because he didn't look his normal self.

'I've needed glasses my entire life,' Greg said, coming into the room. 'Is it a problem? Should I have asked your permission?'

At first Lynda couldn't understand why he sounded so aggressive, but then she remembered their last conversation when he'd wanted to come over to comfort her and she'd told him she wanted to be alone. He'd heard Sarah come back and call out about the fish and chips. The same night Sarah had made a pass at her, but still refused to admit it.

'Of course you don't need my permission. Look, Greg, about the night you called me.'

'Forget it,' he said. 'You made it quite clear I wasn't welcome. No need to drag it up again.'

'No, please, let me explain,' she said and proceeded to fill him in on the situation with Sarah. 'So now I'm stuck with her until I can get her to move out.'

'Why didn't you say when I was on the phone?'

Lynda smiled, relieved to be back on normal terms with

Greg. 'You didn't give me the chance, if you remember. So, tell me, why are you wearing glasses? They suit you, by the way.'

Greg shrugged. 'I usually wear contacts, but my eyes have been reacting to them just recently. You wouldn't have said the glasses suited me if you'd seen me at school. The ones I had to wear back then were so thick I was the target of every bully who wanted an easy prey to pick on.'

Lynda felt the familiar flush of shame when she recalled how Sarah had been tormented over her birthmark.

'That must have been hard to deal with,' she said.

Greg shrugged. 'I didn't deal with it. I turned in on myself just to get through each day. I've had lens implants and laser surgery since then, but I still need contacts or these glasses, so you can imagine how bad my eyesight was when I was at school. It's a wonder I survived. No one from those days would ever recognise me now, but I've never forgotten those who picked on me.'

There was an acid tone in Greg's voice that wasn't normally there.

'I'll tell you my life story one day,' he said. 'It doesn't make for easy listening. Still, I became who I am now, which makes me stronger than all the idiots who tried to destroy me. It's why I founded this charity. I wanted to help others get their lives back. But you know this.'

They worked through the day, answering calls and planning the logistics of the marathon. Lynda would be running in it, so wouldn't be able to be part of the team on the day, but there was still lots she could do to help between now and then. One thing was to get posters printed to advertise it.

'I can also get on to our local radio again. They were really helpful when we needed volunteers,' Lynda said, 'so I'm sure they would give me another slot to drum up entrants for the three races.'

'I believe Cassie and Amanda came over to your place during the week,' Greg said. 'Did you cover everything, or are they still coming in today?'

'Cassie is, but I don't know about Amanda. In fact, I think I hear Cassie's voice outside.'

A few seconds later the door opened and Cassie came in. 'Only me today,' she said. 'I just called Amanda, but she says she's going out to lunch with her husband. There's little more she can do until the website goes live and start getting entries anyway.'

Lynda stood up. 'OK if Cassie and I go through to the other room, Greg?'

He nodded. 'No problem at all. I can handle the calls on my own. Take as long as you need.'

Lynda followed Cassie into the other room and closed the door. Cassie put her laptop on the table and opened it up.

'I've pretty much finished all the back-end work, but I'd like you to take a look at the front end to make sure I've covered everything we talked about in the week.'

'I'm sure you did,' Lynda said. 'You've done an incredible job. You and Amanda both have been amazing.'

Cassie shrugged. 'I don't know if Amanda will stick with it.'

'What makes you say that? She seemed to be keen enough in the week.'

'It's something she said to me when we were leaving your place,' Cassie said. 'Please don't think I'm talking out of turn, but I . . . never mind. Let's get on with the website.'

'Is it something the charity could help with?' Lydia asked.

Cassie shrugged. 'Look, this has to be in complete confidence, but I think she's being abused by her husband. He keeps such a tight watch on everything she does. I've only known her since we both came here in response to your television interview, but I've spent a bit of time with her as we needed to coordinate on the website and accounts.'

'And?' Lynda said.

'Let's just say I had a lot of experience dealing with abusive and controlling men when I was younger. Amanda's husband fits the bill in every respect. She has to tell him where she's going, who with and how long for. She can't go out without him, even just with girlfriends, not that I think she has any, to be honest.'

'Would it help if Greg or I talked to her?'

Cassie shook her head. 'No! You can't tell her what I've said. She trusted me and I shouldn't have said anything. I've only told you now because I think the charity might need to look elsewhere for an accountant. Even if she wants to carry on, I have a feeling her husband will do everything he can to stop her. I bet that's why he picked today to take her to lunch. He knew we'd arranged to come here. Look, I'm not comfortable talking about Amanda. Shall we get on with the website?'

Lynda nodded, but her thoughts were reeling. Surely there must be something they could do to help Amanda.

They spent the next half hour going over aspects of the website with Lynda understanding only about a quarter of everything Cassie said, but it was clear the young woman knew exactly what she was doing.

'When do you think it can go live?' Lynda asked.

'Leave it with me for another week,' Cassie said. 'I just want to test everything to make sure there are no bugs or glitches. What if we meet up here again next week? If we're both happy, it can go live then.'

Cassie packed the laptop away and then paused. 'Please don't mention anything to Amanda. I'm sure she'll let you know if she decides to quit.'

'I might need to tell Greg to look around for someone. The accountant who looks after the charity's affairs has made it clear he doesn't want to take on the books for the race event.'

'Don't tell him yet. Let me chat with Amanda and see how she feels.'

'OK, but I'd really like to get someone in place before we go live.'

'Next Saturday OK? Can you hold off until then?'

Lynda agreed and they both went back to the main office.

'Bye, Greg,' Cassie said. 'See you next week!'

Greg waited until the door closed behind Cassie.

'How did it go? You happy with everything?'

'Yes, Cassie has done an amazing job,' she said, wishing she could prepare Greg for the fact that Amanda might be bailing on them, but she'd given her word to Cassie, so she kept quiet.

'I've made a list of all the things we discussed earlier,' Greg said. 'Do you want to go for a drink later so we can work on the event some more?'

The invitation felt more like an olive branch than a come-on. Lynda smiled.

'I'd love to, but I can't because Jason is coming over tonight. He says it's important, or I'd put him off.'

She saw Greg's expression change. The last thing she wanted to do was upset him again. It had taken most of the morning to get back to their normal easy working relationship.

'Look, what about tomorrow? We could meet for a drink in the evening?'

The moment she said the words, she wished she hadn't. Greg's whole face lit up.

'Great,' he said. 'I'd love that!'

Chapter Twenty-Two

Lynda arrived home still trying to figure out how she'd been stupid enough to offer Greg the encouragement he'd been wanting for so long. As she entered, she automatically put up her hand to straighten the mirror and was shocked to see how out of alignment it was. Up until now it had only needed a tiny touch to put it right after Sarah had moved it, but this time it was way off line. She had to get Sarah out!

She put it straight and then headed to her bedroom. She needed a shower and to relax a bit before Jason arrived. Over her bed, she had two prints of the fens. They were almost mirror images of each other, but both were just fractionally out of alignment. Lynda knew that no one else would have noticed it, but she was certain they had been moved. This was too much!

'Sarah,' she called. 'Have you been in my bedroom?'

A few moments later Sarah appeared in the doorway. 'In here? No. Why would I come in here?'

'These two prints have been moved.'

'Not by me. Besides, they look perfectly straight.'

Lynda shook her head. 'No, they are crooked. Look at them.'

Sarah came and stood next to Lynda. 'Nope, you're wrong. They're dead straight.'

Lynda suddenly felt Sarah was too close and took a step back.

'Maybe you're right,' she said. 'I told you, didn't I, that Jason is coming over tonight?'

'Yep. You said I had to make myself scarce.'

'I never said any such thing.'

Sarah laughed. 'You might not have used those words, but that's what you meant. Anyway, I've got things to do this evening, so I won't be in your way. What do you think he wants?'

'No idea,' Lynda said, but she'd been wondering the same thing. Was it possible they could give their relationship another chance? Is that what Jason was hoping for? It was definitely what she wanted to happen.

She hadn't realised, but while she'd been thinking, Sarah had taken a step towards her. There was barely any space between them. Lynda moved back and found herself up against the wardrobe door.

'I need to have a shower and get changed,' she said, expecting Sarah to move, but she stood her ground.

'What time is he coming?' Sarah said.

Had she moved again? Lynda felt trapped. Claustrophobic. She took a step to the side to put space between them. Sarah reached out and touched Lynda's arm.

'What's wrong?' she asked. 'You look terrified. Are you scared of me?'

'No, of course not,' Lynda said, hoping Sarah didn't hear the tremor in her voice. 'I'm tired. That's all. It's been a tough week.'

Sarah smiled. 'Life is tough,' she said, trailing her finger down Lynda's arm. 'I'll leave you to get ready.'

As she left the room, Lynda wondered if she'd imagined it, but Sarah's smile had looked like a threat.

Lynda was relieved to find Sarah had gone when she came out of the shower. She slipped on some black jeans and a pale blue tee-shirt. As she sat down to put on her make-up, she glanced in the mirror and could see the reflection of the two prints above her bed. This time she wasn't quite as certain. Had they been moved again? If they had, it wasn't by much, she thought, as she got up to straighten them. Surely, after what she'd just said to her, Sarah wouldn't have moved them. Or would she?

She had to get her life back in some sort of order. Sarah had to go so that Lynda could regain her peace of mind.

Chapter Twenty-Three

That evening Lynda opened the door to Jason and had to stop herself from falling into his arms. He looked every bit as gorgeous as when she'd seen him last.

'Hi,' he said, leaning down to kiss her cheek. 'I come bearing gifts.' He lifted up a bottle of Faustino V. 'I take it you still drink this?'

Lynda smiled and moved back to let him come in. 'I do indeed. I haven't cooked, but we could order a takeaway to go with it.'

'Sounds good to me,' Jason said.

She followed him to the kitchen and tried not to get annoyed as he rummaged in the drawer without asking.

'What are you looking for?'

'Corkscrew. It used to be kept in here.'

'No, it didn't,' Lynda said. 'It's always been in the next drawer.'

Jason looked up. 'You sound annoyed. Should I have asked first? I did used to live here.'

Lynda shrugged. 'Used to. Not *do* live here. You moved out, if you remember.'

'Touché,' Jason said. 'Let's not fight. I should have asked. I'm sorry. Is it OK to get down two glasses?'

'Is that sarcasm?'

He smiled. 'No, not at all. It was a genuine question.'

'Go ahead,' Lynda said. 'The glasses are where we always kept them.' She went through to the lounge and grabbed the phone from her bag. 'What do you fancy to eat?' she asked as she came back into the kitchen. 'I fancy Chinese, but we can order whatever you want.'

'Chinese sounds good to me. Want to choose a menu for two?' he suggested. 'You know I'll eat anything, so go for whatever suits you.'

Lynda tapped the app and placed the order.

'It will be here in half an hour,' she said. 'Shall we have a glass while we're waiting?'

It felt so right being in the kitchen with Jason. How on earth had they reached the stage where he'd stormed out? But she knew the answer to that: she'd driven him away.

'Where's this wonderful cat I've heard so much about?' Jason asked. 'I take it that's her bed.'

Lynda sighed. 'She's been gone for almost a week now. I'm starting to worry about her. Georgina, my friend from downstairs, thinks she's semi-feral and has gone off hunting, but she might have a second family somewhere to share her affections with, although the state she was in when I found her didn't point to that being the case.'

She wanted to ask if he liked cats, but thought it would sound as if she was inviting him back to live. Although she wanted that more than anything, they weren't at that stage yet.

'Let's go and sit in the lounge,' she said. 'We can come back here when the food arrives.'

Jason picked up his glass and the bottle. Lynda let him go through first. She wanted to see where he chose to sit. As she'd guessed, he went straight to the armchair that used to be his.

'How are things with you?' he asked. 'I was surprised to hear you had that old school friend of yours living here.'

'She was once my closest friend, but I hadn't seen her in about fourteen years. Her moving in here wasn't exactly my choice,' she said, 'but I felt I owed her.'

'For what?'

Lynda told him about Hazel and the bullying and how she hadn't been there for Sarah when she'd promised to be.

'I didn't feel I had any option other than to offer her a place to stay, but now it feels like she's been here forever. She's taken over my life. I'm convinced she's been moving things just to wind me up.'

Jason looked as if he wanted to say something, but the intercom sounded.

'That must be our food,' Lynda said. 'Hold your thought. You can tell me what it was you wanted to say while we're eating.'

She opened the door and ran downstairs to the main entrance. The smell of the food made her hungry the moment the driver handed over the bag.

'Thank you,' she said, slipping him a tip.

Upstairs, she put the various cartons on the breakfast bar and took out two plates.

'Bring the wine and glasses through,' she called out.

'Wow! It's just as well I'm hungry,' Jason said as he settled himself on one of the stools.

'I know,' Lynda said, thinking how good it was to have him there. 'It's only meant for two, but there's enough here for four people, I think.'

Silence reigned while they helped themselves to the food, then Lynda touched Jason's arm.

'You wanted to say something, but were saved by the bell. What was it?'

He put his head on one side. 'Promise not to take offense?'

'I'll try not to, but I'm not offering any guarantees.'

Jason sighed. 'It's about Sarah moving things. Are you sure she's doing that?'

'I'm not certain, no, but . . . oh, I see what you're getting at. You think it's like it was between us.'

Jason swallowed what was in his mouth. 'You did accuse me of some outlandish things,' he said.

Lynda sighed. 'I know,' she said, 'but this is different.'

'In what way?'

'To start with, I should have told you before, but I've been in therapy for a while now.'

Jason looked surprised. 'I'm glad,' he said.

'It made me realise that I've been really unfair to you. I blamed you for things that had nothing to do with you. Accused you of stuff I now know you would never have done.'

He picked up his glass and took a sip. 'You were grieving. I should have been more understanding, but the effect the grief had on your OCD tendencies pushed me further and further away.'

Lynda reached over and touched his hand. 'I know. I also

144

know now that I was experiencing survivor guilt, but didn't understand that at the time. I also resented you still having your family. I don't mean I wanted you to lose yours, but I was angry that I'd lost mine and somehow angrier that you hadn't. That doesn't even make sense, does it?'

'Yeah, it does. In a funny way I got it and really wanted to help you, but you seemed to blame me even for breathing at times.'

'I know, but as I said at the beginning, the way I blamed you for everything is not the same way I feel about Sarah. I really think she is messing with my mind.'

'By moving things?'

Lynda nodded. 'That and other stuff. I can't explain it, but sometimes she scares me.'

'In what way? Is she threatening you?'

'Not exactly, but she crowds me. She invades my personal space. I wish I could find a better way to put it into words. I just feel uncomfortable with her being here.'

'Then tell her to leave.'

Lynda wished Jason could see things from her point of view. 'I have asked her to move out, but she hasn't been able to find anywhere in her price range. I can't just put her out on the street. Don't ask me why, I just can't.' She smiled. 'Let's not waste any more time talking about Sarah. You said you had something to discuss with me. What is it?'

'I've been offered a promotion,' he said.

Lynda was genuinely pleased for him, but couldn't see why he needed to talk about it with her. 'And you're telling me because?'

Jason laughed. 'Trust you to get straight to the point. I was presented with the opportunity of taking over the London office and I jumped at it.'

'Wow! That's brilliant news, but I'm going to come back to my original question. What's this got to do with me?'

'Nothing at the moment, but maybe . . . Let me start again from the beginning.'

Lynda smiled. 'Now that's a good idea. I might understand you then.'

He laughed. 'You're right. OK, here goes, I was offered the position a couple of weeks ago and of course I'm going to take it. In fact, I start on Monday. I'll be one of the daily commuters heading off to the Smoke bright and early each morning, but that's not something I want to do for the rest of my life.'

'What other option is there?' Lynda asked.

Jason shrugged. 'This is where you come in.'

'I don't see how,' she said.

'I'm thinking of moving to London to live, but it hit me – that would mean the end of any chance for us to get back together. If there's even a small hope, I would rather continue to commute, but if we're completely over then I'll start looking for a place to live in London. So, my question is this: is there a chance for us? Should I commute or move?'

Chapter Twenty-Four

The question was so out of the blue Lynda felt as if she'd been punched. Of course she hoped there was a chance they could get back together, but this felt too much like a gun to her head.

'I can't make that decision for you. It's not fair of you to ask me.'

'I'm not asking you to make the decision,' he said. 'I'm just asking if there was a chance for us. That's not the same thing at all.'

'Jason, I love you. I don't think I'll ever stop, but you can't throw the move or commute question at me and expect an instant answer. What do *you* want to do?'

He shrugged. 'I don't know and that's the honest truth. I really hope we could try again, but when I think of the way we parted I kinda feel there's no point. We made each other miserable towards the end. I don't know if it would be the same if we got together again, or if we'd be more like we were in the beginning. What do you think?'

'About what? You moving to London, or us making each other miserable?'

'About me moving to London or commuting,' he said.

'I think you should do whatever feels right for you. If we're meant to be together, we'll find a way. If we can't manage it, then maybe it wasn't meant to be.'

He raised his eyebrows so far they almost disappeared into his hairline.

'That's a bit fatalistic,' he said. 'What happened to your certainty about everything? There was a time when you would make a statement and then stick to it doggedly even when you must have known you were in the wrong.'

Lynda wanted to tell him to get stuffed, but she was honest enough to know he was telling the truth.

'I've sort of lost my sense of certainty about everything at the moment.'

'Because of this Sarah woman?'

She nodded, wanting to tell him about the cards, the weird phone calls and the feeling of being watched whenever she left the apartment, but now wasn't the time.

'I don't know what to say. I wish I could put it right for you.'

She felt tears filling her eyes and looked at him through a blur.

'I know. You always did have the knight in shining armour syndrome lurking.'

He sat up straighter. 'What's that supposed to mean?'

'I didn't mean anything by it, but you do have a tendency to believe in the male being the protector of the species.'

'There's nothing wrong with that,' he said.

'Except it can be a bit irritating to be made to feel incompetent.'

'I have never made you feel that way!'

Lynda laughed. 'You really believe that?'

He looked angry for a moment, then joined in with her laughter. 'OK, I admit I can come across a bit heavy-handed at times, but I never meant to make you feel incompetent. Let's change the subject. Are you still running? I miss our regular runs together. It's not as much fun going out on my own.'

She smiled. He was right. It used to be a shared pastime; now that she was running on her own she had to admit it did sometimes feel a bit lonely.

'I haven't run as much as I should.'

'Oh, why's that? You were always the one who forced me to get up and go.'

Lynda laughed. 'I did not!'

'Yes, you did, but that doesn't answer my question. Why aren't you running as much as you should?'

Lynda told him about the weird man in the car who'd tried to follow her a few times, although she really didn't want to go into the details of everything else that was troubling her.

'You shouldn't be running on your own. I think I should come over and run with you. I'd soon sort out whoever the idiot is. I'd teach him to leave you alone.'

'And here you go again with your Superman attitude. Don't you think I can deal with this myself?'

'Well, obviously you can't or you wouldn't have mentioned it.'

She clenched her fists. 'My turn to ask: what's that supposed to mean?'

Jason frowned. 'Isn't it obvious? You brought it up, so it must be bothering you. If it's bothering you, it means you haven't dealt with it.'

'And you want to swoop in like my saviour and protect me from the nasty man? Why do men always think women can't fix their own problems? I don't want a bodyguard, thank you very much.'

'Well, what do you want? You wouldn't even give me a straight answer when I asked if you wanted to give us another chance.'

She jumped to her feet. This was so unfair. 'No, you put a bloody gun to my head and tried to get me to decide if you should commute or move to London. You want an answer? Here it is. Move to London.'

Jason stood up. 'You've made your feelings very clear. I should have known you weren't ready to act as a grown-up.'

'Me? At least I'm capable of deciding where I want to live.'

'Yes, here on your own. You've now made sure I know that!'

'I never said anything like that, but since you've raised it, yes, I want to live here on my own.'

She looked up and could see the hurt on his face. 'Jason, I didn't mean that. Let's not fight. I'm sorry. I shouldn't have said those things about you having a Superman complex.'

'Why not? It's obviously what you think.'

She could feel the tears welling up again. 'I don't know what I think at the moment. I'm not even sure I'm capable of thinking.'

He took a step towards her and held out his arms. She melted into them.

'I didn't mean to present you with an ultimatum,' Jason said. 'I want you to know that I love you and would give anything for us to make a go of things, but we're clearly too far apart at the moment. I'm going to commute for a couple of months.

Maybe we can go on a few dates. Get to know each other all over again. Let's see what happens. How does that sound?'

Lynda hugged him. 'I'd like that. I'm sorry I snapped at you.'

He leaned down and kissed her forehead.

'I'm going now, but maybe we could go out for a meal tomorrow night. What do you say?'

'I can't tomorrow. I have a meeting with Greg from the charity.'

'Can't you change it?'

Although there was nothing she'd rather do than put Greg off, she knew it wouldn't be fair to him.

'We could have lunch,' she suggested.

Jason shook his head. 'I promised my mum I'd go to hers for Sunday lunch.'

She was about to point out that since neither of them could change their arrangements maybe they should put it off for a week, when she heard the front door open.

'It's only me,' Sarah called out.

'Want me to deal with her? Superman to the rescue,' Jason whispered and winked.

Lynda laughed. 'That won't be necessary.'

They moved apart as Sarah came into the room.

'Sorry, am I interrupting something? I'm Sarah, and you must be Jason.'

Lynda felt the atmosphere change. It was almost like a Mexican stand-off, so clear that each of them had taken an instant dislike to the other. Jason said hello and then turned to Lynda.

'I'd best be off. We'll sort out a good day for that dinner. No need to come to the door. I know my way out.'

Chapter Twenty-Five

Lynda went to the door anyway. She didn't want him to leave without a proper goodbye. She didn't know whether to be annoyed or relieved that Sarah had come back when she had. She and Jason had a lot to sort out, but for the first time she felt there was a chance their broken romance could have a positive outcome.

'Take care of yourself,' he said. 'If you're ever in need of Superman, you have my number.'

Jason leaned down and kissed her gently on the lips. Only the knowledge that Sarah could appear at any moment stopped her from grabbing him and dragging him into the bedroom.

'You take care, too,' she said, longing to call him back as he walked to the stairs. She closed the front door feeling more hopeful than she had in a long time.

She went through to the lounge where Sarah was sitting on an armchair with her feet tucked under her. She looked so comfortable Lynda was irrationally annoyed.

'So that's the gorgeous Jason,' Sarah said. 'No wonder

you're still mooning over him. If my tastes ran to the male gender, I think I might fancy him myself.'

Lynda wasn't sure how to take Sarah's words. Her voice had an edge to it.

'Did you have a nice evening?' she asked, determined to change the subject. She had no intention of discussing Jason with Sarah.

Sarah waved her hand in a dismissive gesture. 'It was OK. I just wandered around Stamford. It's not easy to have a good time when you have no money and no one to be with. I'm not as lucky as you with all the stuff going on in your perfect life.'

There it was again. That edge to Sarah's voice.

'I don't have lots going on and my life is far from perfect,' Lynda said, picking up the glasses and wine bottle.

Sarah got up and followed her through to the kitchen.

'You've got more going on than I have,' she said.

'Maybe,' Lynda said, thinking of the way her life seemed to be spiralling out of control, 'but not all of it is good.' Lynda wanted to scream at Sarah about the pain she felt about losing her family, while Sarah still had hers, about how she'd give up everything she owned to have them back, but then she remembered Sarah's family situation wasn't exactly the happiest, so she bit her lip and kept quiet.

'Some people are never satisfied. You've got a well-paid job, do all that charity work to make you feel great about yourself and you have a nice man hanging around like a puppy dog searching for someone to love.'

'Don't speak about Jason like that. There's nothing puppy dog about him.'

'It sure looked like it when I came home,' Sarah said.

Lynda heard the word *home* and wanted to yell that this wasn't Sarah's home. She was a temporary and now very unwelcome guest. Nothing more.

Lynda shook her head, but didn't answer. She started loading the dishwasher and clearing away the debris from the meal she'd shared with Jason, hoping Sarah would get the message and leave her alone.

'So is the big romance back on?'

'Not exactly,' Lynda said.

'But it could be?' Sarah asked.

Lynda had the feeling the answer meant more to Sarah than a simple yes or no. Not for the first time, she wondered if Sarah had deliberately made herself homeless so that she could move in with her.

'It could be, but we haven't reached a decision yet. Jason's going to be working in London and commuting over the next couple of months while we try to work things out. Look, I don't want to talk about this right now. I just need to get this place cleaned up and go to bed.'

'I'll give you a hand,' Sarah said. 'It's too early for me to go to bed. I wouldn't mind if I had someone to jump in with me. You should have kept hunky Jason back to keep you company.'

'Look, Sarah, I really don't want to talk about Jason, OK?'

'Sure! Keep your hair on. I was only making conversation. Jeesh, you're snappy.'

'I'm sorry. I'm feeling a bit sensitive about the situation with him at the moment.'

She put the last piece of cutlery in the dishwasher and

looked round to see if there was anything else. As she scanned the kitchen she became aware of the way Sarah was looking at her and had never felt more under a microscope.

'Why are you staring at me like that?' Lynda said.

'Like what?' Sarah asked, her face breaking into a smile. 'I was just amused at how tidy you are. Everything has a place and that's where it has to go, even in the dishwasher. I've noticed anything I put in you move to a different place. Do you ever lighten up?'

'It's just who I am. This is the way I like to live.'

She bit her lip to stop the words *leave if you don't like it* from being spoken.

'You've always been like this,' Sarah said. 'Even back when we were in school you had to have everything just so. God forbid if your books weren't in the right order or someone moved your pen.'

'Like you used to?' Lynda said. 'No one else touched my things, but you used to get a big kick out of shifting my stuff around so that I couldn't find anything I was looking for.'

'Yeah, but that was only after you'd fallen for Mark and left me to face those bitches on my own. You deserved a bit of payback then. Who knows, maybe you still do!'

'What's that supposed to mean?' Lynda said.

'Oh nothing, keep your knickers on, Lynda,' Sarah answered. 'But sometimes you're so concentrated on yourself that you've no idea about what goes on in other people's lives. It's always you, you, you.'

Chapter Twenty-Six

As Lynda lay in bed Sarah's words kept repeating over and over. She tossed and turned, trying to find a comfortable position. Her head was pounding, her body sweaty, and her mouth was dry. Maybe if she got up and had a drink of water she'd feel better.

She padded through to the kitchen, poured a glass of water and downed it in one. As she headed back to her bedroom, she could hear Sarah whispering. She must be on the phone to someone, she thought. Lynda looked at her watch: 2.30 a.m. Who would she be talking to at this hour of the morning?

Half wanting to tiptoe to the door and listen, Lynda instead continued on towards her own room. Whatever Sarah was doing had nothing to do with her. She was about to close her bedroom door when she heard Sarah's voice raised in anger.

'I told you! It's not what you think!'

Lynda paused, but then continued closing the door. She had no intention of getting caught up in Sarah's problems. She climbed into bed, convinced she wouldn't be able to sleep, but woke up in fright when her alarm blared out. She usually ran on Sundays, but this morning couldn't face the idea of getting out of bed. Maybe if she closed her eyes and snuggled down she'd manage another hour or so of sleep.

Half an hour later she gave up. Coffee was what she needed. She got up, slipped on her dressing gown and walked to the kitchen, only to find Sarah already there.

'Morning,' Sarah said. 'There's coffee in the pot if you want some.'

Sarah looked exhausted, as well she might, Lynda thought, knowing she had been awake at least as late as the early hours of the morning.

'Thanks,' Lynda said. 'You look tired. Rough night?'

Sarah smiled. 'Me? Nope. I slept like a baby.'

'Oh,' Lynda said. 'I was up late myself. I thought I heard you on the phone in the early hours.'

Sarah shook her head. 'Not me. You must have dreamt it. Maybe you were sleepwalking and imagined voices.'

Lynda wanted to push the point, but realised there was nothing to be gained by arguing over something that really wasn't that important. If Sarah didn't want to admit she'd had a late-night conversation, that was her business.

'Not running this morning?' Sarah asked.

Lynda walked over to the cafetière and poured herself a cup of coffee. 'No, I don't feel up to it today. I'm going to have a lazy day and then go to meet Greg this evening to discuss some charity stuff.'

'I'll be out for most of today. You'll be pleased to know I'm going flat-hunting.'

'You've got viewings booked?' Lynda asked, hoping she didn't sound too eager.

'Not actual viewings. I thought I'd go round the local estate agents' windows to get a feel for what's out there. You know, get some idea of what I might need to pay in rent.' She walked over and put her cup in the sink. 'I'm off to shower. Don't worry; I won't use all the hot water.'

Lynda watched her saunter out. Thank goodness she'd have the place to herself for most of the day. It seemed incredible that Sarah had only been with her a week. It felt like an eternity. She could put up with her for a few more days. Once Sarah moved out, Lynda's life would return to normal. Well, as normal as it could be.

An hour later she was on the couch reading when she heard Sarah leave. She looked at her watch; there was plenty of time to spare before she needed to start getting ready. She adjusted the cushion behind her back, lifted her legs onto the couch and settled down to figure out the culprit in her favourite author's latest book.

Lynda woke two hours later as her phone rang. She reached out for it and pain shot across her shoulders. She must have fallen asleep lying in an awkward position. Looking at her phone, she saw the number was withheld. Deciding to ignore it, she knew she needed to move around to loosen up.

Standing up, her back on fire, she walked to the lounge window. From there she had a clear view of the street below. On the pavement opposite was a dark patch. Lynda stared. Her hand went to her throat. She felt sick. Was it? Could it be? Deep down, she knew. It was Lucky. The bundle of fur was twitching. She ran to her bedroom and threw on the first clothes she found. Not bothering with socks, she slipped her feet into her running shoes and headed for the door.

Lynda ran down the stairs and wrenched open the street door. She rushed over and dropped to her knees next to Lucky. There was no blood. She hadn't been knocked down. So what had happened to her?

She scooped Lucky up and carried her across the road. Tears were streaming down Lynda's face, but she made no attempt to wipe them away. Staggering inside, cradling Lucky, she hammered on Georgina's door.

'Oh no! What's happened to her?' Georgina asked as she opened the door. 'Has she been knocked down? I didn't hear anything.'

Lynda shook her head. 'I need to get her to the vet. Can you call them to say I'm on my way?'

'Of course, which vet do you use?' Georgina asked.

'Stamford Animal Hospital,' Lynda said through her tears.

'You aren't safe to drive. I'll take you,' Georgina said.

Lynda waited, quietly sobbing, while Georgina went into her flat to grab her car keys. She was just finishing a phone call as she ran back out again.

'Come on, let's go. The vet will be waiting for us.'

Lynda sat next to Georgina in the vet's waiting room, unable to think clearly. Had the phone call just before she'd seen Lucky come from the same person as before? Did that person have anything to do with what had happened to her cat? The poor thing had shuddered and heaved all the way to the vet.

The door leading to the surgical rooms opened and Dr Meadows came out looking grave.

'I'm sorry,' he said, 'but it looks as though Lucky has

ingested a poisonous substance. We've done all we can, but there is no hope she will recover.' He sighed. 'I feel the kindest option is euthanasia.'

Lynda gasped. 'There must be something more you can do.'

He shook his head. 'We really have done everything possible. Lucky isn't likely to live for more than a few hours and she is in terrible pain. I need your permission before I can put her out of her misery.'

Lynda nodded. 'I'll sign whatever you need. Can I see her?' she asked.

'Of course.'

She followed the vet down the corridor to the operating room. Lucky was stretched out on the table, unmoving.

The nurse looked up and shook her head.

'I'm so sorry,' Dr Meadows said, 'it seems she hadn't the strength to hold on.'

Lynda felt her eyes fill with tears. She hadn't even had chance to say goodbye.

'Do you think she was deliberately poisoned?' Lynda asked.

He shook his head. 'I assumed she'd eaten something that might have been put out for rats. I'm afraid I see far too many domestic pets who've ingested poisonous substances left out to deal with a rat problem.'

'Could an autopsy prove that?'

He shrugged. 'It would prove she'd ingested poison, but not where or how. Would you like me to conduct an autopsy?'

Lynda shook her head. There was no point if all it proved was that Lucky had been poisoned, but didn't point to who had done it.

'Sorry to have to ask this,' Dr Meadows said, 'but how

would you like to dispose of her body? I can arrange a cremation.'

Unable to take any more, she nodded. All she wanted now was to get out of the vet's to deal with her loss. She went back along the corridor to find Georgina waiting for her with open arms.

'You poor thing,' she said. 'Come on, let's go home.'

'I'm going to report Lucky's death to the police,' Lynda said.

'You also think it was deliberate? The thought went through my mind,' Georgina said. 'Who would do such a thing to a poor defenceless animal?'

'I don't know, but I'm not going to let this pass without reporting it.'

'Good!' Georgina said. 'I'll go with you.'

When they arrived home, Lynda parted with Georgina in the hall, saying she'd knock on her door as soon as she could. She went upstairs to shower and dress in something more suitable for a visit to the police station. The cards and phone calls were one thing, but killing her cat put everything into a different league. As she showered, all she could think about was poor Lucky. Who would do something so cruel to an innocent animal just to get at her?

As she leaned forward to pull on her trainers and lace them up, tears fell, dripping down onto her fingers. She promised herself she'd find whoever did this and make sure they were punished.

Once she was ready, she went downstairs and tapped on Georgina's door. It opened almost immediately.

'Hi,' Georgina said. 'Are you OK? No, of course you're not. What a stupid question. I'm sorry. I guess I'm more upset about Lucky than I'd realised.'

'I've been thinking,' Lynda said. 'I should take the rosemary plant with me to the station. I think Lucky's death is connected to that in some way.'

'Oh no,' Georgina said. 'I don't have it any longer. I binned it because it suddenly hit me that it might upset you if it was staring at you every time you came to chat.'

Lynda realised she hadn't seen the plant the last few times she'd been in Georgina's kitchen.

'That was kind of you,' she said, 'but it would have been good to take it with us today.'

'I didn't know we would be going to the police station,' Georgina said. 'My only thought was to protect your feelings.'

Lynda smiled. 'I know that and it was good of you to think of me.'

Georgina grabbed Lynda's arm. 'You don't need the plant. You have the card, which is far more important when it comes to proving someone is out to upset you. Also, I'll be there, so I can tell the police the plant existed.'

'You're right,' Lynda said, not wanting to go into why she had no intention of showing the card to the police.

Georgina kept up a non-stop stream of platitudes as Lynda drove. Although she realised it was to stop her from thinking about Lucky, by the time Lynda parked outside the station she had never been closer to losing her temper with her young friend.

'You didn't need to come with me,' she said. 'I can do this on my own.'

'I know you can,' Georgina said, 'I'm just here to support you and be a witness. But, if you like, I can wait in the car. I didn't mean to intrude.'

Realising she'd offended Georgina, Lynda shook her head.

'I'm sorry. I didn't mean to sound so ungrateful. It's just . . . I don't know what I'm feeling, to be honest. I need to tell the police everything from the beginning and they're going to think I'm nuts.'

'No, they won't. I saw the plant, remember. And Lucky is dead. Neither of those are figments of your imagination.'

'You're right,' Lynda said. 'Come on, let's get this over and done with.'

Lynda locked the car and looked over at the police station. It was bigger than she'd expected for such a small town. It could almost have been taken for a country house. She wondered if people were peering at her from the three windows either side of the central doorway.

Georgina was slightly ahead of her and had stopped dead in front of the door.

'I don't believe this,' she said. 'It's closed!'

Lynda looked at the sign. 'It's only open three days a week. What happens if there are crimes committed on the other days?'

Georgina pointed to the sign. 'We can go to one of the other stations.'

Lynda felt wiped out already without trawling around the other towns trying to find a police station that was open. 'What time does it say they're open tomorrow?'

'From half nine until five.'

'Fine,' Lynda said. 'I'll leave work early tomorrow and come back in the afternoon.'

'It wouldn't take us long to go to one of the other towns,' Georgina said.

'No,' Lynda said firmly. 'I said I'll come back tomorrow and that's what I'll do.'

She saw Georgina getting ready to argue and knew she didn't have the strength to fight back.

'Please, Georgina, let it go. I'll deal with it tomorrow,' she said, heading back to her car. 'Come on. I'll treat you to a coffee and cake on the way home.'

Lynda leaned back against the padded seat and tried to relax. As soon as the waitress had put her usual coffee and carrot cake in front of her, she'd felt a rush of nausea and had to run to the bathroom where she'd dry-heaved, but nothing had come up.

'Sorry for rushing off like that,' she said, moving her bag off the table where she'd dumped it before fleeing. 'I don't think I've ever felt as stressed out as I do right now.'

Georgina reached across and touched Lynda's hand. 'You don't need to apologise to me, but maybe you do to yourself.'

'What do you mean?'

'You have so much going on at the moment that you can't control. We don't know who is out to upset you like this, but we absolutely know who is making your life a misery at home and that's something you can control. Why don't you simply tell Sarah to get out?'

Lynda tried to put into words why she couldn't do that, but even as each thought came to her mind, another seemed to follow on contradicting the one before.

'She went out today to flat-hunt. I think she is determined

this time to find a place. I really hope so as she's freaking me out with all the stuff she keeps moving.'

'You mean the mirror and your hoodie?'

Lynda nodded. 'Yes, but it's more than that. You know those two prints over my bed? She moved them, just fractionally, but I knew she'd done it and then she swore blind she hadn't touched them.'

'She's gaslighting you. If you can't tell her to sling her hook, would you like me to do it for you?'

Lynda smiled. 'I told Jason off for having a Superman complex. There's no way I could let you handle Sarah. Don't worry, I'll deal with her. I just need to find the right way to do it.'

Georgina shrugged. 'OK, fair enough. Now, the other thing you can control is when to report to the police. There's still time for us to drive to one of the other stations.'

Lynda felt such a flood of weariness wash through her that the mere thought of arriving at another station only to find it might be closed was too much to contemplate. She shook her head.

'No, I'll go to Stamford tomorrow. Now, let's enjoy our coffee and cake.'

Later, when she was getting ready to go out to meet Greg, Lynda mulled over the conversation she'd had with Georgina while they were having coffee. She'd seemed annoyed that Lynda wasn't prepared to travel to Bourne or Market Deeping. She hadn't wanted to drive all over the county as upset as she was. They could have gone to Lincoln, but that would have taken over an hour in each direction. Tomorrow, though, she'd leave work early and report everything at the Stamford station.

She finished putting on her make-up and stood up. A quick drink with Greg to discuss the details of the marathon and then home for an early night. She was exhausted after getting so little sleep the night before. That reminded her. She knew she had definitely heard Sarah on the phone, so why had she lied and said she'd been asleep all night? Maybe it was a call to Maria and she didn't want to talk about it. That was fine by Lynda. As soon as Sarah moved out, she didn't want to know anything about her life. She'd wanted to atone for her past, but now she'd had enough.

She came out of her bedroom and heard a noise in the kitchen. Sarah must be back, she thought. Could she leave without being heard? No, why should she creep around in her own apartment?

Lynda went through to the kitchen to find Sarah sitting at the breakfast bar staring into space.

'Everything OK?' Lynda said.

Sarah jumped. 'Oh, sorry, I didn't hear you. Yeah, I was miles away wondering how I was ever going to get enough dosh to rent somewhere. From what I could see in the estate agents' windows, most of them want a month's rent in advance, plus a month's rent as a deposit. Some of them are asking for two months' rent as deposit. Where am I going to get that much money from? I'm really sorry, Lynda. I would never have moved in with you if I'd known I was going to be staying for so long.'

Lynda could feel the blood draining from her face. No way

was Sarah staying with her a second longer than was absolutely necessary.

'How much would you need?' she asked.

Sarah shrugged. 'The cheapest place looks as if I'd have to cough up well over a thousand and that's just for a studio. If I tried to go for a one bed, I'd be looking closer to two grand.'

Lynda did some mental arithmetic. She could lend Sarah the money, but would she ever get it back again? On the other hand, did that matter? Maybe this was the penance she needed so that she could forgive herself.

She moved over to Lucky's bed cushion and scooped it up. She'd need to get rid of it, but in the meantime she'd put it in the hall cupboard so that she wouldn't be constantly reminded of her loss.

'What are you doing?' Sarah asked, following her into the hall. 'I thought you said your cat always came back.'

Lynda shoved the bed into the cupboard and slammed the door.

'Lucky won't be coming back. Someone killed her.'

'What? How? When?' Sarah asked.

'I don't know what happened. I found her dead in the street this morning. The vet asked if I wanted an autopsy, but there was no point. It was obvious she'd been poisoned.'

'Poisoned? What makes you so sure?'

'Because the vet said she'd eaten something really bad.'

'You know I don't like cats, but that's a shit thing to happen. I really am sorry for you.'

'Are you?'

'Why are you looking at me like that? I didn't have anything to do with the cat's death.'

Lynda stared at Sarah, trying to work out her expression. 'I didn't say you had.'

'Well then, stop looking at me as if I'm someone out of a horror film.'

'Am I? Sorry, I didn't mean to. Anyway, that's a matter for the police to deal with. I'm going to report Lucky's death and the other stuff.'

'What other stuff?'

'It doesn't matter. Look, Sarah, I have to go out to meet Greg, but I need to talk to you when I get back. Maybe we can come up with a way for you to afford your own place.'

Sarah laughed. 'What am I supposed to do? Rob a bank?'

'Not that, no, but I might be able to help you.'

She left before Sarah could ask any questions about what she had in mind.

Greg was already at the Rose and Crown when Lynda arrived. Judging by the empty pint glass in front of him, he'd been there for a while.

He jumped up as she approached the table.

'Hi,' he said. 'You look lovely. What can I get you to drink?'

'I'll have a tonic with ice and lemon, please.'

'No gin?' he asked.

She shook her head. 'I'm driving.'

Lynda sat down, wishing she'd insisted on discussing the marathon in the charity office. The way Greg had looked at her had made her feel even more uncomfortable than usual.

He came back with her tonic and another pint for himself.

'I take it you're not driving,' she said.

'I live a few streets from here. This is my local, so I don't need to worry about having one too many. I can always stagger home regardless. If you want, I can show you where I live when we've had our drinks.'

Determined to bring the conversation back to business, Lynda shook her head.

'Not tonight, I'm afraid. I have to get home to sort out some work stuff.'

'Maybe another time?' he said, looking hopeful.

Lynda smiled, but didn't answer. 'Now, about the marathon. What was it you wanted to discuss?'

To be fair to Greg, Lynda realised he really wanted to go over all the finer details of the event. He reached over to the seat on his left and picked up a thick folder.

'I've got everything to do with the event in here,' he said. 'Shall we go through it all bit by bit?'

Two hours later Lynda was convinced the race weekend would be a big success and could raise enough money to keep the charity going for another year at least.

'You have brilliant organisation skills, Lynda,' Greg said. 'Look, it's still early. Why don't we go somewhere for dinner? Get to know each other better outside of the charity stuff?'

Lynda knew she had to put a stop to this. 'Greg, thank you for the invitation, but you should know that it's possible Jason and I might be getting back together. He came to see me last night and we're . . . well, we're . . . not really anything at the moment, but there's a chance we could be in the future.'

'He's moving back in with you?'

'Not yet, no. He's been promoted and is going to take over the London office.'

'You're moving to London?' Greg asked.

'No. I'm fixed here for the foreseeable future. Jason is going to commute for the next few months. After that, who knows?'

His face fell. 'I see. So there really is no hope for me?'

She shook her head. 'No, but we can still be friends. That doesn't need to change, does it?'

For a brief moment his expression was almost one of anger, but it disappeared immediately, to be replaced by his usual kindly appearance.

'If that's what you want, then OK, but if things don't work out for you with Jason, I'll be here, even if it's just as a friend.'

Chapter Twenty-Seven

On Monday afternoon, Lynda pulled into the police station car park, relieved to spot signs of life this time. As she got out of the car and looked across at the building, she could see shadows of movement behind the windows and the front door was open. She locked the car and walked towards the building, trying to sort out in her mind how to explain her concerns without coming across like a neurotic imbecile.

Lynda approached the officer at the front desk, but when he looked up and asked how he could help her, all her prepared thoughts flew from her head.

'I don't know,' she said and burst into tears. Horrified, she gulped for air and tried to pull herself together. 'I'm so sorry.'

The officer smiled. 'Don't worry. Take your time.'

She sniffed back the tears. 'I think someone is stalking me,' she said. 'And whoever it is killed my cat.'

'Take a seat over there. I'll get someone to come and talk to you.'

After a few minutes, a man approached. 'I'm Detective Constable Fredericks. I believe you have reason to think someone is stalking you. Would you like to come with me so I can take down a few details?'

Relieved to be able to put everything into the hands of the police, Lynda nodded. She got up and followed him along a hallway and into a small room.

'It's a bit cramped in here, but the other rooms are in use. Please, take a seat,' he said, pointing towards a small desk with a single chair on either side.

Lynda sat down and waited until the officer got out a pad and signalled he was ready to listen.

'First, can you give me your full name?' He wrote that at the top of the page. 'Now, tell me why you think you're being stalked.'

Unable to find the right words at first, and after stumbling a few times to get started, Lynda poured out all her concerns. Every so often the officer made a note on his pad, but didn't ask any questions until she'd finished.

'Do you mind if I use your first name?'

'No, of course not,' she said. She pointed to his pad. 'It's Lynda with a y, not an i.'

'OK, Lynda,' he said, picking up the pen and changing the spelling of her name on the paper, 'let me see if I have this right. You have an old school friend staying with you who you don't like and don't trust. If you think she's playing mind games with you, why not tell her to leave?'

'It's complicated,' Lynda said. 'She has nowhere to go, but she said she'll leave as soon as she gets the money together.'

'Could she have hand-delivered the plant and the card?'

'She might have done,' Lynda said, beginning to wish she'd never come to the station.

'So where is this plant?'

'I told you: I didn't want it in my flat so I left it with my neighbour. She threw it away. She didn't want it to upset me every time I saw it.'

'And this card that you mentioned came with the plant – what was on it?'

'As I told you –' Lynda paused, trying to rein in her mounting irritation '– I-I can't remember.'

'You can't remember?!'

'No, I can't remember.'

'OK, and where is it?'

'I don't have it any more.'

'How come?'

'I-I . . . I threw it away. I found it too upsetting.'

'You found it upsetting but you can't remember why? Pity! Miss Blackthorn, I'm sorry to say that even if you'd kept this . . . card . . . that you said came with the plant, I doubt it would have been enough for us to launch an investigation.' He smiled. 'The hangman's noose drawing you've shown me could have been done by anyone.' He pronounced his words slowly as if he doubted her mental faculties. 'As upsetting as it is, it's not a crime. It could simply be a prank in very poor taste.'

Lynda felt as if she was sinking in quick sand. 'And the car that has followed me on my runs? Shouldn't that be taken seriously?'

'You haven't been able to provide us with any details of the car. Not the make or the number plate. Without those, we have nothing to go on.'

Lynda wondered if he thought she was hysterical. She might as well go all in.

'What about Lucky?'

'Ah yes, this cat of yours. You say you think your cat was poisoned?' he said.

'She was! There wasn't a mark on her body and her face was all screwed up as if she was in terrible pain.'

'How long have you had her?'

'A few months. Why is it relevant?'

'And she wasn't in your flat?'

'No, she goes hunting when I go out for a run in the morning.'

'Oh, you allowed her out?'

'Well . . . yes.'

'I see, so she could have picked up something anywhere.'

'No . . . I know she was poisoned.'

'How? Did the vet say it had been deliberate?'

'Yes . . . well, no . . . but . . . he did say she'd eaten something poisonous!'

'As I said, she could have eaten something dodgy outside. It's not infrequent with cats that are allowed outdoors. I'm sorry, but so far there doesn't seem to be anything concrete for us to go by. You had your cat cremated, and refused to pay for an autopsy, is that correct?'

'I didn't refuse to pay! I just didn't see the point at the time, but you're right, that's what I should have done. I was too upset to think straight.'

'Either way,' he said, 'it means we have nothing to go on in that regard. Well, taking everything into consideration, I'm not sure how you think we can help.' He stopped speaking and looked at her, obviously annoyed for having his time wasted and clearly hoping she'd get the hint and leave.

Lynda felt as if she was being dismissed, but couldn't blame him. She stood up and thanked the officer, glad to be able to get out of the room, which had become claustrophobic. She felt like she was suffocating. He walked with her to the front door. Lynda wondered if he was concerned she might not leave unless he was there to make sure she did.

Heading back to her car she replayed the conversation in her mind. He hadn't taken her seriously, that was for sure. To make matters worse, he'd been condescending. Did he think she was simply neurotic and seeking attention? Even if Georgina had been with her he would have probably reacted in the same way.

Lynda walked up the stairs, thankful that Georgina hadn't heard her come in. She'd bring her up to speed later on her visit to the police station. The last thing she wanted right now was to relive the humiliation. She opened her front door and gasped. The mirror was once again skewed. Why was Sarah doing this? She reached up to straighten it, calling out for Sarah.

'I'm in the bathroom,' she answered. 'I won't be long.'

Lynda went through to the kitchen and saw that Sarah had yet again left her cup in the sink. Why couldn't she put it in the dishwasher, or wash it by hand?

Flicking the switch on the kettle, she decided to get changed while it was boiling. As she went into her bedroom, the first thing that hit her was that the two fenland scenes had been swapped over. The birds in the pictures were flying the wrong way. Instead of appearing to fly towards each other, they were now heading in opposite directions.

She was about to yell for Sarah to demand she swap them back when her front doorbell rang. She went through the hall and opened it.

'Georgina! Sorry, now isn't a good time,' she said.

'Oh, OK. I just wanted to find out if you went to the police station.'

'I did,' Lynda said. 'I'll come down and tell you about it in a bit. Right now, I have a problem to sort out.'

Georgina smiled. 'No worries. Come down when you're ready.'

Lynda shut the door and turned back just in time to see Sarah go into the kitchen. Lynda followed her in.

'I have some news to make you smile,' Sarah said. 'I got a job today. It's only a temp position, but at least I'll be earning some money. You'll never guess where I'll be working! Do you want me to make some coffee?'

Anger such as she'd never known before washed over Lynda's body. 'No, I bloody don't want you to do anything other than put my prints back the way they should be!'

'What are you talking about? What prints?'

Lynda grabbed hold of Sarah's arm and dragged her to the bedroom. 'Those,' she said, pointing to the wall above her bed. Stunned, she saw that they were back the way they should be.

'What about them? I haven't touched them. Why would I?'

'You've put them back again. Why are you doing this? Is it to mess with my head? Did you steal my hoodie? Did you kill my cat?'

'You are not well. You know that, don't you?' Sarah yelled, wrenching her arm free. 'You need to get better professional help. That therapist you're going to isn't doing anything for you.'

'How do you know I'm seeing a therapist?'

Sarah grinned. 'I didn't. It was just a good guess that someone with as many issues as you would be in therapy. You are OCD-centric. The slightest movement of anything drives you insane.'

'You leave my OCD out of this. You've been messing with me. Don't deny it. Every time I come home the hall mirror is askew. You shift things around and then pretend you didn't. I want you out of here. Go on, get out. Find some other idiot to take you in. I've had enough!'

Sarah glared at her. 'You're actually going to throw me out? I have nowhere to go.'

'Too bad! I want you out of here. Now!'

Lynda watched as Sarah stormed down the hall and wrenched open the door.

'I'll be back for my things when I've found somewhere to stay.'

As she slammed the door behind her, Lynda crumpled into a heap and sobbed. She was still on the floor crying when the doorbell rang. Dragging herself to her feet, she went to answer it, knowing it was probably Georgina. The last thing she wanted was to talk about what had just happened, but with the noise Sarah had made as she left, Lynda knew Georgina would be concerned.

She opened the door and stood back to let her friend in. 'You obviously heard Sarah leaving,' she said. 'Come through to the kitchen and I'll tell you all about it.'

Lynda waited until Georgina had settled herself at the breakfast bar before moving over to sit on the other stool.

'I think I've finally got rid of my unwanted guest, but not in a nice way. I feel really bad.'

'I heard part of the argument,' Georgina said. 'From what I could tell, you did the right thing.'

Lynda sighed. 'I know, but I could have handled it better. I told you, didn't I, that she's been shifting things just slightly and then lying about it? Well, this time she went too far and actually swapped the two prints over.'

Georgina shook her head. 'There's something a bit off with the way she manoeuvred you into taking her in. It was almost as if she wanted to upset your life. But that's another story. Tell me,' she said, 'how did it go at the police station?'

Lynda laughed and could hear the hint of hysteria rising in her voice. 'It didn't go terribly well. The very polite young officer who dealt with my concerns made it quite clear he believed I was being hysterical. He made it sound as if Lucky dying was my fault because I allowed her out, if she did exist at all, since I'd already had her cremated instead of taking her body to show him.'

'We should have gone to one of the other stations yesterday,' Georgina said. 'Let's go back tomorrow. I can tell the officer about the plant and Lucky.'

Lynda shook her head. 'Even with you swearing to those things I don't think they would do anything. I'm sorry, Georgina, I know I should offer you something to drink, but I'm wiped out. Can we talk more tomorrow?'

Georgina stood up and smiled. 'Of course.'

Lynda stood up and went with Georgina to the door, stunned to see Sarah coming up the stairs.

'Want me to stay?' Georgina asked.

Lynda shook her head. 'Don't worry. I can deal with this.'

'Can we talk?' Sarah said, moving to one side to let Georgina pass her.

Lynda shook her head. 'No. You went too far this time. I'm not stupid. I know what you've been doing. If you need to get something from the spare room, go ahead, but you're not staying here any longer.'

'Fine!' Sarah yelled, shoving past Lynda and heading to the bedroom.

A few minutes later she came out carrying a small overnight bag.

Lynda took an involuntary step back at the look Sarah gave her.

'I hope you rot in hell,' Sarah spat as she stormed past.

As the door slammed behind her, Lynda stumbled into the kitchen. She'd never seen such a look of hatred on anyone's face.

Chapter Twenty-Eight

When Lynda arrived at work on Tuesday morning she was stunned to come face to face with the last person she wanted to see. Sarah was seated at the receptionist desk. She hesitated in the doorway, then remembered Sarah saying the night before that she'd found a temp job. *Not here*, she begged silently, *please, not here!*

'What are you doing here?' she said, walking to the reception desk.

'What does it look like?' Sarah said. 'My first day at work and I couldn't even shower before I came in. I slept in my car last night, thanks to you.'

Lynda leaned forward and whispered. 'This is not the place to discuss personal matters.'

'You're such a bitch,' Sarah said.

'What did you just call me?'

The phone rang and Sarah answered it. 'Colforth Management Solutions,' she said, flicking her fingers in a gesture of dismissal that made Lynda want to slap her.

Lynda managed to get through two meetings without

messing up, but she couldn't stop thinking about Sarah being in the building. She felt sick just knowing she was downstairs. Would Sarah leave if she offered her the same amount of money as she would earn here for a week? It was worth trying. Anything was better than having her so close at hand.

As she approached the ground floor, Lynda could hear Sarah's voice. She was talking to someone so maybe now wasn't the right time, but then she heard her name mentioned. She ran down the last flight and saw Pauline standing next to Sarah's desk. Of all the people in the office she could have spoken to, Sarah had found the one person who had disliked Lynda from the moment she had joined the team.

'And then she kicked me out. I've barely closed my eyes all night.'

'I can imagine. Sleeping in your car must have been the pits. Look, since my flatmate moved to the US last month I have a spare room in my house,' Pauline said. 'If you can put something towards the mortgage and bills, you could stay with me until you find a flat of your own.'

Lynda saw Sarah smile and glance in her direction. 'Well, look who it is. The person who's caused all this chaos in my life.'

'Are you two talking about me behind my back?' Lynda demanded.

'How could we be doing that when you're right here in front of us?' Sarah said.

'Pauline, don't you think it's unprofessional of you to discuss me like this with Sarah?'

'What do you mean?' she asked. 'I wasn't discussing you, but it does seem as if Sarah is in a tough spot because, well, because . . .' She took a step towards Lynda. 'I hope you're not going to report me to HR.'

'What? No!' Lynda said. 'Why would you think any such thing?' As she said the words she saw a smirk on Sarah's face and realised she must have put the idea in her head. 'I was just pointing out that you should not be talking to Sarah about me in a place where anyone could overhear. Which I just did, by the way. Sarah, did you tell Pauline the reason I asked you to leave?'

'Yes, I did. I told her you accused me of messing with your stupid prints which I didn't touch! I also told her about your OCD issues.' She turned to Pauline. 'She imagines things have moved and then swears I moved them, but in truth nothing has been moved at all!'

Lynda knew she shouldn't rise to the bait, but couldn't help herself. 'Things were moved in the apartment and you were the only person who could have done it.'

'You are paranoid,' Sarah said. 'I am so glad I don't have to put up with you any longer. Even if I did have to sleep in my car, it would be better than living with you. Instead I'm going to stay with Pauline for a bit. Isn't that right?'

Lynda waited for Pauline to speak, but she looked as if she hadn't realised until that point quite what she'd got involved with. She swallowed a few times and then nodded. Sarah smiled like the cat who'd got the cream. Lynda felt sorry for Pauline. She had no idea what a viper she was letting into her home.

Sarah moved her smiles from Pauline to Lynda. 'I'll be over this evening to pick up my things. I take it that's OK with you?'.

Lynda managed to nod and turned towards the stairs. Yet again she'd been put in the wrong. Pauline must see her as unhinged.

Still, she thought, mounting the stairs, at least after this evening she would no longer have to worry about having Sarah in her home.

Chapter Twenty-Nine

Somehow Lynda got through the rest of the day. She got in the car and as she clicked the seatbelt into place ready to leave, she tried to picture how relieved she would be once Sarah had collected her belongings and left for good. That thought reminded her that she needed to call in on Georgina once she got home. She felt bad that she'd fobbed her off the night before, but other than filling her in on the fact that Sarah had gone, she really hadn't been up to talking.

She drove home carefully; she was well aware that her concentration wasn't as solid as she would have liked, but with so many thoughts spinning through her mind, it was hardly surprising she was struggling to focus.

As she let herself into the downstairs hallway, she was looking forward to a long hot shower, but that would have to wait until Sarah had been and gone. First though, she needed to have a chat with Georgina.

She rang the bell and waited for the door to open. If Georgina was working, she wouldn't leave her computer until she'd saved her work. A few seconds passed and then Georgina appeared.

'Hi,' she said. 'Come in. Have you got time for tea? Or would you prefer a glass of wine? I know which I intend to have.'

Lynda followed her into the kitchen. She loved the warmth of the pale lemon walls and right now she needed the lift the room always gave her.

'So, what's it to be?' Georgina said, waving the bottle of pinot grigio in Lynda's direction.

'A glass of that, please. I have a minor event to celebrate this evening.'

'Sounds good. What is it?'

Lynda raised her glass. 'Me getting my life back,' she said.

'I'll definitely drink to that! I take it you are now completely rid of Sarah?'

'Not quite, but I will be after she collects her belongings this evening,' Lynda said.

Georgina turned and opened a drawer. She rummaged inside and then handed Lynda a key.

'Here, I won't be needing this any more.'

Lynda took her spare key and felt tears about to fall. She tried to compose herself. 'I never thought I'd miss a cat as much as a human, but I do. In some ways she's left an even bigger hole in my life than Jason.' She wiped her eyes on a tissue. 'I didn't tell you last night because, well, because it was an upsetting day, but Jason and I are getting on much better.'

'Oh, I am glad. Do you think he'll move back in?'

'Not for a while. We're going to take it slowly and see how

things work out. He's been promoted and he'll be commuting to London Monday to Friday, so we won't see much of each other during the week, but maybe weekends will be looking up for me.'

Lynda finished her wine and stood up. 'Thanks for the drink. I think I'd best get upstairs and wait for Sarah. Take a guess where she's going to live for a while.'

Georgina laughed. 'I can tell by your voice it's not somewhere I'd ever think of, so put me out of my misery.'

'She's moving in with a colleague from work. Pauline has no idea what she's letting herself in for.'

'How does she know anyone from your workplace?'

'You won't believe it, but she signed on with the temp agency we use and they booked her for this week with us. I've already spoken to them. When the week's up we'll be getting someone else. I just hope this time it's someone who is capable of doing the job.'

She put the key in her pocket. 'Thank you for all the times you took care of Lucky.'

Georgina waved her hand. 'I enjoyed doing it. I just wish she was still with us.'

Lynda opened her front door and immediately looked to see if the hall mirror was out of alignment. It wasn't, but she still lifted her hand to straighten it. At least she wouldn't need to deal with Sarah's mind games any more.

She walked through to the kitchen. Should she have another glass of wine now or wait until Sarah had been and gone? Deciding she'd enjoy the wine more once she had the flat to

186

herself, she filled the kettle and flicked the switch. She'd have a cup of tea while she waited. She should have given Sarah a definite time to come over instead of leaving it up to her, but then again she would probably have come whenever it suited her regardless of what arrangement they'd made.

She took her tea into the lounge and had just sat down when her mobile rang. She'd left her bag in the kitchen, so went back to get it. As she got there, the ring tone stopped. She lifted the phone out of her bag. She'd missed a call from Jason.

Walking back to the lounge, she touched the screen to call him back.

'Hi, sorry, I didn't make it to the phone in time,' she said when she heard his voice. 'Did you need me?'

He laughed. 'Is that a leading question?'

'It could be.'

Lynda realised it was a long time since they'd been comfortable enough with each other to tease. It felt good to be close again.

'Where are you?' she asked.

'I'm at King's Cross waiting for the Peterborough train. It's been a long day. I wondered if you wanted to meet me in Peterborough for dinner. I haven't planned anything. We could go wherever you fancy.'

'I would've loved to,' she said, 'but Sarah's coming to collect her belongings this evening and I don't know what time she'll be here.'

'Hey, that sounds very positive. You finally turned her out. How did you manage that?'

'I'll tell you all about it when I see you. If she comes early, I could probably get to Peterborough before your train gets in, but I don't want to make any promises.' She could hear the station's background sounds. 'It's noisy there,' she said. 'A far cry from our sleepy neck of the woods.'

'You just heard the tannoy announce the arrival of the Peterborough train. I'm going to find a seat. If Sarah gets done early, give me a call. If not, maybe we can make a plan for tomorrow evening. What do you say?'

'I think that's a great idea.'

'OK,' Jason said. 'If you can't make it tonight, we have a date for tomorrow.'

'A date,' Lynda said. 'I like the sound of that.'

Jason said goodbye and the line went dead. Would they be able to be a couple again? She had no idea, but really hoped so.

An hour later Sarah still hadn't turned up. Lynda had tried her number several times, but it just went to voicemail. Clearly there was no way now she'd be able to get to Peterborough this evening, but at least she would have tomorrow night to look forward to.

She was just about to try Sarah's number again when she heard the door open. Lynda jumped up and went into the hall.

'I'll get out of your hair as soon as I can,' Sarah said, 'but it's going to take me a while.'

'Would you like me to give you a hand?' Lynda said.

'I don't want you anywhere near my stuff,' Sarah said. 'You might plant something on me, like your stupid hoodie, and claim I was stealing it.'

Unable to think of a response that wouldn't sound like she was apologising for something she had no intention of apologising for, Lynda walked back into the lounge, furious and relieved at the same time.

It took the best part of an hour and a half before Sarah came to the lounge to say she was ready to go.

Lynda stood up. 'I'm sorry it didn't work out,' she said.

'No, you're not,' Sarah answered. 'You made it quite clear from the moment I arrived that you only took me in because you felt you had to. Believe it or not, I tried not to upset your weird ways, but no matter what I did you found fault with me.'

Lynda thought about Sarah using all the hot water, never cleaning up after herself, moving things that she knew Lynda didn't want moved.

'Look,' she said, 'let's just call it a day. You're right, I only invited you because I let you down in the past, but if you'd only tried to fit in with how I like my home to be, it might have been OK. I'm not saying it would've been perfect, but we might have got on better.'

Sarah laughed. 'I doubt anyone could live with you.'

As she turned to leave, Lynda called out. 'I need your keys.'

'I've left them in the bedroom,' Sarah said. 'Don't worry. I won't be back. This hasn't exactly been the happiest of times for me, you know. Not once did you ask me how I was feeling after breaking up with Maria. You think you're such a great person with all your charity work, but when it comes down to it, you're a self-centred cow. You aren't really doing any of those things for charity because you want to help others. You're doing them so that you can polish your halo and see yourself as Saint bloody Lynda. Even that poor sucker running the charity will find out in the end that you only care about yourself. I bet he wouldn't be sniffing around if he knew what you're really like.'

Lynda stood rooted to the spot as Sarah left, once again

slamming the door behind her. Was Sarah right? Was she self-centred and only thinking of herself? During one of their many arguments a long time ago, Jason had said something similar.

She no longer felt like celebrating with a glass of wine, or anything else. She would have a long hot shower and climb into bed. The picture Sarah had painted of her had hurt. There was just enough truth in what she'd said to hit home. She'd started running to raise money to combat bullying out of guilt for the damage she'd caused. But was that such a bad thing?

Lynda didn't feel much better even after her shower. She climbed into bed and pulled the duvet over her head, wishing she could hide away from the thoughts going round and round in her mind.

Chapter Thirty

On Wednesday morning Lynda woke bleary-eyed once again after a fitful night. Fragments of her dreams came back but without enough clarity to remember everything. She'd been in the back next to Sean as the car approached the bend. Dad was yelling and then he'd swerved, going through the barrier and the car plunged into the river. There was something important that happened before the car swerved, but what was it? If only she could remember! Maybe if she stopped trying so hard, or thought about something else, it would come back to her.

She lay for a few moments thinking about what had been said the night before when Sarah was leaving. Sarah's words had touched a raw nerve. Lynda wanted more than anything to ignore them, but she couldn't. Sarah had always had a spiteful streak and had known exactly where to aim her barbs. Nothing had changed.

She got up and dressed for her run, automatically looking round for Lucky to let her out, only to receive a punch in the gut when she remembered Lucky was gone forever. She tiptoed down the stairs and opened the main door as quietly as she could. As she ran, she could feel the tension leaving her body. Her footfalls seemed to beat out a tattoo: Sarah is gone, Sarah is gone. Her spirits lifted and she found herself running freer.

A cyclist slowed down as he passed her and gave her a friendly thumbs up. She realised she hadn't seen the man in the car for a few days. Life was on the up.

When she went into the office an hour and a half later, there was something else to add to her good feelings about the day. A stranger was sitting at reception. Lynda walked over to say hello to a woman in her sixties. The agency must have acted immediately to get someone to replace Sarah.

'Hi, I'm Lynda. I work up on the first floor. Welcome to the office.'

The woman smiled. She looked so much like an image from a children's book depicting someone's favourite grand-mother, Lynda couldn't help but return her smile.

'Good morning,' she said. 'I'm Barbara. The agency called me this morning as a matter of urgency. Apparently the person you had working here couldn't make it. I've been told this is a maternity leave situation, so I'm hoping to be here for a couple of months at least.'

Lynda felt a grin spread across her face. 'I hope you'll be happy. If you need anything, please call me,' she said, giving Barbara her extension number.

She headed up to her office almost skipping up the stairs. Maybe life really was looking up. She had a date this evening with Jason and it seemed that Sarah was completely out of her life.

Lynda sailed through her work. Even Pauline was more cooperative than usual and seemed to enjoy working with her on the new client project. Maybe, Lynda thought, even after just one night she was finding Sarah more of a pain to have in her home than she'd anticipated.

As she was getting ready to leave the office, her phone rang. She saw from the display it was Cassie.

'Hi, Cassie,' she said. 'All OK with the website?'

'Yes, that's why I'm calling. I think we'll be able to go live this weekend. Any chance of meeting at the charity on Saturday?'

'That sounds exciting. What time did you have in mind? Want to make it lunchtime and we'll order in some food to celebrate?'

'Sorry,' Cassie said, 'that would've been great, but I'd like Amanda to be there to check I've got all the account details correct and in the right places. She's going out for the day with her husband so has asked for an early-morning meeting. Any chance we could meet at half nine? I know you usually get there for ten, so it's only half an hour earlier.'

'Yes, of course,' Lynda said. 'See you then.'

She drove home singing along to the radio, planning what to wear on her date with Jason. Nothing too flirty, but definitely something dressier than the usual jeans and tee-shirts she seemed to live in over the weekends. A shower, fresh make-up, perfume and spending time on her hair was in order.

As she turned into her street she saw she'd be able to park in her favourite spot. It seemed as if life had decided to give her a few breaks one after the other.

Chapter Thirty-One

Lynda climbed into the taxi that evening and gave the restaurant name to the driver, making sure he knew the address. She'd never eaten at Amore before and wondered if Jason had chosen the place for its name or its reputation for superb Italian food. Either way, it seemed he was doing all he could to make the evening special.

As the taxi pulled up in Cheyne Lane, she saw Jason walking towards the restaurant. She paid the driver and climbed out, just as he reached the doorway.

'If this is a sign of how perfect the evening is going to be, then I'm a happy man,' he said as he leaned down to kiss her hello.

Lynda grinned. 'I feel as giddy as I did on our first date.'

'Good,' Jason said, squeezing her hand. 'So do I. Let's go eat.'

Once they were seated and had been given menus to study, Jason reached across the table to take Lynda's hand.

'Shall we celebrate with a bottle of Contarini Prosecco?'

'You remembered!' Lynda said.

'How could I forget?'

Lynda felt as if she'd floated into another realm. She was with the man she had always loved, in a fabulous restaurant, holding hands across the table. This was all she had ever wanted. How could she have been so crazy as to drive him away?

Forcing herself to concentrate on the menu, she looked down to choose her main course.

'I think I'm going to have the Pollo Crema e Funghi,' she said, laughing at her attempt to pronounce the dish with a passable Italian accent.

'Tender chicken breast cooked in a brandy, wild mushroom and garlic creamy sauce,' Jason read. 'Sounds good, but I'm going for a steak with green pepper sauce, or Filetto al Pepe Verde as the Italians call it.'

The evening passed in a haze. As they sipped the last of the wine Lynda couldn't recall an evening she'd enjoyed more.

'Lynda, I love you. You know that, don't you?'

She nodded. 'Of course I know it. I've always known. I love you too.'

'Then won't you tell me what's worrying you?'

'What do you mean?'

'I can tell you have something troubling you. You're here with me, but a tiny part of you is not. I don't want to pry, but I also can't bear to see you unhappy, and I think there's something going on that's upsetting you.'

Lynda thought of everything she'd been keeping from him and wished more than life itself she could let go and be honest, but after the way she'd behaved towards him before they split up, he might think she was going off the edge again. She couldn't bear it if he thought she was imagining someone was persecuting her. She couldn't show him the messages without also telling him what she'd done to Mark.

He reached across and took her hands in his. 'You look so sad. Please don't be. I'm not going to press you, but just remember I'll always be here for you.'

She managed a smile. 'How can that be when you're planning to move to London at some point?'

Jason squeezed her hands. 'I'm so pleased you raised that because I have a proposition to put to you.'

'Oh,' she said, laughing, 'I'm going to be propositioned. Sounds like fun!'

'It could be,' he said. 'Why don't you move to London with me when I eventually go?'

She took her hands away. 'How can I? My job, my charity work, all my life is here.'

But even as she said the words, the thought occurred to her that there were other jobs, other charities. What was there to keep her in Stamford? It hit home to her that she wanted her life to be wherever Jason was.

'I'm not asking you to make a decision tonight, but I wanted to put the idea in your head. Your company has offices in London. Is it possible you could transfer?'

'I could,' she said, thinking how badly she'd been doing at work recently. Still, before Sarah had come back into her life, she'd been doing OK. She wouldn't have been promoted and given an exciting new account to work on if she hadn't been.

'But what about the charity? The race event was my idea. I talked Greg into it. I couldn't walk out and leave him high and dry.'

'I wouldn't ask you to do that. As I said, I don't want you to make a decision tonight. I just want you to think about it.'

Lynda thought about leaving behind all her troubles and smiled. 'I don't need to think about it. I want us to live together again. As long as I can stay until after the race weekend, I'd love nothing more than to move to London with you.'

'I'd call for another bottle of wine to celebrate, but I have an early start tomorrow. I have to drive to Cardiff for a series of management meetings. As the new head of the London office, I can't miss it, otherwise right now I'd be sweeping you off your feet and booking a room for tonight in The George.'

'Let's do that when you get back,' Lynda said. 'How long will you be away?'

'I'll be away for at least a week, maybe ten days, but for certain we'll celebrate properly the moment I return.'

Lynda went home with more hope for the future than she'd believed possible just a few weeks earlier. Thinking back over the evening, the only point where things could have gone wrong was when he'd picked up she was troubled over something.

As she got out of the taxi, she tried to work out in her own mind why she'd kept herself from telling him everything. Was it because she didn't want to ruin the evening, or was it because she didn't want him worrying about her state of mind? In the past she'd come out with some pretty outlandish accusations. She couldn't take the chance he might think she was going through another episode like that.

She smiled, thinking of the long lingering kiss they'd shared while waiting for her taxi.

'We can make a go of this,' he'd said, gently running his fingers down her arm, 'but you can't hide things from me. If we're going to be together, then anything that worries you is going to worry me.'

She'd opened her mouth to tell him everything and then closed it without saying a word.

'Fine,' he'd said. 'Let's leave it at that for now. When you're ready to tell me, I'll be ready to listen.'

Had he been too annoyed to ask again, or was he just giving her space? Lynda wasn't sure, but hoped it was the latter.

She let herself into the downstairs hall, catching sight of something white just inside the doorway. Even before picking it up she knew it must be from the same person who'd delivered the last envelope.

With shaking hands, she reached down and picked it up. As before, the envelope carried just her first name in capital letters.

She opened the envelope and pulled out the card. Someone had laser-printed a cat. Underneath was a message: *Suffer, bitch, suffer!*

Chapter Thirty-Two

Lynda had no intention of going out for a run on Thursday morning. She'd hardly closed her eyes all night and knew there was no way she had enough energy to get into her running gear, far less cover five kilometres. Even though she'd locked up the apartment like a fortress before climbing into bed, she'd still jumped at the slightest sound. Even the rustle of leaves shifting in the breeze had kept her on edge. The least noise made her sit upright in bed listening for footsteps, or worse, the sound of someone breathing. Her mind ran rampant – should she go to the police again or was there no point? When she'd gone before the officer had made it clear he thought she was wasting his precious time, and the message could have been printed on any computer by any person. She knew in her heart it was probably Sarah, but maybe ignoring her was the best way to go.

She dragged herself out of bed and headed for the kitchen. There was no way she could drink coffee when she was already on edge, but her throat was dry, so she needed something. She opened the fridge, pulled out the carton of orange juice and filled a glass. That would do.

The message was clearly a threat, but what would Sarah do next? Lynda didn't trust her not to have made a copy of the apartment keys. Whether she had or not, Lynda decided she'd have more peace of mind if she had the locks changed. She picked up her phone and searched Google, pressing the call button when she found the service she needed.

'Fortune Keys Locksmith. How can I help you?'

Once she'd arranged for the locks to be replaced that day, she knew she needed to make sure Georgina would be around to let the man in.

Lynda quickly showered and got ready for work, calling in at Georgina's on the way to explain about the latest note.

'I just don't feel comfortable knowing she might have keys to get in. Are you around today? The man said he'd be here in about an hour, so I can stay home if you need to go out.'

'I'm not going anywhere and I think you're doing exactly the right thing,' Georgina said. 'Of course I'll take care of that for you. Tell me, before you rush off, how did your big date with Jason go last night?'

Lynda explained the plans she and Jason had made.

'Of course, I won't be leaving for a few months yet. I wouldn't feel right leaving the charity in the lurch when the race weekend was my project. I'll need to tell Greg and the others on Saturday, but I really feel Jason and I can make a go of it this time.'

'I'm sure you can,' Georgina said. 'I'll miss you when you leave, but I'm really happy for you.'

'We'll still be friends,' Lynda said. 'You can come and visit us once we're settled in London.'

Georgina smiled. 'That's something to look forward to. I haven't been to London for years.'

Lynda looked at her watch. 'I must go or I'll be late for work. See you later.'

As Lynda arrived home on Thursday evening, she finally felt the tension leave her body. Somehow she'd coped with work and meetings throughout the day, but hadn't been able to put the message out of her mind. Lucky had definitely been poisoned and the killer had wanted her to know.

Relieved there wasn't another envelope waiting for her in the hall, she walked across and rang Georgina's bell. She needed to get her new keys before she could let herself into her flat.

'Hi,' Georgina said, 'I've been listening out for you. Would you like a drink before you go up?'

'No, thanks. I've had one hell of a day,' she said. 'I just want to get inside, kick my shoes off and put my feet up for an hour or so.'

'That bad?' Georgina said.

Lynda nodded, too drained to explain exactly how bad the day had been.

'Come through. Your new keys are in the kitchen.'

Lynda walked behind Georgina, so thankful she hadn't had to stay at home to deal with the locksmith.

'Here you are,' Georgina said, holding out two sets of keys. 'He replaced both locks and said the main one is the most secure you can have. You won't need to worry about anyone breaking in.'

Lynda took the keys. 'Thanks,' she said, 'but it wasn't someone breaking in that worried me; it was knowing Sarah could let herself in whenever she wanted.'

'Do you still worry about her?' Georgina asked.

'I didn't show you this morning because I was still feeling a bit fragile about it, but I found this in the hall when I came home last night,' Lynda said, passing the envelope to Georgina.

She watched as her friend pulled out the paper and read the words.

'This is really nasty,' she said. 'I hope you're going to take it to the police.'

'And say what?' Lynda said. 'I have no proof it came from Sarah. The policeman I dealt with before as good as accused me of wasting police time. He made it clear he wasn't going to do anything unless I had something more to show him.'

'But you have!' Georgina said. 'You have this.'

Lynda sighed. 'I know, but don't you see? The cat image and the words are printed. There's nothing about it to show who it came from.'

'I know that,' Georgina said, 'but it's still a threat. You can't let her get away with it.'

Lynda took the envelope back and put it in her bag. 'You're right. I should show this to the police, although I'm kind of hoping that Sarah will leave me alone now.'

Chapter Thirty-Three

When she woke on Friday morning after another bad night, Lynda realised she had to follow Georgina's advice. Sarah couldn't be allowed to get away with what she was doing. Yes, Lynda owed her for not standing up to the bullies on her behalf when they were at school, but that was fourteen years before and she'd done her best since then to make up for it by trying to help others.

What about Mark? Have you done enough to make up for what happened to him?

She pushed thoughts of Mark from her mind. That was something she would regret to her dying day, but there was nothing she could do to change anything now.

She showered and dressed quickly, determined to go to the police station before she had time to rethink her decision.

As she drove, she planned exactly what to say. She would present the police with the facts and hope they believed her sufficiently to at least give Sarah a warning. Pulling into the station car park, she made another decision. Next weekend, she would tell Jason everything, holding nothing back. She'd even tell him about Mark and why he'd committed suicide. It was time to face up to her past so that she could finally be happy with Jason.

She walked into the station trying to convince herself that reporting the latest message was worth the effort involved. A different sergeant was sitting at the desk, so she had to explain herself all over again.

'Take a seat, please. Someone will be out to speak to you shortly.'

With a feeling of déjà vu, she sat in the same place as her last visit. The feeling was intensified when Detective Constable Fredericks came forward.

He smiled. 'Miss Blackthorn, would you like to come through?'

She stood and followed him and wasn't at all surprised to see they were going to the same interview room as before. She just hoped the outcome would be different.

'How can I help you today? Do you have more information on who might have sent you the previous messages?'

'I don't have any proof, but I think I know who it was,' she said. 'I had an old school friend staying with me and I think it was her.'

'I recall you mentioned her before,' he said, picking up a pen. 'Can you repeat her name?'

'Sarah Coulsdon.'

'And what reason do you have for believing Miss Coulsdon is responsible?'

Lynda explained all that had happened since Sarah had come back into her life.

'I'm a little confused over the timeline of events,' he said.

'You received the plant and card before she moved in with you, but the hangman's noose drawing arrived shortly before she moved out? Why would she send the plant to threaten you if she wanted to move in with you? And why would she send the drawing if she didn't want to move out?'

Lynda shrugged. 'I have no idea. None of it makes any sense. She took great delight in moving things just enough for me to notice, but not sufficiently for it to be noticeable to anyone else.'

'And yet you say she swapped the position of two prints in your bedroom?'

'Yes, but she moved them back again before I could confront her.'

'You said she didn't like cats. Is this why you feel she sent the card?'

'Yes! She wanted to upset me because I threw her out.'

'I'm afraid this sounds more like two ex-friends having an extended argument than anything we can take action on.'

'Not even about my stolen hoodie?' Lynda asked, realising how stupid it sounded even to her own ears.

He shrugged. 'We can make a report on it, but I'm afraid it falls under the level of crime needed for us to take action.'

'So you can't or won't do anything?'

'Miss Blackthorn, we're not in the habit of employing police resources to investigate a missing hoodie when there are more serious crimes in need of police attention. You've made your friend move out of your home, so the chances are you won't have any more trouble.'

Lynda stood up, angry with herself for bothering to come to the station.

'Thanks for nothing,' she said, heading for the door.

'Before you go, Miss Blackthorn, I want you to know that I would really like to help you, but you have to bring me something I can use.' He smiled, not unkindly, but it still grated on Lynda. 'After you left on your last visit, I looked up the case details regarding the accident you mentioned.'

She stopped and turned to face him. 'And?'

'At the inquest you were very vocal about what you called the police indifference to the account you'd given, but in fact your words had been taken seriously. The scene of the accident, from where the car left the road to where it was retrieved from the river, was searched in minute detail to find evidence to corroborate your story that someone else must have been involved. There was no obvious damage to your father's car other than that which would have resulted from going through the barrier. No other vehicle was indicated on the report. No sign of another car's paintwork having connected with your father's car. As you know, that particular bend has an unfortunate history with far too many accidents taking place there.'

'What's the point of you telling me all this?' Lynda said. 'Do you think I don't know the police found nothing? I am well aware I was regarded as an unreliable witness because of my memory lapse and lack of evidence to back up my belief that Dad was forced off the road, but I'll say now what I said back then. My dad was a good driver and would not have taken that bend too fast. Something caused him to leave the road. I just wish I could remember what it was!'

She turned and walked out. There was no point in trying to argue with someone who'd already made up his mind she was wasting precious police time.

Lynda started her car, furious with the officer, but even angrier with herself for not being able to put into words the fear she felt. Even though Sarah was out of her apartment, she still felt unsafe.

She arrived at her office feeling as if climbing the stairs to her own floor was going to take more effort than she was able to manage. As she walked into reception, her boss looked up from some papers he'd been studying on the counter. He glanced at his watch and frowned.

'I'm sorry I'm late,' Lynda said. 'There was somewhere I needed to go before coming in.'

Don Frankam frowned. 'And that was more important than this morning's meeting?' he asked in anything but a friendly voice.

Lynda stopped dead. The new account! She'd totally forgotten she was due to make a presentation.

'I'm so sorry,' she said. 'I left a message with Barbara to say I was running late. Were you able to reschedule? Shall I phone the client and apologise?'

His frown deepened. 'That won't be necessary. Fortunately, Andrew was able to step in at the last minute and make the presentation. He made an excellent job of it. So good, in fact, that the client has insisted he wants Andrew to continue as his liaison contact going forward.'

Lynda knew the presentation was good. She'd prepared it. Her colleague had helped, but she had spent long hours working on the client's instructions. Andrew must have downloaded all the files and necessary presentation details from her computer. She wanted to make excuses, but knew deep down that the fault was hers. She wasn't concentrating on her job. How could she with everything else that was going on?

'I'm sorry,' she said again.

Don Frankam shrugged and moved towards her, lowering his voice so that only she could hear.

'I'm sorry too, Lynda. I hope I didn't make a mistake promoting you over Andrew. I honestly believed you were the best person for the job, but now I'm not so sure. It's up to you to prove to me and everyone else that you deserve the position you are currently holding.'

Chapter Thirty-Four

Lynda could barely hold back the tears as she waited for Penelope to call her in. Other than how things were going with Jason, there didn't seem to be any part of her life that wasn't falling apart.

Was this some kind of karmic payback for the teenager she'd been? She couldn't control the questions bombarding her mind and had no answers to any of them. She wanted so much to go home and climb into bed, but what good would that do if she was awake for half the night and experiencing dimly remembered nightmares during the other half.

Penelope's door opened exactly on the stroke of seven. At least something in her life was running correctly.

'Come through, Lynda.'

As she stood up, a wave of fatigue flooded her body and she had to clutch at the wall to keep her balance. Penelope rushed over.

'Here, take my arm. Let me help you,' she said.

Holding on to Penelope, Lynda was able to walk the short distance to the therapy room without stumbling, but wondered how she would manage when it was time to leave. She probably shouldn't be driving. Maybe Georgina could come and pick her up.

'Settle yourself down,' Penelope said. 'Are you unwell? Should you be at home in bed?'

Lynda tried to smile, but felt the tears welling up. 'I needed to come,' she said. 'I don't know what's happening any more. Everything is going wrong. Even my job is a disaster. I think I've been put on notice.'

'But you're not sure?'

'I'm not sure of anything!' Lynda said, horrified to hear her voice sounding close to hysteria.

'Lynda, listen to me. You need to take a few deep breaths and then tell me slowly what has happened to cause this level of distress.'

Lynda struggled to slow her breathing and for some time the only sound in the room was her laboured gasps, but eventually she was able to get her emotions under control. She looked at Penelope.

'I am so sorry,' she said. 'I know I have to get myself together, but so much has happened since I last saw you. I'm scared witless.'

'Lynda, let's stop there and do some calming exercises.'

Lynda nodded, unable to speak.

'Close your lips and inhale through your nose. One, two, three, four. Now hold your breath. One, two, three, four, five, six, seven.'

Lynda followed Penelope's instructions, feeling a bit calmer as she went through each stage.

'Now exhale through your mouth. Let me hear a nice

whooshing sound. One, two, three, four, five, six, seven, eight.'

Lynda felt her breathing become more manageable.

'Let's go through it a few more times,' Penelope said.

After another three repetitions Lynda felt more at peace.

'Are you ready to continue?' Penelope said.

Lynda nodded. 'I went to the police station this morning before I went to work, but I might just have well not bothered. The officer I've been dealing with has made it perfectly clear he thinks I'm wasting their time. The only good thing that's happened is that I've had the locks changed.'

'On a practical level, I'm very pleased you've done that. It should give you some peace of mind and level of security. Let's examine the issues step by step. What happened with Jason?'

Lynda gave what sounded to her own ears as a hysterical laugh.

'Jason and I are planning to get back together.'

'But that's excellent news,' Penelope said.

'Is it?' Lynda asked. 'What if I tell him all that's been happening? Won't he think I'm back to the same state I was in when he left?'

'You haven't told him about the threats?'

Lynda shook her head. 'We're planning to live together in London. I'm hoping that once I move, Sarah will leave me alone.'

'You will need to tell Jason at some point. Keeping a secret this big would put a strain on any relationship.'

'You're right. I should tell him,' Lynda said, 'but not now. He's in Cardiff for the next week at least. Sarah's actions are not something I want to talk about over the phone. I think

Jason and I need to be face to face so that I can see whether or not he believes me.'

The next part of the session was spent talking about her work situation, which Lynda knew without needing to be told was going to improve only once she'd sorted out this situation with Sarah.

By the time they had covered her nightmares and gone over the techniques Penelope felt might help her to recover her lost memories, Lynda felt she had her emotions almost back under control, but she must have still looked shaky because Penelope suggested getting someone to come and pick her up.

Lynda smiled. 'I was thinking the same thing,' she said. 'I'll go downstairs and call my friend.'

She said goodbye and went down to the street. Taking out her phone she was about to touch the screen on Georgina's name, but changed her mind. It wasn't fair to put that on her and drag her halfway across town when she might be busy. Lynda vowed to drive very carefully and make sure she didn't fall asleep at the wheel.

Lynda was relieved to arrive home safely after her therapy session. Penelope always had a calming effect on her, which she'd really needed after her day had started so badly at the police station, and then gone from bad to worse the moment she'd arrived at work. She thought over Don's words. Had he threatened her with the sack, or had he been simply saying to pull herself together? Looking back on the day, it seemed as if everything she'd touched had created problems for her or someone else in the office. The really galling thing was

Andrew sailing around the place totally in control of every situation and tidying up all the messes that led back to Lynda. If she heard 'oh, thank you, Andrew, we couldn't have done it without you,' one more time she'd scream.

But she knew that wasn't fair to him. All the mistakes had been hers. She hadn't been able to concentrate properly for days. She walked up the stone steps and opened the door, wanting to go upstairs and crash, but knowing she should tell Georgina she'd been to the police station.

She rang Georgina's bell and waited. After a few moments the door opened.

'You look all in,' Georgina said, frowning. 'Bad day at work?'

'Bad day all round, starting with my visit to the police this morning.'

'That doesn't sound good,' Georgina said.

'It wasn't. I could see the officer dismissed my concerns as the ravings of a lunatic. I gave him Sarah's details and he said he'd look into it, but I think he was just humouring me. I doubt they'll do anything at all.'

'Want to come in and offload?'

Lynda shook her head. 'Not right now,' she said. 'I've had the worst day at work, and although my therapy session was helpful, it hasn't stopped me from feeling as if I've been run over by a tractor. I'm going upstairs to shower, climb into bed and hide under the duvet until tomorrow.'

She waved at Georgina and continued upstairs. Sorting out her new key should have given her a sense of security. There was no way anyone could have been inside, but she still opened the door cautiously and peered into the hallway before going in.

The place no longer felt like home. There was no sense of joy in being here. She reached up to straighten the mirror and laughed. There was a touch of hysteria in the sound. Even she could see it was already perfectly aligned, but that didn't stop her needing to touch it to assure herself it didn't need adjusting. If she couldn't control that urge, how was it going to work if she moved to London with Jason? She'd drive him mad.

Chapter Thirty-Five

On Saturday morning as she ran, Lynda vowed to tell Jason everything that had happened since Sarah had turned up at the charity. She wouldn't hold anything back. More than anything, she wanted their relationship to work. As Penelope had said, keeping such a massive secret would drive them apart. This time, she wouldn't allow her insecurities to come between them. As soon as he was back from Cardiff she'd open up about her fears. With him on her side, she could cope with anything.

She pushed herself to the limit as she ran and arrived home breathless but at peace. Whatever happened from now on, she was going to take charge of her life.

When she opened her front door she heard her phone ringing and rushed through to the bedroom where she'd left her bag, but the ringtone stopped before she could reach it. Grabbing the phone, she saw she had a missed call from Jason and was about to call him back when a text message pinged.

Sorry I missed you. Hope you had a good run. Going into a meeting now. No rest for the wicked. Will call you this evening. Love you so much. J xxx

She quickly texted back: *Love you too – don't work too hard. L xxx*

Stripping off her running gear, she headed for the shower singing a very loud but very off-key rendition of 'I Will Always Love You'. She laughed as she mentally apologised to Whitney Houston and any of her neighbours unfortunate enough to hear her.

By the time she reached the charity office she'd decided to tell Greg she would be moving to London. Her future was with Jason. The sooner she committed to that, the better. When she went inside she was surprised to see Cassie and Amanda with him. All three looked up as she came in. She thought they looked awkward. Had they been talking about her? Why would they?

Then she remembered. She'd arranged to meet them all this morning to go over the remaining details so that the website could finally go live. Amanda had asked for the early start because she was going out for the day with her husband. How could she have forgotten?

'I'm so sorry,' she said. 'I know I should've been here half an hour ago. I'm afraid I've a lot going on at the moment and it slipped my mind.'

'I can't stay much longer,' Amanda said. 'My husband is coming to pick me up in half an hour. That's why I asked if we could meet earlier.'

Throwing her bag onto the nearest desk, Lynda apologised again. 'Let's go through to the meeting room,' she said.

Lynda was in awe of the fabulous job Cassie had done.

'This is amazing, Cassie,' she said. 'It looks so professional. If we'd tried to do it ourselves it would have ended up a dog's dinner.'

'Amanda has set up all the payment options for those entering the three races, as well as the pricing for race merchandise, as sourced by Greg.'

'You are all shining stars,' Lynda said. She took a deep breath, knowing she had to let them in on her future plans.

'I've something to tell you all because it will impact on my volunteer work in the future. I know you're aware I've been hoping to get back together with Jason. Well, it's going to happen. We're planning to move in together in a few months.'

'That's great news,' Greg said, although his expression told her he thought it was anything but good. 'But I'm not sure how it will affect the charity. You're not planning to stop coming in, I hope.'

'Not immediately,' Lynda said, 'but eventually, yes. Jason is away in Cardiff for another week, but when he gets back he'll be commuting from Peterborough to London every day. That's not something we want him to do long-term, so he's going to search for an apartment for us to move to in London.'

'When?' Greg asked.

'I don't know yet, but I won't be moving in with him until after the race weekend. I wouldn't leave you all in the lurch, but I felt I should let you know now, rather than drop it on you at the last minute.'

'I'm happy for you,' Cassie said.

'Me too,' Amanda said.

Lynda turned to Greg. He looked stunned and her heart went out to him. She knew he had been hoping for something more than friendship, but even if she hadn't got back with Jason, that wasn't going to happen.

Amanda looked at her watch. 'I need to get going.'

As they went through to the main office, the charity door burst open and Sarah stormed in.

'You bitch!' she screeched, pointing her finger at Lynda. 'You got me fired from that temp job. Don't try to deny it. I know it was you. You didn't care that I was left penniless. You just couldn't bear the thought that people liked me more than they liked you.'

Lynda stood frozen to the spot, unable to speak.

Greg took a step forward and put up his hand. 'I think you should stop right there. Whatever you have to say to Lynda should be said in private. Perhaps you could go into the meeting room. I'm sure Lynda would be happy to discuss your grievance with you.'

Sarah laughed. 'You think so? You don't know the first thing about your precious Lynda. Has she told you why she volunteers here? You think it's because she's so good? Well, let me tell you, she's far from good. She only does it to make herself feel better about what a cow she was when we were younger.'

She turned to Lynda. 'Go on, tell them what a first-class bitch you were back then. Tell them how you turned your back on me and let everyone bully me about my birthmark.'

'Sarah, I . . .'

'That's right, you can't even get the words out, can you?'

218

Lynda felt everyone's eyes boring into her. She wanted to defend herself, but how could she? Everything Sarah was saying was the truth. She *had* told the agency to send someone else. She *had* left Sarah defenceless when they stopped being friends.

If only Sarah hadn't been so jealous of Mark, they could have continued to be friends, but Sarah had done everything she could to drive a wedge between her and Mark. It was only after they'd had a massive argument over him that the rift had appeared. And was the argument worth it? No, because after breaking her friendship with Sarah she hadn't done what Mark had begged her to do. He'd committed suicide because of that. She'd driven him to it.

Greg, Cassie and Amanda were all staring at her. Especially Greg, who was looking shocked.

Sarah laughed. 'Well, now you know the real Lynda Blackthorn.'

She turned and walked out, leaving behind her a silence so loud Lynda felt deafened by it.

Greg stood up. 'I know Lynda better than either of you and whatever she may have done in the past, the person she is now is all that matters. We've all got skeletons in our closets. None of us are saints.' He whirled round, pointing at each of them in term. 'Can you honestly say there's nothing in your past lives that you wouldn't be horrified for the rest of us to know?'

He waited. Cassie and Amanda stayed silent.

'I thought not,' he said. 'Lynda, whatever that woman said has nothing to do with the person I have got to know over the last couple of years.'

'Thank you,' she said, 'but much of what Sarah said was

true. I'm not going to deny it. She was bullied over that birthmark. I was her only friend and used to protect her, but then I met someone, a boy, and fell in love. Sarah was jealous. She felt left out and tried to come between us. During that time, I wasn't there for Sarah. She was badly bullied, but one day she fought back and seriously injured the main bully, Hazel. She was expelled and I never saw her again until she came in the same day as the two of you,' she said, turning to Cassie and Amanda.

Amanda looked at her watch and then picked up her bag. 'Thank you for telling us,' she said. 'I'm sorry, but I have to go. My husband doesn't like it if I'm late when he's planned a full day out for us.'

Cassie picked up her laptop case. 'Wait for me, Amanda. I'd best be off as well. I'll let you know as soon as the site is live, Lynda. I'll be doing it over the weekend.'

Lynda watched them go, wishing she could turn back the clock so that they never had to hear about her past.

Greg smiled. 'Want a coffee?'

'I'd love one, thank you,' she said. 'And Greg, thank you for your words of support.'

'No bother,' he said. 'I meant it. We all have things in our past we never want to see the light of day. You were just unlucky that Sarah decided to out you.'

Except, thought Lynda, she hadn't outed her worst secret, but then again maybe Sarah didn't know Lynda had driven Mark to commit suicide.

Chapter Thirty-Six

It was amazing, Lynda thought, how much lighter she felt after finally telling someone, other than Penelope, that she'd allowed Sarah to be bullied. She'd been too distracted, too wrapped up in her own young love fourteen years ago, she hadn't been able to stand up for Sarah when the others had mercilessly mocked her birthmark. They'd eventually pushed Sarah to the verge of a breakdown. What Sarah hadn't mentioned in the charity was what had happened the last day she and Lynda had seen each other. Lynda had arrived late for the time she'd promised Sarah she would be there for her.

Lynda could remember as clearly as if it had happened yesterday the look of joy on Sarah's face as she'd stood over the screaming Hazel. Teachers had come running, one taking the rock from Sarah. Another teacher had lifted the injured girl, blood seeping through her fingers as she held them to her face.

Sarah laughed. 'I hope it leaves a deep scar so that you'll know what it feels like to be mocked.'

There had been a court case, but Lynda couldn't recall the details. For a full year she'd been too distraught over Mark to have time for anyone else, but she did remember being told that Sarah had been sent to an institution. Her parents had obviously thought they'd had no choice but to have her sectioned. Or maybe it was court ordered.

Much of Sarah's accusation about why Lynda had supported the charity was true. She had given her time for the wrong reasons. She'd wanted to feel better about herself, but it had never worked.

In the next session with Penelope, she planned to be more honest about her past. She would finally tell her about what had happened with Mark. She looked at her watch. Jason would be calling soon. She'd open up more with him as well. If their relationship was going to work, she needed to trust him with some of her secrets.

Realising she still had enough time to make a cup of tea, she went through to the kitchen, instinctively looking at where Lucky used to sleep. Was Sarah disturbed enough to kill a cat? Lynda had no idea, but she couldn't shift the thought from her mind that Lucky had gone missing the day Sarah had moved in.

She flicked the switch on the kettle and began her tea-making ritual. As she took the mug from the cupboard and reached for the teabags, she decided to do things differently. Instead of making sure the mug was in exactly the right place, she moved it an inch to the left, then another inch, and another, until the mug was far from where it should be. Forcing herself to take deep breaths, she continued making her tea with the mug in its strange new position. It felt wrong, so very wrong, but she controlled the urge to move the mug back to where it should be. Changing the order of making the tea itself was a step too far, but she knew she'd passed a milestone just by moving the mug. If she could break just one of her rituals, she knew she stood a chance of changing her life.

Lynda took her tea through to the lounge, feeling as if she'd conquered Everest. When the phone rang she was feeling so pleased with herself she almost sang when she said hello.

'And hello to you, gorgeous,' Jason said. 'You sound happy.'

'I am,' she said. 'I've just broken one of my rituals. It was hard, but I did it.'

'Wow! I don't know what to say to that, other than just . . . wow! What made you decide to do it?'

'It's been a combination of things. Partly the therapy and partly having to confront something from my past. Well, two things from my past.'

'Am I allowed to ask, or would you rather not tell me?'

Lynda heard the pensive note in his voice and sighed. 'I'd rather not tell you, but I'm going to. You've been asking me what's wrong and I keep telling you nothing, but that's not true. Do you have time to listen, or should we talk later? I mean, do you have to go off for another meeting or dinner or anything?'

'Lynda, even if I was supposed to be somewhere else, being on the phone right now with you is where I want to be. If you feel up to telling me, then I'm here to listen.'

She began by telling him about Sarah at school and then how she'd been manipulated into allowing Sarah to live with her.

'So when I said you should throw her out,' Jason said, 'you didn't feel you could. You felt you owed her because, in your mind, you'd let her down in the past?'

'That's exactly the reason,' Lynda said.

'But I don't understand why you're still stressed out,' Jason said. 'Now that she's gone, the problem is solved, or is there more to it?'

Lynda sighed. 'There's more to it.'

She told him about the plant, the messages and how she'd found poor Lucky.

'And the police aren't prepared to do anything?' Jason said.

'Apparently I don't have enough proof. None of the messages are handwritten, so there's nothing to show who they came from. The police officer didn't exactly say it, but I got the feeling he thought I might have been making stuff up for attention.'

'Why didn't you tell me any of this before? Didn't you trust me?'

'It wasn't that,' Lynda said. 'It was that I didn't want you to think I was imagining things, like I did before. You know, after my family died.'

'I know,' Jason said, his voice little more than a whisper. 'You were hurting so badly and I didn't know how to comfort you. I hate the thought of being so far away. Shall I come back? I can tell my boss I have a family emergency.'

'No,' said Lynda. 'There's no point. I'm doing fine now. I'm more in control of my emotional state than I've been in a very long time. I know what Sarah's doing and I understand why she's doing it, but I can't see any way she can hurt me now. If I find another card I'll just throw it away.'

'I love you,' Jason said. 'I love you so much. Just keep away from the mad woman as much as you can.'

'After this morning's episode I don't think I'll be seeing her again.'

'What happened this morning?'

She told him about Sarah coming to the charity.

'And, of course, Amanda was there.'

'Who's Amanda?' he asked. 'Sorry, I'm trying to keep up.'

'Hmm, you might not like this story, but I promise you I was innocent of any wrongdoing. Well, not completely innocent, but I didn't know about Amanda.'

She filled him in on what had happened at university.

'But that was years ago,' he said. 'She's still mad at you?'

'Not at all, but I still feel bad about it. Tell me how things are going with you?'

Jason laughed. 'I came here thinking I was the bees' knees because I now run the London office. I've since discovered that not only am I just a small cog in a massive wheel, but that I am one of the tiniest of all the cogs. London is not, as I'd thought, the centre of the universe. In our company it's barely on the map, but I have some great ideas to change all that.'

The rest of the conversation was taken up with their plans for the future. By the time they'd said goodbye ten times each, Lynda was smiling so hard her face ached.

She put the phone on the side table and reached for her tea. It was stone cold. Who cared? She could always make another one, either by following her ritual or by breaking it. Life was good.

As Lynda got up to go to the kitchen, her front doorbell rang. She put the mug back on the side table and went to open the door.

'Hi,' Georgina said. 'I don't know about you, but I find myself at a loose end and wondered if you fancied a takeaway and a movie.'

Lynda grinned. 'Come in, you must have read my mind. I was wondering what to do with myself tonight.'

Georgina followed her into the lounge and sat down in the armchair opposite Lynda's. 'Shall we order in and watch something on Netflix, or go out and watch a film on the big screen?'

'I think I'd rather stay in. I don't feel like getting dressed up to go out.'

'Sounds good to me,' Georgina said, waving her phone. 'What do you fancy to eat?'

'I haven't had a pizza in a long while,' Lynda said. 'I'll go with anything as long as it doesn't have anchovies or pineapple on it.' She stood up. 'Fancy a glass of white? I've got a couple of bottles in the fridge.'

Georgina nodded and gave Lynda a thumbs up, then began tapping on her phone. Lynda went through to the kitchen and opened the wine. She slipped an ice cooler sleeve on the bottle and carried it with two glasses through to the lounge. Putting everything on the coffee table, she sat down.

'So, what are we having?' she said.

'Barbeque pizza,' Georgina said, 'with a side order of salad.'

Lynda laughed. 'The healthy option!'

'As long as we have something green then that wipes out all the calories in the pizza. It's a fact! Tell me, have you heard from Jason?'

Lynda filled her in on the call she'd just had and explained her plans for when Jason came back.

'He's coming straight here from Cardiff a week tomorrow. When he arrives, I'm planning a seduction second to none. Good food, good wine, sexy me. No way is he going home on Sunday night.'

Georgina grinned. 'Lucky you, but doesn't he have to go to work on Monday?'

'He has to commute to London early Monday morning, but that's OK; he can shower and change here, then pick up his suitcase when he gets back in the evening.'

'Sounds like you're finally getting your life back into order. I wish I could do the same.'

'Is Steven still giving you grief?'

Georgina shook her head. 'No, but I need to get myself out into the dating world again. I like living on my own, but it would be nice to have some male company from time to time.'

Lynda thought about the many nights she'd felt the same and her heart went out to her young friend. Why was it that the good ones seemed to attract the wrong type of men?

'You look thoughtful,' Georgina said. 'I hope you're not worrying about me.'

Lynda shook her head. 'No,' she said. 'I was thinking about what happened this morning.'

She told Georgina about Sarah coming in and causing a scene.

'You know,' Georgina said, 'you might not be worrying about me, but with that woman determined to hurt you, I worry about *you*.'

Chapter Thirty-Seven

As Lynda sat waiting for Penelope on Friday she couldn't help but compare the way she felt this week to her previous sessions. A whole week had gone by with nothing more worrying than a few minor work issues. There had been no threatening messages, no nasty phone calls, not a word from Sarah. She suppressed a laugh that threatened to bubble up in her throat as she wondered if there was even any point in being here.

Penelope opened the door into her office and beckoned Lynda in.

'How are you feeling this week?' Penelope asked once they were both seated in their usual positions.

'Better than I've felt in a while,' Lynda said. 'For once, I have good things to talk about.'

Penelope smiled. 'That *is* good news. I thought you looked more at peace with yourself when I opened the door. What has happened since I saw you last?'

'I suppose the most positive thing is how well Jason and I are getting on. He's still in Cardiff, but he's due back on Sunday.

He's coming straight to my place and I'm hoping he'll stay overnight.'

'That's quite a change from our previous discussions. Do you feel you're ready to live together again?'

Lynda shook her head. 'Not fully. I know I've still got a long way to go, but I've been working on the techniques you taught me and I've had what is for me a major breakthrough.'

She explained how she now never put her mug in the same spot twice in a row.

'I know that's almost a different kind of ritual, but before, if it wasn't exactly in the right place, I couldn't bear to look at it, far less make myself a tea or coffee.'

Penelope made a note on her pad, but didn't comment.

'Am I right in thinking this is an improvement?' Lynda asked. 'It feels as if it is.'

Penelope nodded. 'Two things. Firstly, you have recognised an issue, and secondly, you are learning to deal with it.'

Lynda smiled. 'That's not all. I told you about my obsession with the hall mirror?'

Penelope nodded again.

'I am still fixated on it, but I've trained myself not to touch it every time I pass through the hall. If I think it might be slightly out of alignment, I stand back without touching it and make myself study it properly. If it really is crooked, like after I've dusted, then I straighten it, but I no longer feel that compulsion to do it all the time.'

'That is a definite breakthrough,' Penelope said. 'I know you believed that your house guest was deliberately moving it to mess with you. Do you still think that?'

Lynda nodded. 'Yes, I do. I believe she was running a

vendetta against me. I know that sounds paranoid, but you know the old saying: just because you're paranoid, doesn't mean there isn't someone out to get you,' she said, laughing.

'And have you seen her since she moved out?'

'Unfortunately, yes,' Lynda said and explained what had taken place at the charity the week before.

'You seem to be making progress in many areas,' Penelope said.

Lynda shrugged. 'I am, but I still don't feel any closer to remembering what happened the night of the crash, although I did have a very vivid dream about it this week. I woke up drenched in sweat, convinced I knew what had happened, but when I tried to remember, the details faded away.'

'Do you want to explore what you can remember of the dream?'

Lynda nodded. 'Yes, although there isn't much to tell. My father's car was a metallic red Peugeot 408, but in the dream it was a much smaller version. At least, it was on the outside, but not on the inside.' She looked over at Penelope who was busy making notes. 'You know how in dreams weird stuff seems normal? Well, we were all in a car that was bigger on the inside than it was on the outside.'

'Like the Tardis?' Penelope said.

'Yes, but not that extreme,' Lynda said. 'I can remember seeing Dad's car from the outside as if I was looking at it from a distance and it was this tiny car compared to how it should have looked, but at the same time I was inside the car and it was the proper size.'

'What happened next?' Penelope said, pen poised above her pad.

'Then my dream morphed into the usual one where we went through the barrier, but when I woke up my brain was screaming at me that something important had happened in the dream, but whatever it was, I couldn't drag it into my conscious mind.' She sighed. 'Do you still think one day I'll remember those missing moments before Dad drove through the barrier?'

Penelope nodded. 'Yes, it seems your subconscious is trying very hard to fill in the gaps. I feel one day you will get the answer you need, but it might still take some time.'

Chapter Thirty-Eight

The next morning Lynda went out for her normal five-kilometre run, remembering when she and Jason used to run together in the mornings. It would be great to have someone running with her. She'd missed him in the apartment since he'd left, but she realised as she reached her comfortable pace and settled into a rhythm how much she'd enjoyed running with him.

Hard on the heels of that thought came the realisation that she hadn't seen the man in the blue car for a couple of weeks. Maybe he'd given up tracking lone women or he could have found someone else to annoy. Either way, she no longer had him to worry about. It meant she could concentrate on her breathing and simply enjoy the run.

She arrived home, out of breath, but happy. Looking at her watch she saw it wasn't one of her fastest runs. In fact, if anything, it was one of her slowest. It must have been because her mind had been more on the thought of Jason coming home tomorrow than pushing herself. She laughed. She'd need to up her pace once she started running with him.

An hour later, having showered and dressed, she was pulling up outside the charity. She hadn't seen or heard from Cassie or Amanda since the showdown with Sarah the week before, so she wasn't sure if they'd be in today, or how they would react to her if they did come in. The group of young men were in their usual spot. Lynda wondered why they'd picked this particular street to hang out in. There didn't seem to be anything here to attract them.

Lynda pulled on the car's handbrake and reached for her bag. Whatever happened, no matter how embarrassing, she was glad at least one of her guilty secrets was out in the open. At least now she didn't have to pretend she had nothing to hide. *Apart from Mark*, her treacherous brain reminded her.

She got out of the car and crossed the road, ignoring the cat calls. As she opened the charity door she heard Greg's voice on the phone. He was counselling a caller, so she simply waved as he looked up.

She headed for the kitchen and put the kettle on, certain Greg would need a coffee as it sounded like a difficult call. Sometimes the callers just wanted someone to listen; other times they were in desperate need of advice on how to stop the bullying. That was always harder to deal with because bullies didn't play by any set rules. The advice given to one youngster being victimised wouldn't necessarily work in another situation. From what she could hear from Greg's end, the caller had tried just about everything and Greg was talking them down from a possible suicide state.

Eventually, she heard the tone of Greg's voice change. He must have got through to the caller that life is always worth living. If she'd known that Mark would take her rejection as he did, would she have done anything different? Hard to know. She'd barely turned sixteen at the time. What Mark had asked of her she couldn't give, but she hadn't been honest with him. She'd let him believe they had a future together until it came to the point where she had to act on that promise.

Stop it! Stop thinking about Mark and what happened to him!

Mechanically, she made two cups of coffee and carried them through to the office. Quietly, she put Greg's down on the desk and smiled when he mouthed a silent thanks.

She moved over to the other desk just as Greg ended the call.

'That sounded like a tough one,' Lynda said.

Greg sighed. 'It was. Poor child is being picked on at school and online. He feels there's nowhere safe. The worst of it is he thinks he deserves it. The bullies have completely destroyed his self-belief. I know exactly how he feels.'

It was so rare for Greg to open up about his own life that Lynda wasn't sure how to react.

'Is that what happened to you?' she asked.

Greg nodded. 'At least I didn't have the online bullying to deal with. I could go home and lock myself in my room. It was the only place I felt safe. Youngsters today have no safe places. Trolls on the internet can get them wherever they go.'

'Were you able to help your caller?'

Greg shrugged. 'I hope so, but I don't really know. He sounded better, but it could take a word to destroy him again.'

'Is there something you want to ask me, Greg?' Lynda said.

'What makes you say that?'

'The expression on your face. I think I know you well enough by now to tell when you have a question.'

He laughed. 'You're right, but I wasn't sure if I should ask.'

'Go ahead, fire away,' she said.

'Have you seen Sarah since last week? I've been worried about you. She clearly blames you for everything bad in her life.'

'I haven't seen her or heard from her. I feel a tremendous amount of guilt over what happened, but I don't think I can put it right now. I think it's best if we stay away from each other.'

'And how are things with Jason?' he asked, far too nonchalantly for Lynda to believe he wasn't desperately hoping things were not going well.

She was about to answer when the phone rang. Picking it up, she prepared herself to help the caller.

The phone lines were busy for the next couple of hours, so it was almost lunchtime before Lynda was able to take off her headset. Shortly afterwards, Greg did the same.

'Fancy a pasty?' he asked. 'I'm buying.'

'I'd love one,' Lynda said, 'but it's my treat this time. I'll go.'

Greg stood up. 'No, better if I go. I haven't had chance to tell you but Cassie and Amanda are both coming in today. Cassie says there's been a glitch with the new site so she had to take it down. The changes she has to make impact on the accounting side of things, or something like that. To be honest, when Cassie gets all techie, I lose interest.'

Lynda smiled. 'She is quite intense, but very good at what she does.'

'I know,' Greg said, 'and I'm prepared to take her word for anything she feels needs to be done. I just don't want to hear how she does it.'

He picked up his jacket from the back of his chair and headed for the door. 'I'd best get enough for all of us. I won't be long,' he said.

Lynda sat at her desk waiting for another call, but none came in. Just as she was about to send a text to Jason to see if he was free to speak, the door opened and Amanda came in, closely followed by Cassie.

As the last time she'd seen them had been so awkward, Lynda felt the need to put them both at their ease.

'Hi, you two. Look, about last week. I'm really sorry about everything. It must have been very embarrassing and upsetting for both of you.'

Cassie looked uncomfortable. 'It was a bit, but what Greg said about us all having skeletons in our past hit home. None of us are perfect, although I come pretty close,' she said, grinning.

Lynda turned to Amanda, who reached out to put her hand on Lynda's arm. As she did so, her sleeve rode up and Lynda saw her wrist was a mass of black and green bruising.

'Oh my God, Amanda, what happened to your wrist?'

As soon as she said the words she wished she'd bitten them back. From the look on Amanda's face and the way she was pulling at her sleeve it was obvious she didn't want attention drawn to her arm.

Silent tears were streaming down Amanda's face. Cassie came and put her arm round her. 'It's OK. You're safe here.'

Lynda took Amanda's hand and gently squeezed it. 'I have a friend who runs a shelter. She'd take you in immediately. Shall I call her?'

Amanda shrugged off Cassie's arm and pulled her hand out

of Lynda's grasp. 'I have no idea what you're talking about, either of you. I shut my wrist in the car door. Now, can we get on with whatever it is we need to sort out so that I can go home? I have a lot to do today.'

'Sure,' Lynda said, wishing she could do something. It was clear those bruises had not been caused by shutting her wrist in a car door or anything else. She had clearly seen the imprint of fingers, as if someone had closed their hand on Amanda's wrist and squeezed hard enough for bruises to form. 'We'll have to have our discussion in here until Greg gets back so I can man the phone if needed. That's the problem with us having so few volunteers: if something comes up we don't have people to call on for cover.'

'OK,' Cassie said, 'this is where the problem lies.'

Half an hour later Amanda and Cassie both seemed satisfied, but Lynda's head was spinning. She hadn't followed even half of what had been said by either of them, but as long as they knew what they were doing she supposed she didn't need to understand it all.

'I can make the changes overnight and bring the final version to you tomorrow,' Cassie said, 'as long as you don't mind me breaking into your Sunday. Or, I'm in Peterborough on Monday, so we could meet at lunchtime. Which would suit you better?'

'Do I need to be there?' Amanda asked.

'No,' Cassie said. 'We've already sorted everything to do with the accounting side of things.' She looked over at Lynda. 'Which would you prefer, tomorrow at any time to suit you, or Monday at about one thirty?'

'Can we leave it until Monday? Jason is coming back from

237

Cardiff tomorrow. He's been away all week, so I'd like to spend time with him. He's not looking forward to commuting every day to London, but he'll have to do it until we find a place and move.'

'Which will only be after the race weekend, right?' Greg said.

'I didn't hear you come in, Greg,' Lynda said, wishing she hadn't mentioned Jason. 'I won't be moving to London until the event is done, dusted and cleared up afterwards.'

'I have lunch for everyone,' he said, sounding upbeat, but Lynda could see by the hurt look on his face he was covering up how he was really feeling.

Chapter Thirty-Nine

On Sunday morning, bright and early, Lynda stood in the kitchen surrounded by the ingredients she'd carefully collated for the special celebration meal she'd planned for that evening. She didn't really need to start her preparation for a couple of hours, but she'd woken up early and was too excited to go back to sleep. She'd tried to get interested in her latest book, but found herself reading the same paragraph over and over.

Glancing at the clock on the oven, she laughed. It was only 7.35 and she was already chopping vegetables for dinner! She thought over her menu; nothing says seduction like a home-cooked meal by candlelight. So far Jason had held off coming over to her place as he hadn't wanted to stay overnight until they were both sure they were doing the right thing. He'd said he didn't want to do anything to jeopardise their future. Lynda had decided that tonight was the night they would find out if the spark they used to have in bed still existed. *Of course it does*, she chided herself, remembering how she'd quivered after their last long, lingering kiss.

Concentrate, she ordered, as the knife slipped and she almost lost a finger. The sexy thoughts needed to wait until she was no longer holding a lethal weapon.

Preparation complete, she wondered how on earth she was going to pass the time until Jason arrived mid-afternoon. She hadn't planned to run this morning, but she could waste an hour by going for an eight-kilometre jog. Longer, if she ran slowly and took in her surroundings.

She went to the bedroom and got ready, smiling at how good her life was now that Sarah had given up tormenting her.

At half three Lynda heard the sound she'd waited all day for. The intercom rang to let her know someone was downstairs.

'Hello, gorgeous,' Jason said when she answered the call.

'Come on up,' she said, clicking the button to release the downstairs lock.

Lynda opened her apartment door and waited for Jason to climb up to her floor. As he appeared round the bend in the stairs her heart flipped. He was everything she'd ever wanted in a man. This time she would make it work. No more driving a wedge between them over crap that hadn't even happened.

She opened her arms as he reached her landing. Jason dropped his bag and walked straight into them.

'God, I love you,' he said.

Too choked to speak, Lynda could only squeeze him tighter in response. He let go of her and turned back to pick up his bag. The look he gave her as he straightened up sent shivers through to her core. Kicking the door closed behind them, Jason dumped his bag in the hall and cupped her chin in his hand. Lifting her face to his, he smiled.

Lynda's plan had been to seduce him over dinner, but as he leaned down to kiss her, she knew dinner was going to be much later than she'd anticipated.

Snuggling up to Jason in bed an hour later, Lynda smiled.

'That was quite some hello,' she said.

He pulled her closer. 'Hellos are always fun, but if we don't say goodbye, we can't have another hello.'

'We could try *au revoir*, or *hasta luego*, or *ciao*. None of those actually mean goodbye, do they?'

'I have no idea,' he said. 'Languages were never my strong point.'

She laughed. 'I know all about your strong point,' she said, stroking the hairs on his chest.

'You'll know even more about it if you carry on doing what you're doing.'

'Oh good,' she said. 'I was hoping you'd say that.'

Much later, Lynda couldn't help comparing the way she felt as they worked together in the kitchen with how she used to react when they lived together. Back then, she hadn't allowed him to touch anything if she was preparing a meal. It used to drive her insane if he moved anything, but today she felt totally at peace as he passed her the ingredients and implements as she needed them.

'This is going to be a banquet,' Jason said. 'We have enough food here to feed a rugby team.'

She laughed. 'It does seem to be quite a lot. Oh well,

whatever we don't eat today we can have as leftovers during the week.'

'Is that an invitation to come back again?' Jason said, sounding more serious than she'd heard him that day.

Lynda put down the wooden spoon she'd been using to stir the mushroom sauce and turned to face him.

'That sounds like a deeper question than asking if you've been invited back to share the leftovers. What are you really asking, Jason?'

She held her breath, waiting for him to answer, not sure of what she wanted him to say, or how she would respond if he was going to suggest moving back in.

'I'm asking if we need to wait until we move to London to be together. I want to live with you now, not in a few months' time. How would you feel about that?'

'You want to move back in here?' Lynda asked.

He nodded. 'Or you could move in with me, but as you know I only have a bedsit, so here would be more comfortable for us. Are there too many unhappy memories here from those terrible months before we parted?'

'I don't know,' she said, 'and that's the most honest answer I can give you. I'm so happy you're here and we're together, but I really don't know if you moving back into this apartment would be good for us or not. Can I take a couple of days to think it over?'

Jason dropped a kiss on her forehead.

'Take as long as you need. This time we're going to do it right.'

Chapter Forty

Lynda woke with a wonderful sense of wellbeing. She turned on her side and gazed at Jason still sleeping. At any moment now her alarm would sound and he'd wake. She reached out to her phone and turned the alarm off. She had a much better idea of how to wake him than the shock of music blaring.

Jason came out of the shower with a bath towel wrapped around his waist. He grinned at Lynda.

'Any chance that could be your regular wake-up method?' he asked. 'It sure beats anything else I've tried over the years.'

He came and sat on the edge of the bed.

'Don't worry, I didn't intend to put you on the spot over my question yesterday. I meant what I said. We're going to move at the pace that suits you, but I wanted you to know how much I love you and want to be with you.'

She reached out and took his hand. 'I love you, too. I'll think hard over the next few days. I just want to make sure we're doing the right thing moving in together and living here. Look, why don't you come here when you get back to Peterborough this evening? Stay the night? We can try out a few days and nights before making a commitment. What do you say?'

'I say, yes,' he said. 'Now I need to get a move on or I'll miss my train.'

Lynda watched as he got dressed, admiring the leanness of his body and remembering how it had felt to have him in bed with her. Why was she so nervous about him moving back into the apartment when she had no qualms about setting up together in London? She knew the answer, though. There were so many bad memories here that they might get in the way of them being happy.

'Damn!' Jason said, picking up his phone. 'I hadn't realised the charger wasn't properly connected. My phone is as flat as a pancake. I'll have to charge it on the train.'

He came over to the bed and leaned down, smelling deliciously of shower gel and aftershave.

'*Au revoir,*' he said.

'*Hasta luego,*' Lynda answered, touching her lips to his.

'*Ciao, bella.*' Jason ran his fingers down her face and then stood up. 'I'll call you later when my phone has charged up a bit.'

Lynda watched as he left the bedroom and then snuggled down under the duvet when she heard the door close. She had a few more minutes before she needed to get up and she intended to make the most of them.

After Lynda had showered, she came back into the bedroom and looked at the time on her phone. Ten to eight. Jason would already be on the train to London. In fact, he'd be there in under half an hour. His phone should have some charge by now, as long as he'd remembered to plug it in.

She tapped on his name. The call went directly to voice-mail. Either he hadn't yet had a chance to charge the phone, or he'd forgotten to do so, which was much more likely. While living together, his constantly asking to use her phone because his battery was dead had been another recurring source of annoyance. Would she feel like that again, or would she be more tolerant and understanding? She shrugged. There was no point in worrying over something that hadn't yet happened.

She got dressed and was about to leave for work when she decided to try Jason's phone again. Once more it went straight to voicemail. This time she decided to leave a message.

'Hi, sexy, I just wanted to let you know I'm still tingling from this morning. Call me when you get this and I'll tell you more.'

She laughed and threw the phone on the bed. *I wonder how red his face will get if he listens to that while he's in a meeting.* It was strange that his phone was still switched off but it was always possible the charger point next to where he was sitting was faulty. Maybe the train was in a bad signal area. Yes, that was probably it. She would call him later in the day.

Lynda's morning was taken up with client meetings and discussions with Andrew. The hours seemed to fly by. She looked at her watch, realising she needed to rush to get to the local coffee bar where she'd arranged to meet Cassie.

She grabbed her phone to check for messages, but there was nothing yet from Jason. He had said he'd be tied up for most of the day, bringing the London team up to speed on what had been decided in Cardiff. It had sounded as if there were lots of changes to be made. The London office needed to raise its game to match the standard of the other branches around the country. Clearly that was why Jason had been given the promotion. They had needed a new broom prepared to sweep hard.

Dropping her phone in her bag, she rushed outside. Fortunately the café was just a couple of streets away, so she wouldn't be late if she ran. She arrived slightly out of breath, but right on time. As she entered the café, she saw that Cassie was already seated at a table against the wall. Her laptop was open and she was clearly intent on whatever she was doing as she didn't look up.

Lynda walked over to the table. 'Hi, Cassie.'

'Oh, sorry, I didn't see you come in. One of my clients has a problem with his website and I was just trying to sort it out for him. Can you give me a moment?'

'Sure, no problem,' Lynda said. 'I'll grab a coffee. Can I get you anything?'

Cassie shook her head and pointed to her empty cup. 'No, thanks, I've just finished one.'

Lynda waited at the counter for the barista to make her a cappuccino and then headed back to the table. It looked as though Cassie had finished whatever she'd needed to do as she was looking in Lynda's direction.

'Sorry about that,' Cassie said, as Lynda sat opposite her. 'This particular client is a pain, but he pays well.'

'They're the best kind,' Lynda said, taking her phone from her bag and putting it on the table. 'Shall we get to it?'

Cassie slid her laptop round so that it was between them and they could both view the screen. She began to go through the various changes she'd made, but Lynda couldn't follow a word of the jargon. As for the website, it looked identical to how it had appeared on Saturday.

'So, you see,' Cassie said, 'I think this is now the best and, I hope, final version. With your OK I can set it to go live this afternoon. What do you think?'

'It looks great, Cassie. You've put so much work into this that it can't possibly be anything other than a success,' Lynda said.

She picked up her phone and glanced briefly at the screen, but there was still nothing from Jason.

'Can I get you something to eat?' Cassie asked. 'I had a meeting scheduled with a new client in the offices along the road, but he had to reschedule, so I'm free for the next half hour or so.'

'That would be lovely, but it's my treat,' Lynda said. 'You're giving your time free of charge. There's no way I'm going to let you buy me lunch!'

After studying the menus, Lynda went over to the counter to order their food – a prawn baguette for her and a tuna melt for Cassie.

'We'll bring the food over,' the barista said, taking Lynda's money.

As she returned to the table, Cassie pointed to Lynda's phone that she'd left on the table.

'I think you just received something. Your phone buzzed.'

Lynda snatched it up, but there wasn't anything from Jason.

It was a message from Andrew saying their client had turned up an hour before he was due and asking if there was any way Lynda could come back early from lunch.

'Cassie, I'm sorry, I'm going to have to run. It's a work emergency.'

'Not to worry,' Cassie said. 'I had to be in Peterborough anyway, so it's not as if I came especially to have lunch with you.'

Lynda went to the counter and asked for her baguette to go. She waved at Cassie and headed back to the office, checking her phone on the way. Still nothing from Jason.

Surreptitiously during the meeting, which ran over its allotted time even though it had started early, Lynda kept snatching glimpses at her phone. As soon as the meeting was over, she went through to her office and tried Jason's number. Yet again her call went straight to voicemail.

Trying not to get irritated at the fact that he'd clearly forgotten to charge it throughout the day, she packed up her things and headed for home.

I will *not* get annoyed when he comes over, she told herself. I will *not* ruin our evening. But she knew she'd have to use every calming technique Penelope had taught her to prevent her exploding as soon as Jason walked through the door tonight.

Chapter Forty-One

She went into the kitchen, dumped her bag on the breakfast bar and had just put the kettle on when her phone rang. *Finally, Jason! It's about time*, she thought. *Stay calm, Lynda, stay calm.* She rummaged in her bag and hauled the phone out. The display showed Carla's name. Why was Jason's sister calling her? She lived in Blackburn, so they hadn't had much to do with each other even when she and Jason were living together. They hadn't spoken at all since Jason had moved out. Maybe he'd told her they were thinking of getting back together.

'Hi, Carla, how are you?'

Lynda heard a sob and someone trying to speak, but no words.

'Carla, you OK? What's wrong?'

'Did you see the news?' Carla said between sobs.

'No, I've only just got home. What's wrong?'

'It happened early this morning, but we've only just been told,' Carla said. 'Mum and Dad are in bits. Mum asked me to let you know.'

'Know what? Has something happened to Jason?' Lynda could hear Carla groaning, but no words came out. 'Carla, what's happened? Tell me!'

'He's dead! He fell in front of a train this morning.'

'What are you talking about? That's not possible . . . I . . . I saw him this morning. Are you sure? It must be a mistake.'

'It's not a mistake. My parents are at the hospital with the police right now.'

Lynda slid down the wall until she was on the floor. She vaguely remembered hearing something on the radio about a major incident which had closed one of the lines at Peterborough station, but she'd been too taken up with work and meeting Cassie to take any notice.

She was aware that Carla was speaking, but couldn't take in the meaning of the words.

'Lynda, did you hear me?'

'No, sorry, what . . . how . . . what . . .'

'I said, we will let you know about the funeral arrangements.' Carla was clearly trying hard not to break down. 'Jason . . . He told Mum you two were getting back together, so you should be there.'

Lynda felt numb. She found herself saying thank you when what she wanted to do was scream that Carla was wrong. Jason couldn't be dead. He just couldn't. He was going to return her calls. He was on his way over. He must be.

She mumbled through a goodbye to Carla and ended the call. Looking at her phone, willing it to ring, to prove Carla wrong; but deep inside, she knew he was gone. She sat frozen, unable to move.

Curling up in a ball, she sobbed until her throat was raw. Picking herself up off the floor, she dragged herself through to the bedroom. Sleep was what she needed.

Hours later she was still awake, staring at the ceiling, wondering if she would ever sleep again.

Chapter Forty-Two

Lynda looked around the meeting room and felt tears well up. Why had she come to work? After last night's news she should have stayed home today, but she'd forced herself to go into the office. Staying home with her thoughts would be worse than being here. She'd completely forgotten to work on the presentation for the new client. Thankfully, Andrew had stepped in yet again to save her from letting the company down. She realised not only had he not used her ideas as she'd thought he would, he'd come up with his own and had put together compelling reasons as to why the client should go with them. He was showing all the qualities she hadn't believed he possessed. No wonder he'd been so disappointed when she'd been promoted over him.

The minutes ticked by so slowly she felt trapped in suspended animation. She should have told Don Frankam about Jason. No! Don't think about Jason. Too late, she felt a tear fall and involuntarily choked, trying to stop herself from sobbing.

All heads around the table turned in her direction.

'I'm sorry,' she said, staggering to her feet and pushing the chair back. 'I . . . Please excuse me.'

She stumbled to the door and wrenched it open. As she closed it behind her, she leaned back against the wall and allowed the tears to flow. Almost blind, she felt her way along the corridor to her office. Once inside, she shut the door and stumbled across to her desk. She had to get out, go home. She couldn't cope.

But right now she wasn't safe to drive. She'd have to pull herself together somehow. She had no idea how long she sat staring into space, but the sound of someone tapping on her door pulled her back into the room.

'Come in,' she called out, praying it wasn't Don. She didn't feel she'd be able to cope with him.

'You OK?' Andrew said as he came in. He closed the door behind him. 'You look as if you need a stiff drink. I can't offer one of those, but I have a shoulder to cry on if you need one. Is there anything I can do to help?'

'Thank you, but I don't think anyone could help me at the moment.'

As she started to tell Andrew about Jason she began to sob again. When she had her tears under control she managed to put her thoughts into words.

'Did you see on the news yesterday about the man who died by falling in front of the train at Peterborough station?'

Andrew looked confused, but nodded.

'He was my boyfriend. We've only just got back together.'

'Oh God, I'm sorry,' Andrew said. 'I had no idea. Have you told Don?'

She shook her head.

'Lynda, you should go home. Would you like me to tell him?'

'Please,' she said. 'I don't think I can.'

'I'll drive you home. Wait a few minutes while I go up and fill Don in on what's happened and then get my stuff together.'

'Thank you,' she whispered. He opened the door. 'Andrew!' He turned back, a questioning look in his eyes.

'That was a great presentation this morning. You deserved the promotion. I realise that now.'

He smiled. 'Thank you for saying that, but you and Don were right. I wasn't ready. It's only because I've had to step up that I've forced myself to do it. If I'd been the one to be given the promotion instead of you, my insecurity would have stopped me from taking it on properly.'

Lynda didn't take in any of the drive home. They seemed to arrive outside her flat in just a few minutes. Normally the drive from Peterborough to Stamford seemed unending, but not today. She thanked Andrew and climbed out of his car. Hers should be safe enough in the office parking area. He lowered his window and called out to her as she walked towards the front steps.

'Lynda, I don't think you should come into work for a few days and Don agrees with me. He said to take as much time as you need. When you feel ready to return, let me know and I'll come and pick you up.'

She turned back, pulling a tissue from her pocket as she did so. It was already saturated, but she wiped her cheeks with it anyway.

'I can't think straight at the moment, Andrew. Can I let you know once I've got my head sorted? I'm not sure how long I'll be off.'

'Of course,' Andrew said. 'No problem at all.'

He waved and drove off.

Lynda climbed the stone steps to the front door and crept through the downstairs hallway. Dragging herself up to her floor, she wondered if she should tell Georgina, but right now she needed to be alone. She'd barely made it inside when her phone rang. She ignored it.

Reaching up to straighten the mirror, something she hadn't done in over a week, she shuddered at her reflection. No make-up, bags under her eyes, she looked worse than a hag on a bad day. Still more tears flooded her eyes and ran down her face. She made no attempt to stop them.

Turning from the ugliness in the mirror, she went through to the kitchen. Maybe a coffee fix would help her to cope. She filled the kettle and flicked the switch to turn it on, then slumped at the breakfast bar to wait for it to boil.

Her phone rang again. She dragged her bag towards her and rummaged until she found her phone. Looking at the display, she saw Carla's name. Could she cope with Jason's sister's grief? She had no choice.

'Hello, Carla,' she said and stopped. What could she say next? Anything she tried would be wrong.

'Lynda, I'm so sorry, I have more bad news.'

What could possibly be worse than anything she'd already heard, Lynda wondered. She waited.

'The police have been in contact with Mum and Dad. They've viewed the CCTV footage and it looks as though Jason was pushed.'

'Oh God, please, no.'

'The police are going to make a televised appeal for people who might have seen something to come forward. That's why I'm calling you. I wanted you to hear it from me before you saw it on the news on later.'

'Thank you,' Lynda said. 'Do the police have any leads?'

'Not really. The CCTV footage was grainy and not very clear, but they could see enough to know he didn't jump.'

'Did you think he had?' Lynda asked.

Carla sighed. 'No! I assumed it was an accident. I thought maybe he tripped. Why would anyone deliberately push him in front of a train?'

'I don't know,' Lynda whispered, but her mind was screaming it must be because of her. Jason didn't have any enemies – but she did.

'Funeral arrangements are still being organised. I'll be in touch once I have the day and time.'

'Thank you,' Lynda said and ended the call.

Could it have been Sarah? Was she deranged enough to kill? Maybe she should go to the police and tell them more about Sarah's early home life and what she'd done to Hazel, but would that be enough to convince them? Lots of kids were bullied at school and grew up in abusive homes. Some of them even fought back viciously, as Sarah had, but they didn't turn out to be murderers. She had no proof and the officer had made it clear: no proof, no interest, but did she really believe deep down that Sarah could have pushed Jason in front of a train? *What possible reason could she have when she barely knew him? I know the answer to that*, she thought. *If Sarah did it, then it was to hurt me.*

How much more could she take? She'd lost everyone she'd ever loved. Mother, father, brother and now Jason. Even Lucky had been taken from her.

She stood up and walked over to the fridge. With everything going round and round in her head there was no way she'd be able to relax, but maybe a few glasses of wine would help. Sitting back at the breakfast bar she opened the bottle of cold white and filled her glass, remembering the wonderful night and morning they'd spent together. Was it really only two days ago? Was he dead because Sarah had decided to use him as a weapon?

Lynda felt she was toxic. Had everyone she cared about died because of her? Was her family's car crash meant to kill her? But she wasn't even supposed to be in the car that evening. No, that didn't make sense. It had been deliberate, she was sure of that, but *she* wasn't meant to die that night. Draining the glass, she filled it again, knocking it back in one.

When she went to fill her glass again she was angry to find the bottle was empty. She opened the fridge. Perfect! There was another bottle. She knew she needed sleep, but her mind was still too active. She wanted to be able to go to bed and pass out.

Knocking back glass after glass to deaden her mind, she went to pour another one, but again there was nothing left in the bottle. She knew there was no more white wine in the fridge and she hadn't stocked up on any red, but she had a bottle of cooking brandy on the shelf above the breadbin. Levering herself up, she crossed the kitchen to get it; she stumbled and only just stopped herself from falling by clutching the work surface.

Once she was sure she could walk, she grabbed the brandy bottle and went back to the breakfast bar to pick up her wine glass. She looked at her phone. Fuck it, she'd leave it there. Jason couldn't call and she didn't want to talk to anyone other than him. Leaning against the wall for balance, she headed to her bedroom. Tripping as she went through the door, she landed face first on the bed.

Forcing herself upright and turning to sit on the edge of the bed, she realised she still had a bottle in one hand and a glass in the other. Perfect! She unscrewed the bottle, spilling brandy over her leg, but managing to fill the glass to the top. She dropped the bottle, and watched with fascination as the golden liquid flowed across the floor.

'This one's for you, Jason,' she garbled, upending the glass and swallowing half the contents.

She turned towards the bedside cabinet and managed to put the glass down without spilling the contents.

'Well done, me!' she slurred.

Dragging off her clothes, she fell back onto the bed. Half sitting up, she reached for the glass and drained it.

'Dear God, let me sleep and never wake up,' she prayed as her head flopped onto the pillow.

Chapter Forty-Three

Lynda woke from a fitful sleep on Saturday morning and cringed as she moved her arm and the stench of her own unwashed body hit her nostrils. When had she last showered? Two, maybe three days ago. She'd gone to bed after Carla's phone call and had only got up to use the toilet or drink water. She sat up and looked around her bedroom. The clothes she'd pulled off were on the floor where she'd dropped them. The curtains were closed and she had no idea what time it was. The room stank of brandy where she'd dropped the bottle and saturated the carpet.

She glanced at her phone but knew it wouldn't give her the information she needed. On one of her trips to the kitchen for water she'd picked it up and brought it to the bedroom, but deliberately not charged it so that she wouldn't have to deal with any calls.

She put her feet on the floor and stood up. She couldn't carry on like this, hiding away from everyone. Picking up the phone, she connected the charge cord, then dropped it on the bedside table. Could she go for a run? She didn't feel like it but instinctively knew she should. Where was her running watch? What did she do with it? Had she left it in the lounge with her laptop?

That was a mystery for later. The clock on the oven in the kitchen would tell her the time.

Padding through, Lynda tried to convince herself running would at least take the edge off the screaming grief currently threatening to engulf her, but knew she was probably too weak to even walk the five kilometres of her normal route, far less run it.

The oven clock showed it was just after seven. She was suddenly hungry and took down a bowl from the cupboard. Maybe some breakfast cereal would give her a bit of energy. Did she have milk? She opened the fridge, relieved to see a nearly full bottle. She took the top off and sniffed at the contents. It would do.

After the first bowl, Lynda was still hungry, so polished off a second helping. She sat at the breakfast bar and tried to work out exactly how long she'd been in hiding from the world. However many days it was, something inside told her it was too long. She felt like going for a run after all. Maybe she could manage a couple of kilometres if she took it easy.

She put the bowl and spoon in the dishwasher and went through to the bathroom. Normally she wouldn't bother showering before running, but there was no way she was going anywhere before she'd cleaned herself up.

As she got dressed after the shower, she could hear her phone pinging to let her know about all her missed calls and messages. Oh hell, there were bound to be some from

Penelope. She'd not gone to her Friday-evening session and hadn't called to let her therapist know she wasn't coming.

Although tempted to pick up the phone, she decided to leave it until she got back from her run, just in case there was something that might upset her. She went to the lounge, relieved to find her watch was still connected to the laptop and fully charged. She put it on, not that she planned any record times, but she felt wearing it was a step in the right direction.

Lynda closed her front door as quietly as possible and lightly ran downstairs. Outside the apartments the fresh air felt amazing. She set off on her usual route, but planned to turn back when she felt she'd done enough on this first outing. Arriving home, she looked at her watch and saw she'd covered nearly three kilometres. Better than she'd hoped.

She opened the door to the apartments and almost walked into Georgina.

'Hi,' Georgina said. 'I'm so relieved to see you. I've been up to your door so many times. I heard you go out earlier. I've been really worried. Are you OK? You've not answered any of my calls or messages.'

The concern on Georgina's face made Lynda feel guilty for ignoring her. She'd heard her at the door several times while she'd been hiding away from the world, but hadn't been able to face speaking to anyone, not even a friend.

'I'm really sorry,' Lynda said. 'I just . . . I just couldn't bear the thought of talking to anybody. I'm trying to deal with it now, but I just couldn't face it. I'm sorry.'

'I saw on the news that Jason had died and guessed that was why you didn't answer the door,' Georgina said, gently stroking Lynda's arm.

Lynda barely managed to hold back her tears. 'Someone pushed him under a train. How could anyone do that?'

'I don't know!' Georgina said. 'I saw reports on the news earlier in the week, but at first had no idea it was your Jason they were talking about. Then, when they showed his photo, I came up immediately. Oh, Lynda, I am so, so sorry. Is there anything I can do? Have you heard when the funeral is going to be? Would you like me to come with you?'

Thinking of all the messages that must be waiting for her on her phone, Lynda shrugged.

'I put my phone on silent and then let the battery die. There's probably a message waiting for me upstairs.'

Georgina took hold of Lynda's hand. 'Why don't you come in for a drink this evening?'

Every fibre of her body wanted to say no, but Lynda knew she couldn't hole herself up forever.

She nodded. 'I was going to go to the charity today, but I just can't.'

'I can understand that,' Georgina said, 'but don't hide yourself away. I'll be here all afternoon if you need company before tonight.'

Once upstairs, Lynda looked at the list of missed calls and messages. Two voicemails from the police. Could she face talking to them? She'd have to, but not right now. There were also two from Penelope. She quickly sent her a text apologising and promising to attend the next Friday-evening session. She'd explain why she'd missed last night when she got there and could talk to Penelope face to face. Jason's murder felt too raw to try to put it into words in a text message, but she knew she had to try.

She did the same with Greg, as sending him a message was easier than talking to him. Within moments his reply pinged back.

I can't imagine what you're going through. I'm here if you need a friend.

That evening, sitting in Georgina's kitchen, Lynda found it so hard to put into words why she'd hidden away, but knew she owed her friend some sort of explanation. Before she could frame the sentence, Georgina spoke.

'I saw on the television today that the police are looking for someone in connection with Jason's death. I hope they find whoever did it.'

Lynda shook her head. 'I suppose I should have realised it would make the headlines, but I haven't seen it. I've deliberately not looked at the news. When Carla, Jason's sister, called me to tell me he'd been pushed I drank myself into a stupor. I pretty much stayed in one for the next few days.'

Georgina reached out and touched Lynda's arm. 'So you didn't know they were showing the CCTV coverage?'

'What? No! Surely they aren't showing the moment he was pushed? That's barbaric.'

Georgina shook her head. 'No, of course not. What the clip shows is the person they believe pushed him.'

'So they can see the person's face?'

Georgina shook her head again; her lips were compressed as if to prevent any words from escaping.

'What is it?' Lynda said. 'I can see by the look on your face there's something more. Tell me!'

Suddenly, Lynda felt the air leaving her body. The room

263

was spinning. She was vaguely aware of Georgina jumping up and grabbing her.

'Do you need to lie down?'

'No, I'm OK,' Lynda said. 'I'm not sure what happened there. I became a bit lightheaded.'

'Are you sure you're OK?'

Lynda nodded. 'I'm fine.'

Georgina went back to her own stool and sat facing Lynda. 'The station was crowded, and on the CCTV it's hard to make out even if the person was male or female, because whoever it was had on a hoodie.'

There was something in the way she'd said the words that put Lynda on edge.

'There's more, isn't there?' she said.

Georgina nodded. 'You know that hoodie you love? The one you said Jason bought for you?'

Lynda nodded, dreading what was coming next, but knowing before Georgina spoke again what she would say.

'From what I could make out, the hoodie in the CCTV footage looks very much like yours. Same design on the back.'

'Sarah!' Lynda said.

Georgina shrugged.

Sarah was clearly deranged and needed to be locked up.

'She saw me wearing it while she was with me and commented on the unusual design. I told her it had been a special gift from Jason.'

'Watch the news clip and if you think it's your hoodie, you have to tell the police you recognise it and who you think might have taken it.'

'Georgina, they didn't believe me about the other stuff. Do

you really think they'll take me seriously if I say I think Sarah pushed Jason in front of that train?'

'I don't see why not. Aren't they appealing for anyone with information to come forward?'

Lynda sighed. 'You're right. I'll go.'

Chapter Forty-Four

On Wednesday morning Lynda put down the paper she'd been trying to read. There was no way she could concentrate. Yet again, her thoughts went to the visit she'd made to the police at Georgina's urging. At first, she'd seen the same officer who'd stopped short of rolling his eyes when she'd put forward Sarah's name again. He probably thought she had some hidden agenda. To be fair, he had said he'd follow up on it, but in such a tone of voice it was obvious he didn't expect anything to come of it. Even when she'd pointed out the similarity to the design on her hoodie, he'd been sceptical, but had at least brought in his superior, the lead detective on Jason's case, who had taken her far more seriously.

Twice yesterday and again earlier today when she'd left the office to try to clear her head, she was convinced she'd seen Sarah in the distance, but when she'd looked more closely she was nowhere to be seen. Maybe the police officer was right and she was building Sarah up in her mind as some sort of monster when she was nothing of the sort.

She picked up the report again. If she didn't get her mind

back on what really mattered, she'd not only be demoted, she'd be out of a job. Don Frankam had allowed her a great deal of slack, most of which Andrew was taking up, but there would come a point when she would have no choice but to quit. As it was, she owed Andrew an enormous debt. He'd been so kind and helpful and she really wasn't sure she deserved it.

She'd read the same page three times without taking in any information when there was a tap on the door and Pauline stuck her head round it.

'Have you got a moment?' she asked.

'Sure, of course,' Lynda said, glad of the interruption.

Pauline came in and shut door, but didn't move towards the desk to sit down. She looked a bit sheepish.

'Something wrong?' Lynda asked.

'I don't know, to be honest,' she said. 'This is awkward and I don't really know where to start.'

Lynda smiled. 'Why not start by sitting down?'

Pauline laughed. 'Yes, good idea. Sorry, this is stupid. I don't even know if I should tell you . . .'

'Is Sarah still with you? I know she gave you the victim speech, but really you should make her leave. She isn't stable.'

Pauline shook her head. 'She's not causing me problems, well, apart from not paying anything towards the mortgage or utilities even though she'd promised she would.'

'She still hasn't got a job?' Lynda asked. 'I thought she swore she would be out searching for one every day and that she'd take anything that was going.'

Pauline sighed again. 'She did say that, but I don't think she's even looking. In fact, I know she isn't because of what she *is* doing and that's why I need to talk to you.'

Lynda waited and watched Pauline's expression undergo several changes. There was obviously something important on her mind. She looked as though she didn't want to say whatever it was but felt she had no choice.

'Are you sure you want to tell me?' Lynda said when it seemed as though Pauline wouldn't ever be able to put her thoughts into words.

'Yes, I have to,' she said. 'It's really important you know what I overheard, but I don't want to add to your worries. On the other hand, if I didn't tell you and anything happened to you, I would never be able to forgive myself.'

Lynda sat up straighter. 'What sort of something?' she said.

'Last night the police came to talk to Sarah. I don't know what it was about because they went into the kitchen and closed the door.'

Oh, thank God! Lynda thought. They must have taken her seriously after all.

'It was two officers, both plain clothes, so I knew it must be something quite serious. They were only in there for about twenty minutes and then left. When Sarah came back from showing them out I asked her if everything was OK.'

'How did she look? What did she say?' Lynda asked.

'She looked thoughtful,' Pauline said. 'She didn't answer me straight away. When I asked her again, she said that no, things weren't OK and she had plans to make.'

'Did she say anything else?' Lynda asked.

Pauline shook her head. 'No. She went through to the spare room and didn't come out again for the rest of the evening.'

Lynda frowned. 'But what has that got to do with me? Why are you telling me this?'

'When I was on my way to bed I overheard her talking to someone on the phone. The thing is, Lynda, I think she might be following you.'

'I knew it!' Lynda said. 'I thought I'd seen her a few times this week, but she was too far away for me to be certain. What did you hear her say?'

'She said: "I'm watching Lynda all the time now."'

'Any idea who she was talking to?'

Pauline shrugged. 'Not at all, but I thought you should know what I heard. Whether or not it's got anything to do with the police visit, I really don't know, but it's clear she's watching you.'

Pauline hesitated, then nodded, as if making up her mind to something. 'I think you should let the police know what I heard. Or do you think I should do that?'

'I'll tell them,' Lynda said, 'but if they need you to corroborate what I've told them, you will back me up, won't you?'

'Of course,' Pauline said, 'but I can only say what I heard. I have no idea who she was talking to, or why she's watching you.'

After Pauline left, Lynda sat staring into space, her words revolving in her head. What was Sarah up to? On the one hand, Lynda was relieved to know the feeling of being watched wasn't her imagination, but on the other, why was Sarah following her? And who the bloody hell had she been talking to?

When Lynda left work that evening she tried to look around for Sarah without making it obvious that was what she was doing, but didn't spot her. Now that she knew Sarah really was on her tail, she'd be more on her guard. She climbed in her car and put on the seatbelt. Even though she'd not achieved much at work, it was better to be there than hiding at home as she'd done last week.

She drove out of the office car park and was about to turn left when something made her look to her right. In the distance she thought she could see Sarah, and turned the car in that direction to make sure it was her but by the time she reached the spot she was nowhere to be seen.

Was there any point in telling the police as she'd told Pauline she would? Probably not. More to the point was trying to work out what Sarah was planning to do next.

Chapter Forty-Five

July 2022

Lynda sat down in the therapy room wondering where she should start. There were so many things troubling her. Penelope smiled, but didn't speak. Lynda knew she was giving her time to sort out what she needed most to discuss.

After a few minutes of silence, she tried to put the worst days of her life into words.

'I'm sorry I missed our session last week. Jason . . .' She tried to take a deep breath. Would it ever get easier? 'Jason has been murdered,' she said.

'I got your texts. I also saw the request for information on the television,' Penelope said. 'I wish you had called me. I would have made time for you. Did you have someone with you to help you cope with the news?'

Lynda shook her head, unable to speak for several seconds. Shuddering, she finally managed to find her voice and told Penelope about Carla's call and her own subsequent visit to the police.

'You told them you thought Sarah might be responsible?'
Lynda nodded.

'That is a very serious accusation to make,' Penelope said, writing something on her pad.

'I know, but for once they followed up on what I had to say. Apparently they actually went to ask her some questions.'

'How do you know?'

She told Penelope what Pauline had said. 'And what she overheard proves she's been following me.'

'Have you given the police this additional information?'

Lynda shook her head. 'I thought about it, but decided not to bother. I've told them over and over that Sarah is waging some sort of vendetta against me, but they obviously think I'm hysterical and fixated. The officer was very dismissive, although, to be fair, they did follow up after I told them I recognised the hoodie.'

'Do you feel their attitude might have something to do with your comments at the inquest after the accident?'

'Possibly. Yes, definitely. The officer I've seen recently even mentioned it. I kept telling the police it was no accident, but no one would listen.'

Penelope scribbled something down on her pad. 'We have discussed this in past sessions, but there is still more to deal with. What can you remember of the incident? Could something have run out in front of the car causing him to swerve?'

'That was one of the suggestions at the inquest, but I don't think so. I keep dreaming about Dad's car driving towards us while we're also in Dad's car, but it's all so confused I no longer know what's real and what's simply my imagination running riot.'

Her hands formed into fists and she beat her thighs. 'There's something in the back of my mind, but whenever I try to

272

grasp the memory, it vanishes. I can vaguely remember the fear as the car smashed through the barrier and fell into the river.'

She shivered as she recalled the freezing water pouring in through the open window. She had panicked as she'd desperately struggled to get her seatbelt undone. By the time she was free, the car was full of greenish slimy water. Holding her breath, she'd turned to Sean to free him, but she could see by his staring eyes he was already dead. The water was turning red with blood from the front of the car. She'd forced herself out through the window and kicked for the surface. Gasping for air, she took a moment before diving back down to try to get her family out, but she couldn't get the doors open.

Out of breath again, she kicked upwards once more. Even though she knew it was useless, she took a breath and dived down again. This time she didn't even make it as far as the car before she had to surface again. Again and again she'd tried, each time failing to make it to the car. She only stopped when hands grabbed her and hauled her into a boat.

'I was taken to hospital even though I kept screaming I had to go back into the water. I think I knew my parents and brother were dead, but somehow I'd survived without even a scratch to show I'd been in the car with them. When the police came to the hospital, they implied Dad must have been drunk or something. It was proved later that he wasn't, but to this day they haven't even tried to find out what really happened.'

'Lynda, you came to me after you and Jason had broken up and told me the reason he had left was because you constantly accused him of things he hadn't done. As we have discovered through your therapy, it was your mind trying to deal with

273

your grief which caused you to imagine things that hadn't, in fact, taken place.'

'What are you saying?'

The look of sympathy on Penelope's face was more than Lynda could bear.

'Oh God, please don't say you think I'm imagining things again. I'm not.'

Tears streamed down her face and she dashed them away with her hand. Penelope passed over the box of tissues which had been just out of Lynda's reach. She took one and dried her eyes.

'I believe you are convinced the events happened. However, the possibility of at least some of it being only in your mind, due to the stress you are under, is something we must consider,' Penelope said. 'During your time with Jason the events your mind created felt very real to you. If you remember, you had believed you'd had discussions with him that you later realised had not, in fact, actually taken place. You argued over what had and had not been said and done to the extent that it drove a wedge between the two of you.'

'But it's not the same now,' Lynda said. 'This time I know what's happening to me is not a figment of my imagination. Someone is trying to hurt me and I truly believe it must be Sarah.'

'Lynda, I've asked in previous sessions, but you were not ready to talk about the reason you were late to your appointment with Sarah the day she had chosen to confront the bullies. Would you like to discuss it now?'

Lynda nodded. It was time to get this off her chest. She'd never spoken about it to anyone and the guilt had coloured everything she'd done since Mark had taken his own life.

'Sarah and I hadn't been getting along very well because she didn't like my boyfriend. She said she felt pushed out. Anyway, she'd decided to confront Hazel and her gang head on. For whatever reason, I don't know what it was, but Hazel never used to pick on Sarah when I was around, so Sarah asked me to be there the day she tackled Hazel. She set the day and time and I promised to be there for her.'

She wiped the tears which were now freely flowing.

'Earlier that afternoon I'd promised to meet Mark, but I knew I had plenty of time to get from the railway embankment where we always hung out back to the school for Sarah.'

'But time ran out?' Penelope asked.

Lynda nodded. 'Mark's family were travellers. He kept saying that when his traveller family moved on I should go with them. I'd always agreed, not realising that he actually meant it. That afternoon he told me they would be leaving the following week and that I should move in with his family straight away.'

'You had no idea he was going to suggest this?'

Lynda shrugged. 'He was always saying it, but I really didn't take it seriously. It was one of those "one day" things that would never actually happen. I was only sixteen! That afternoon, when it hit me that he truly expected me to leave my own family to travel with his, I told him I couldn't go through with it.'

'What did he say?'

'He begged me to change my mind. He was devastated, said he couldn't live without me. He accused me of deliberately lying to him, of leading him on, and he was right. I had been by saying "yes" every time he said about running away

275

with him, but I was so young, just a child really. I thought I was so grown up.'

She shuddered, not wanting to finish the story, but now she'd got this far she had to go through with it.

'The argument went on and on. Then I realised what the time was and told him I had to go because Sarah needed me. His last comment to me was that he couldn't live without me. He begged and begged me to stay.'

'So that is how you were late for Sarah?'

'Yes, but that's not the worst thing that happened. The next day Mark committed suicide by jumping in front of a train. I'd allowed him to believe I would go with him and then I let him down. But he meant what he'd said. He'd rather be dead than live without me.'

She took another tissue and blew her nose. 'So, you see, I have plenty to feel guilty about. I didn't show you the cards, but whoever is targeting me knows about Mark. Somehow I have to get through Jason's funeral. After that, I'm going to find out once and for all who's trying to ruin my life. I'm not going to roll over and be a victim.'

But even as she said the words, her treacherous mind whispered: *You don't want to be a victim? What a hypocrite you are.*

Chapter Forty-Six

Lynda shivered as rain dripped down the back of her neck. The weather forecast had predicted sunshine, but it seemed fitting somehow that a sudden downpour should appear to match how she felt. She was standing next to Jason's sister and his parents at the graveside, but felt totally alone. Her grief was different from theirs; she knew that from losing her own family and had no intention of intruding. She watched as his coffin was lowered into the ground and she then moved forward to take her turn to drop a handful of soil into the muddy void. As her offering hit the water which had collected on the top of the coffin a wave of despair rushed through her body and her legs buckled. She felt Carla grab her arm and looked round to whisper her thanks. Jason's parents had enough to cope with without watching Lynda tumble into his grave.

As suddenly as it had started, the rain disappeared and sunshine took its place. The blueness of the sky felt like an affront. Today the sky should be grey and dismal, with all hope gone. Not bright and full of promise of better days. After the priest had intoned the final words of the service, the mourners began to move away from the grave. Through eyes blurred with unshed tears, Lynda saw Jason's mother approaching.

'Are you coming back to the house? You'd be very welcome,' she said.

Lynda smiled and the movement released the tears which ran down her face in silent streaks.

'Thank you,' she said, grateful for the invitation.

'Jason told us he had real hopes of the two of you getting back together. He would have wanted you to be with us at this time.'

'We were making plans,' Lynda said.

She wanted to ask if the police had made any progress in finding out who had pushed Jason, but didn't want to raise the possibility that he might have been killed because of her. His family were being kind and embracing her in their grief. Would they feel the same if they knew about Sarah? The police had made it clear to Lynda that they didn't put much store in her accusations, but she was convinced Sarah was to blame, even if she couldn't bring herself to picture her pushing Jason from the platform.

The gathering at the house was more painful than she'd expected. Those relatives who knew she and Jason had split up, but didn't know they had reconciled, mainly ignored her. If they did speak, it was in a grudging tone to make it clear they were only being polite. Or was she imagining that? Maybe they were simply grief stricken. Jason had been so easy to love. She wouldn't be the only one here who felt as if a light had been put out.

Lynda took the first opportunity to seek out Carla.

'I'm going to leave so that the family can properly grieve,' she said.

Carla put her hand on Lynda's arm. 'You don't have to go. Why not stay for a little longer?'

Lynda forced up a smile. 'It might only be in my mind, but I feel as if some of Jason's aunts and uncles would prefer it if I weren't here.'

She nodded her head in the direction of a cluster of older people gathered in a corner. Every so often one of them looked in Lynda's direction. Without doubt, none of the glances were friendly.

'They're probably wondering how I've had the nerve to show up, considering Jason and I separated some time back.'

Carla shrugged. 'What they think is their problem, not yours. If you want to stay, please do, but if you feel uncomfortable and want to leave, I promise you I understand.'

Lynda looked over to where Jason's mother was being consoled by an ancient-looking woman. His father was at her side looking as if he, too, was about to collapse.

'Your mum and dad are barely holding themselves together. I wish there was something I could do.'

As she said the words, the thought came into her mind that she had done enough. She had no proof, but why would Jason have been pushed if it wasn't connected to her? The messages had let her know she was going to suffer, but it had been kind and loveable Jason who had been selected as the means to make that happen.

She took a step towards Jason's parents to thank them for inviting her, but as she did so his mother collapsed into his father's arms. Now was not the time to go over to them. It would feel like an intrusion. She turned back to Carla.

'Please tell your mum and dad I'll be in touch, and say I said thank you for allowing me to be here today.'

'Don't be silly,' Carla said. 'We've always looked on you as family. Of course you should be here. Take care of yourself, Lynda. Please excuse me, I must go to see what I can do for Mum.'

'Of course,' Lynda said, eyes flooding with tears at the kindness in Carla's voice. She managed to say thank you once again and made her way to the door without bumping into anyone. Once outside, she leaned against the wall of the porch and let the tears flow.

She eventually pulled herself together and went to find her car. She knew she needed to be extra careful driving. It had been hard enough to concentrate driving to the cemetery, but after the trauma of seeing Jason put into the earth, she was barely able to hold it together. Nerves on edge, she made it home.

As she parked the car, she planned how to get through the next few hours without breaking down. A bath with scented bubbles followed by a glass or two of wine might give her the lift she needed. Although she had stopped drinking after that last disastrous bout, right now she felt the need of something to help her relax.

She opened the downstairs door and straight away spotted an envelope on the floor of the entrance hall. It didn't have an address, just her full name printed on the front. It was in a different font from the others she had received, but she was still nervous about what might be inside. She picked it up and peered in at the contents. It was clearly a condolence card.

Not wanting to read it until she was inside her apartment, she carried it up the stairs and opened her front door. Still holding the card in one hand, she reached up to straighten the hall mirror, something she'd all but cured herself of before Jason's murder. Penelope seemed to feel she would once again be able to stop her repetitive compulsion, but Lynda wasn't sure she believed her.

She went through to the kitchen, took off the black jacket she'd bought especially for the funeral and slung it over one of the stools before sitting at the breakfast bar to take out the card. The words on the front were standard expressions of sadness for her loss. She looked inside to see who it was from and dropped the card onto the breakfast bar.

Surely even Sarah wouldn't send this? Pulse racing wildly, she reached down and snatched it up again.

R.I.P. Lynda Blackthorn. Will anyone miss you?

Chapter Forty-Seven

Lynda barely held herself together over the next two days and was in desperate need of Penelope's calming influence. She arrived in the waiting room on Friday evening a full half hour early for her appointment.

'I'm sorry, Miss Blackthorn,' the receptionist said, 'but I'm afraid you'll have to wait until your appointment time.'

Lynda nodded. 'It's fine. Is it OK if I sit here and wait?'

'Of course. Help yourself to a drink from the dispenser if you'd like one.'

Lynda thanked her and headed for the sofa on the other side of the room. Getting here so early was stupid, she knew that, but for some reason she felt she was safer here than anywhere else. Even though nothing had happened since receiving the card, she sensed danger everywhere she looked.

Leafing through the magazines on the side table, she tried to find one that would hold her attention for longer than two seconds, which was about her attention span these days. *Architectural News*, *Fishing Today*, *Candle Making for Money*. Why were the magazines in waiting rooms always on topics few people would enjoy? She picked up the six-month-old copy of *Architectural News* and tried to interest herself in the ten best modern buildings around the world.

The time passed slowly, but eventually Lynda heard the sound she longed for. Penelope was calling her. Replacing the magazine she'd been staring at without absorbing anything for the last twenty-five minutes, she stood up and followed Penelope into her inner sanctum.

'Why do you have such an odd range of magazines?' she asked as she settled herself opposite Penelope.

'Various people from all walks of life donate them. I suppose that's why it's such a disparate range of subject matter, but you haven't come to talk about the magazines. How are you coping?'

Without warning, Lynda felt such a wave of anger sweeping through her she could hardly breathe.

'I . . . want to . . . kill . . . Sarah,' she gasped.

'That is a very extreme statement. You still believe she is to blame for what happened to Jason?'

Lynda nodded. 'Yes, and I think she sent me this.' She passed the condolence card to Penelope. 'She used some sort of stencil to print the words, so I can't prove it was her, but who else could it have been? If I could push *her* under a train, I would do it in a heartbeat.'

Penelope wrote on her pad and Lynda had to stop herself from yanking the pen out of her hand. She pressed her nails into her palms to prevent herself from screaming.

'Lynda, before we go any further, I feel you would benefit from some calming exercises. Shall we begin?'

Five minutes later Lynda felt calmer, but still murderous.

She'd never hated anyone as much as she hated Sarah. Her mind was so taken up with thoughts of revenge that she missed whatever it was Penelope had said.

'Sorry,' Lynda said. 'I didn't catch that.'

'I asked if you had taken the card to the police,' Penelope said.

'I didn't see the point. As I said, I can't prove who sent it and I doubt they would believe me anyway. I think I need to confront Sarah. Get her to admit what she's done.'

'Lynda, I really don't feel that would be in your best interest. I strongly advise you to take the card to the police. Leave it in their hands. If she is guilty, you have to trust they will discover proof of it.'

'Penelope, you don't understand, I've taken them proof. She stole my hoodie and wore it when she pushed Jason off the platform. Even knowing that, they didn't arrest her. She's out there somewhere just waiting for the opportunity to get *me*. I'm not going to let that happen. I'll kill her first.'

'Lynda, you are overwrought. This is natural after all you've been through, but you cannot throw out wild accusations and suggest you want to commit murder. Please, let me help you with some more calming exercises.'

Swallowing the words bubbling in her throat, Lynda nodded. 'OK,' she said. 'Sorry, I got carried away. You're right. I'm overreacting.'

As Penelope counted the breaths in and out, Lynda followed her lead, but her mind was far from calm. Sarah didn't deserve to live.

Chapter Forty-Eight

When Lynda arrived at the charity the next day she was surprised to see Amanda and Cassie standing in the kitchen next to Greg.

'Lynda,' he said, looking up as she came in, 'I was so pleased to get your message you were coming in today. I mentioned it to Cassie and she suggested we all get together this morning to celebrate getting the first entrants on board for the marathon.'

'I've brought cake!' Cassie said, pointing to a Black Forest gateau on the work surface. 'The website is working really well. We've got entries for all three races, all fully paid up, and the money is in the race PayPal account.'

'Don't forget the merchandise orders,' Amanda said. 'The entrants and their supporters are snapping up the tee-shirts, caps, water bottles and even keyrings with the race logo.'

Lynda knew she should feel something, anything, after all she'd put into getting the race event off the ground, but she could only summon enough energy to smile.

'You've been amazing, both of you. I can't thank you

enough,' she said, hoping her voice didn't sound as flat as she felt.

'It was your brainchild,' Cassie said. 'Greg told us how hard you'd worked long before we arrived on the scene. To you goes the honour of cutting the cake!'

They all looked so pleased, Lynda knew she had to force herself to be part of the celebration. It wouldn't be fair to infect their mood with hers. She picked up the knife and carefully cut four slices.

While Cassie and Amanda had been speaking, Greg had made four cups of coffee. He handed them out and then lifted his in salute.

'To the race weekend.'

'To the race weekend,' they all chorused.

Lynda looked at her slice of cake and tried to convince herself she could swallow a bite if she tried hard enough, but as the fork neared her lips she felt as if she would throw up.

'Would you mind if I took mine home to have later?' she asked, looking at Cassie. 'I haven't been feeling very well recently.'

Amanda stepped forward and touched Lynda's arm. 'I was so sorry to hear about your boyfriend. I can't imagine what you're going through.'

'We were all so shocked,' Cassie said. 'I hope it doesn't seem insensitive to want to celebrate the race success. We thought it would, I don't know, maybe give you something to feel good about. Oh damn, I'm making such a mess of this. Like Amanda, I am so sorry for your loss.'

The kindness in their voices almost undid her. Lynda felt tears flood her eyes. 'Thank you. It's been hard.'

'I know I haven't been fair to you over what should have stayed in the past, but if there's anything I can do,' Amanda said, 'please just ask.'

'Me too,' Cassie said. 'If you need company, I can make time for you. You shouldn't be alone.'

'Thank you, but I'll be fine. I have a wonderful friend who lives downstairs. She's there for me whenever I need her.'

Her phone rang and she saw with shock that the caller was Sarah. Hands shaking, she accepted the call.

'What do you want?'

'To clear the air,' Sarah said.

'How? I mean why?'

'Because it's time you knew the truth.'

'What about?' Lynda said.

'Meet me tomorrow and you'll find out. I can come over to your place.'

'No!' Lynda said. 'I don't want you in my home.'

'Well, I can't say come to mine because, thanks to you, I don't have one.'

'I can meet you at Ringo's,' Lynda said.

'No, what I've got to tell you I don't want anyone to overhear.'

Was Sarah going to admit pushing Jason? Why else would she be worried about anyone hearing what she had to say. If she could get her to confess and record it, then she could take proof to the police.

'Why not come to the charity tomorrow afternoon?' Lynda suggested.

'I told you, I don't want others to be able to hear what I have to say.'

'I can make sure nobody else is here. I can ask Greg to let me use the offices for a couple of hours. He can divert the calls.'

Sarah went silent.

'Well?' Lynda said. 'It's here or nowhere.'

'OK, tomorrow at three?'

'Tomorrow at three in the charity office,' Lynda said, ending the call.

Greg had taken his cake and coffee over to his desk to take a call, but Lynda saw he'd removed his headset. She walked over to him, leaving Cassie and Amanda chatting in the kitchen.

'Greg, is there any chance I could use this room tomorrow from three? I know we've diverted the calls in the past. Would it be possible to do that again? It would just be for an hour or so.'

'Of course we can do that. I'm on duty tomorrow afternoon and can take the calls at home, so you could use the rooms any time from one until five. Would that suit you?'

'Absolutely,' she said. 'I've just had a call from Sarah. She wants to clear the air.'

He looked surprised. 'Why do you want to meet here?'

'Neutral ground,' she said. 'She doesn't want to meet in a public place and I don't want her anywhere near my home.'

He looked concerned, but nodded. 'As long as you feel you're doing the right thing.'

'I know I am,' she said.

Lynda went back to finish her coffee and collect her cake. She would stay to answer calls for the rest of the day, but before going home she had a purchase she needed to make.

Chapter Forty-Nine

Sunday morning Lynda woke even earlier than usual, her mind immediately on what she would find out that afternoon. Would Sarah admit she'd pushed Jason? If she did, every word would be recorded.

She headed out for a run feeling mentally stronger than she had for a long time. If it took until the day she died, she would make sure Sarah was punished for what she'd done. She arrived home out of breath, but ready for the challenge ahead.

The day dragged by. It seemed as if every minute took an hour. To pass the time, she went to the Sunday market and found the perfect gift for Georgina's birthday next week. Tucking the hand-printed silk scarf into her bag, she looked at her watch. Damn, she still had hours to go.

She went home again and tried to read, but the lines kept running into each other. She looked for perhaps the fiftieth time at her watch and was relieved to see it was finally time to head over to the charity. She wanted to be there at least half an hour before Sarah arrived to set up the Dictaphone she'd bought on the way home yesterday. It needed to be hidden somewhere out of sight but still close enough that it would pick up everything that was said.

She went downstairs and bumped into Georgina who was coming in.

'Hello, stranger,' Georgina said. 'Everything OK?'

Lynda nodded. 'Yes, I'm on my way to meet Sarah at the charity office. She says she's got things to tell me that she doesn't want anyone else to overhear.'

'You think it's about Jason?'

'What else could it be?' Lynda said. 'All the other stuff she's done isn't bad enough to worry about admitting it in a public place, but saying she pushed Jason is different. She'd want to keep that quiet.'

'But why would she admit to it now?' Georgina said. 'I'm not sure you should be meeting her alone. It could be a trap to get you in a place where she could hurt you without anyone stopping her. Let me come with you.'

Lynda shook her head. 'No, I need to do this alone.' She showed Georgina the Dictaphone. 'I'm going to record everything; besides, she wouldn't dare to try anything when she knows I had to arrange it with Greg for her to come over.'

'I still don't like it,' Georgina said.

Lynda patted her arm. 'I'll be fine,' she said and left.

Lynda parked opposite the charity office. Apart from the usual group of young men further down the road, there was no one in sight. It was the first time she'd been to the offices on a Sunday afternoon and she was surprised how empty and quiet the streets were.

She crossed the road and unlocked the charity door, closing and locking it behind her. She looked at her watch. There was still twenty minutes before Sarah was due to arrive, so she had plenty of time to find the perfect spot for the Dictaphone.

Putting her bag on her desk, she opened the top drawer. Here would be a good place, but Sarah might see it. She moved over to Greg's desk and was about to open the drawer when she heard her car alarm go off.

Those bloody boys must have done something to her car. Leaving the Dictaphone on Greg's desk, she grabbed her bag, ran to the door and unlocked it. Looking out, she saw that, sure enough, her car was surrounded by the group she'd seen earlier.

'What the bloody hell do you think you're doing?' she yelled.

They laughed and took off down the street. She ran across the road, pulled her key fob from her bag and clicked it to shut off the alarm. No matter how many times they reported those boys, the police did nothing more than give them an informal warning as they never caused any actual damage. Frustrated, she went back across the road, hoping they wouldn't pull the same trick again.

She went inside and locked the door, realising she now only had a few minutes before Sarah was due to arrive. She picked up the Dictaphone and put it in the drawer of Greg's desk, leaving it slightly open. Whatever Sarah had to say, Lynda would have a recording she could take to the police.

Going into the kitchen, she made a pot of coffee and took it back to her desk, together with cups, milk and sugar. If her desk was the focus, Sarah wouldn't notice Greg's drawer being open as it would not be in her line of sight.

A minute later, there was a knocking on the door. Lynda went to open it, trying to control the horde of butterflies doing cartwheels in her stomach.

Sarah looked exactly as she always did. She hadn't sprouted horns or turned into The Joker since they had last seen each other. There was no outward sign of glee at the chaos she'd caused in Lynda's life.

'Come in,' Lynda said, pointing to her desk. 'I've just made a fresh pot of coffee.'

Sarah grinned at her. 'That's the friendliest greeting you've given me in weeks. I wasn't expecting you to be so welcoming after everything that's happened.'

'Help yourself,' Lynda said.

Sarah poured a cup of coffee. 'You not having any?' she asked.

Lynda nodded. 'I will in a moment. First, I need to ask if you're going to tell me the truth about what you've been doing. If you're not, there's no point in you being here.'

Sarah smiled. 'Sure, why not? Go ahead and ask your questions. Girl Guide's honour I'll tell you the truth.'

'You never were a Guide.'

Sarah laughed. 'I know, but I promise I'll answer every question truthfully even if I wasn't ever a Girl Guide, but first I want to see your phone.'

'Why?' Lynda asked.

'Because I'm not stupid,' Sarah said. 'I might decide to tell you something that could get me put away for a long time. No way am I going to let you record what I have to say.'

Lynda took her phone from her bag and passed it to Sarah who turned it off.

'OK,' Sarah said, 'what do you want to know?'

Lynda wanted to go straight into asking about Jason, but thought she might get more out of Sarah if she started with the stuff she was likely to admit to.

'Did you keep shifting my hall mirror?'

Sarah nodded. 'And I switched the prints in your bedroom. In fact, while I was living there I moved quite a lot of your stuff. I enjoyed rifling through all your drawers and private papers as well.'

'I knew it! Did you do it because you realised the effect it had on me?'

'In the beginning it was because you were such a complete bitch the first evening you came home when I'd spent all day cleaning the place as a thank you for letting me stay. You didn't appreciate it though. All you did was freak out because I hadn't put your stupid ornaments and pictures back in the exact places you'd had them. After that I thought it would be fun to freak you out by moving things and pretending I hadn't.'

Lynda shuddered. 'That was a shitty thing to do.'

Sarah laughed. 'I know, but you asked for it and besides, it was hilarious watching you get all screwed up about it.'

'As you're being honest at last,' Lynda said, 'when I brought it up, you lied about the night we almost made out, didn't you?'

Sarah smiled. 'Yep, but you so deserved that.'

'Why?'

'Because you led me on and let me think you wanted to go

293

further and then said no. It was like a slap in the face. I thought you should be punished for it. Anyway, that's all in the past. We have other stuff to deal with. Like what happened to Jason. It was terrible what happened to him.' Sarah frowned. 'What a waste of a good-looking man. Did you know the police came to see me to ask if I knew anything about how he'd died? I told them I hadn't a clue, that I had only met the man briefly and had no reason to kill him. They didn't spell it out, but I got the impression you'd pointed them in my direction. Did you?'

'Why would I do that?' Lynda said, unsure of what else to say.

'I can't think why else they would think I was a person of interest.' She smiled. 'You blamed me for everything else, so it seemed natural you'd point the finger at me for Jason being pushed off that platform.'

'So who do you think *did* push him?' Lynda asked, looking directly at Sarah, hoping to see some sign of guilt, but if anything she looked in total control of her emotions.

'I know what you're implying, Lynda – the CCTV wasn't the greatest quality, but I really didn't think it looked like my build. The hoodie was very distinctive, though, wasn't it? It looked very much like the one you said I'd stolen. It must have been terrible for you,' Sarah said. 'I can only imagine what it felt like when you heard. I bet it came close to destroying you.'

Lynda stiffened. 'That's a strange choice of words,' she said.

'Not really. They're exactly the right words. It's what Mark's death did to you.'

Lynda stood up and moved backwards to get as far from Sarah as she could.

'What do you mean?' she said, hoping the Dictaphone was picking up every word.

Sarah shrugged. 'Fourteen years ago you let those bitches bully me and then Mark died. Strange, isn't it, that Jason should have been pushed under a train so that he died in the same way as Mark.'

'Are you saying you did it? You killed Jason?'

'You really expect me to answer that question? As I've already said, I may be many things, but stupid isn't one of them.'

Lynda felt the bile burning the back of her throat and swallowed hard.

'You guessed I was messing with your mind, but you have no idea why I've hated you for over fourteen years. When it comes to it, you're the same naïve idiot you've always been.'

'You're sick,' Lynda said. 'You know that, don't you? You need to get help.'

'Like you? It doesn't look like therapy is doing you any good.'

Lynda realised Sarah still hadn't confessed to anything other than lying and moving things in the flat. She hadn't admitted she'd pushed Jason. Sarah was between her and the door. Had she been an idiot to meet her alone? She wished now she'd let Georgina come with her.

'Pauline overheard you on the phone to someone saying you were watching me. Why were you doing that?'

'Pauline should mind her own business, but as it happens I was talking to Maria.'

'So you were following me?'

'Yes, I was curious.'

'About what?'

'I'll get to that later,' Sarah said. 'Why do you keep looking around as if you need an escape route? Believe me, if I was going to kill you it wouldn't be here where I'd be leaving all sorts of DNA clues around the place.'

'Is that meant to make me feel better?' Lynda asked. 'Or is it a threat?'

'It's neither.' Sarah laughed and stood up. 'You know I could happily murder you, but I don't think you've suffered enough,' she said, moving towards Lynda. 'I want you to suffer as much as I did.'

Chapter Fifty

'Get back over there. Admit what you did. You killed Jason!' Lynda yelled.

'Don't be such a bloody idiot,' Sarah said. 'Haven't you worked it out yet? I didn't kill your precious Jason, someone else did. I'm not going to take the blame for something I didn't do. I've been watching you to see if I can work out who else hates you as much as I do.'

In her peripheral vision Lynda saw the door of the meeting room slowly open and Cassie creep up behind Sarah. She had no idea why she was there, but she'd never been so relieved to see anyone in her life.

Cassie moved quickly, snaking her arm around Sarah's neck and pulling her away from Lynda.

'Let me go, you crazy bitch!' Sarah yelled.

'Shut up!' Cassie screamed, 'or I'll use this.'

Lynda was stunned to see Cassie had a knife in her other hand. She pointed it at Sarah's throat. What was going on?

'She asked you to sit back over here, so that's what you're going to do,' Cassie said, dragging Sarah back. 'Don't worry about this bitch, Lynda, I have everything under control.' She pushed the blade against Sarah's neck.

'Why are you here?' Lynda asked.

'After I heard that you were meeting Sarah today, I wanted to know what it was she was going to tell you.'

'But why?'

Cassie pulled Sarah towards an office chair and forced her into it. 'Well, it's got a lot to do with what happened fourteen years ago.'

As she said the words, Lynda saw Sarah stiffen.

'Do you want to tell Lynda what you did, Sarah? Or shall I tell her? No, I think it's better coming from you. After all, isn't that why you're here? To confess to your crime?'

'What's Cassie talking about, Sarah? What crime?'

Sarah shook her head. 'Please don't hurt me,' she whispered.

Cassie smiled and tightened her hold around Sarah's neck. 'I had hoped to wait until Sarah told you herself, but when she moved to attack you, I thought I'd better come out from hiding.'

'How did you get in? The door was locked,' said Lynda.

'It wasn't locked when you ran over to chase those boys away from your car. I came in then. I paid them to do it, by the way. I wanted to make sure I would be here to hear what this bitch had to say.'

'But why?' Lynda said. 'What has Sarah ever done to you?'

'She ruined my life,' Cassie said.

'How? I don't even know you,' Sarah said. 'Please don't hurt me.'

'Why not?' Cassie hissed. 'It would make me happy to hear you squeal. I'm going to take my time.'

'Lynda, stop her,' Sarah begged.

'Cassie, put the knife down,' Lynda said, fascinated by a small drop of blood running from the knifepoint down Sarah's neck.

'Let's go back in time,' Cassie said, ignoring Lynda's plea. 'Tell Lynda what you did all those years ago. I bet once she knows she won't be so keen to stop me killing you.'

'Please stop, you're hurting me,' Sarah pleaded.

Cassie laughed. 'You did far worse to me. What did you do fourteen years ago?' Her voice was rising.

Cassie moved the blade closer to Sarah's throat and she screamed in pain

'Cassie, stop!' Lynda said as the blood began running a little freer down Sarah's neck.

'Why should I?' Cassie asked. 'I'm going to slit her throat if she doesn't tell me what I want to know. You see, I know what you did, Sarah. You thought you'd got away with it.'

'Fine, OK, OK. I'll tell you,' Sarah sobbed, sweat making her face glisten under the fluorescent light. 'I'll tell you everything.'

'What are you two talking about?' Lynda begged, feeling as if she'd stumbled into a horror story. 'Cassie, tell me what's going on.'

'I thought it was you he was meeting that night, Lynda,' Cassie said, 'but it was her. I only put it together after I saw her birthmark at your place. It's so distinctive, I've never forgotten the one and only time I'd seen it before.'

Lynda watched helplessly as the blade was stroked across Sarah's neck and she screamed again.

'You were there that night, weren't you, Sarah? Tell Lynda what you did!'

Sarah whimpered.

'Tell her!' Cassie snarled.

'Please, I can't bear it,' Sarah sobbed.

'I'm not going to ask again. What did you do?'

Lynda watched with horror as Cassie dug the knife in a little deeper and a spurt of blood shot out. Sarah's scream echoed around the room.

'Cassie, stop. You're going to kill her.'

Cassie smiled. 'Dear Lynda, always worried about others. At least, that's the image you like to portray, isn't it? But the truth is quite different though. Tell me, Lynda, what did you say to Mark the last time you saw him?'

'How do you even know about me and Mark?' Lynda asked. 'What was he to you?'

'I'll tell you both later about me and Mark. You didn't answer my question: what–did–you–say–to–Mark–the–last–time–you–saw–him?' she enunciated as if she was speaking to someone dim.

Lynda raised her voice to be heard above Sarah's whimpers.

'He wanted me to go with him when the camp moved on. But I couldn't do it. I loved him. I wanted to be with him – I really did – but when it came to it, I couldn't face leaving my family behind. I was only a teenager,' Lynda sobbed.

'So you had lied to him. Then what happened?' Cassie asked, but Lynda couldn't bring herself to answer.

'What happened after you told Mark you were dumping him?'

'Mark said he understood. We were going to keep in touch, but then . . .'

'But then?' Cassie said.

'But then, the next day, Mark killed himself,' Lynda said. 'He jumped in front of a train.'

'Ah, that's what I always believed too, but it's not true, is it, Sarah?' Cassie said. She shifted slightly and another rivulet of blood ran down Sarah's neck. 'When I saw her birthmark I remembered where I'd seen it before. You were there the night he died, weren't you, Sarah?'

'Please don't kill me,' Sarah begged.

Cassie stamped her foot. 'Tell her what you did,' she yelled and dug the knife in a little deeper. 'Tell her!' Cassie yelled over Sarah's scream of pain.

'I was . . . furious with you for . . . leaving me to confront Hazel by myself . . . the day before,' Sarah said, her voice barely above a whisper. 'I was going to be . . . expelled and it was . . . all your fault. I didn't know you were going to break up with him. I didn't know . . . you'd said no. I thought you were going to . . . run away together. I thought . . .' Sarah sobbed. 'My life was ruined . . . and you were about to drive into the sunset with him . . . leaving me to face everyone by myself. You abandoned me. You were so . . . besotted with Mark, you'd stopped talking to me.'

'I stopped talking to you because you kept coming between me and Mark. You were so eaten up with jealousy, I couldn't get through to you. What did you do?' Lynda said.

Sarah opened her mouth, but no words came out. She swallowed and Lynda could see the effort it took to speak. 'I . . . I . . .'

'Shall I tell you what this cow can't bring herself to say?' Cassie said. 'Dad was in one of his moods and Mum was drunk, so I sneaked out of our caravan to go and look for Mark. I'd

301

heard him telling his best friend you'd sent him a message and he was going to see you on the embankment, so I knew where to go. I waited for him on the bench where I always used to meet him after he'd been with you so we could go home together, only he never arrived. Someone ran past on the other side of the street. I didn't know who she was, but the birthmark stood out under the streetlight. When I saw your birthmark that night at Lynda's I worked it all out. It wasn't Lynda who sent him a message to meet up. It was you, Sarah, wasn't it?'

'What were you doing on the embankment, Sarah?' Lynda asked.

'Tell her!' Cassie screamed.

'I followed . . . you . . . most nights you were meeting him,' Sarah said. 'So many times I'd heard you two making plans about running away together, him begging you . . . and you agreeing to go.' She swallowed.

Lynda could see how hard it was for Sarah to speak, but she had to know what happened to Mark.

'You didn't . . . deserve a perfect life . . . with . . . the boy you loved . . . after what I'd been through because of you. I wasn't going . . . to let you get away with it scot-free, so I tricked Mark into meeting me. When I heard the train approach I . . . rushed out from . . . hiding and pushed. He fell onto the track . . . as a train was coming.'

'And then you ran,' Cassie said.

'I needed you to pay for . . . what you did to me, Lynda.' Sarah said, 'I wanted you to . . . suffer as I suffered . . . all those months you left me at the mercy of those bullies. I loved you. Really loved you . . . and you turned your back on me. I've hated . . . you ever since.'

'Not as much as I hated you, Lynda,' Cassie said. 'For so many years, I was obsessed with making you pay for killing Mark. I thought he'd committed suicide because of you, but I was wrong. Even if you didn't kill him, it was your fault he died, your fault for bringing this bitch into his life. All of this was your fault and you needed to pay. Even my lousy ex-boyfriend knew how I felt about you, but you were too stupid to let him warn you.'

Lynda felt she was losing her mind. 'I don't even know your ex-boyfriend.'

'You would have done if you hadn't kept running away from him. He told me he followed you when you were out running, but he couldn't get close enough to speak to you.'

'That was your ex?'

Cassie sighed. 'It was. Once I realised what he was up to, I had to kill him. A tragic hit and run accident late one night when he left the pub. I had to deal with him after he left a note under the windscreen wiper of your car, Lynda. Luckily for me I spotted it before you saw it. The idiot wanted you to contact him so that he could tell you.'

'Tell me what?' Lynda sobbed. 'Why didn't he contact me at work?'

Lynda saw Sarah try to stand, but Cassie grabbed her and forced her back down. 'Don't think you're going anywhere,' she hissed. 'You'll leave this chair when I say so and not before.'

Cassie looked back at Lynda and shrugged.

'He didn't know where you worked. He only knew your address after I got it from you that first day. Early in the morning while you were out running was the only time he could try to attract your attention.'

If she didn't do something Sarah could die. How could she stop this? What could she do? The front of Sarah's grey tee-shirt was streaked red with her blood. If only she could get to her phone, but Sarah had put it on the desk behind her. She couldn't even call the emergency services. Sarah's eyes were closed, but Lynda could see her chest moving, so she was alive, but for how much longer?

'Please, Cassie, let Sarah go. She's going to bleed to death.'

'Who cares?' Cassie said. 'You don't even like her and she murdered Mark.'

'Please, Cassie, let her go. Let both of us go. I promise I won't go to the police. I won't say a word, just please, I'm begging you, let Sarah go.'

'I was going to wait to deal with her after I'd finished with you, but you kindly gave me the opportunity to kill two birds with one stone.' She laughed. 'Kill! How apt.'

Lynda heard the rage in Cassie's voice.

'But why?' Lynda wailed. 'Who was Mark to you? I'd never met you before you came to volunteer.'

'I wanted to hurt you so badly, but I thought I'd never be able to track you down. Then a couple of years ago, you got an award for charity fundraising,' she screeched. 'I swore then I'd make you suffer. You and this bitch ruined my life. Mark was all that was keeping me safe until Sarah killed him.'

'I still don't understand,' Lynda said.

'He was my half-brother,' Cassie said. 'He was my big brother and he stopped my father from raping me, but then Sarah killed him and I was left to the mercy of that pig and his friends.'

Chapter Fifty-One

Lynda could see Sarah's head drooping more and more while Cassie was speaking. How much blood could she lose and still survive? There was a steady flow now, keeping time with her sluggish breathing. Her eyes were closed. Lynda knew she had to do something, but what?

'Sarah,' she yelled. 'Sarah, wake up!'

'Let me tell you about my life,' Cassie said, as if Lynda hadn't spoken. 'Mark always said his dad was a bastard, running off and leaving him with our shared miserable mother, but believe me, *my* father would have made Mark's look like a saint complete with a bloody halo.'

'Sarah, please, wake up,' Lynda said. 'Please, open your eyes.'

'Fuck you! Listen to me!' Cassie yelled. 'If you don't, I'll stick this knife deeper into her neck and then slice yours open too.'

Tears streaming down her face, Lynda nodded. 'I'm sorry. I'm listening now, but please let Sarah go?'

Cassie put her head on one side as if considering Lynda's request. 'Nah, I don't think I will. I could, but then I wouldn't get the revenge I've wanted ever since you got that award.

And then you popped up again being the face of a charity, begging for help from the public. You are such a fucking hypocrite.'

'I didn't try to win an award. I just wanted to make up for how I was at school. Please, I'm begging you, put the knife down. Let her go.'

'I don't think Sarah would be capable of walking away even if I did let her go.' Cassie sighed. 'Now you've made me lose my thread. Where was I?'

Lynda wiped tears away with her sleeve. She had to do something or Sarah would bleed to death.

'Lynda!' Cassie shouted. 'I asked you a question. Where was I? If you don't answer me I am going to get very angry. You don't want to make me angry, do you?'

Lynda shook her head. 'No, I don't want you to get angry. I also don't want you to go to prison for murder, so please won't you take the knife from Sarah's throat?'

Cassie laughed. 'Oh, I'm not the one who's going to prison, you'll see. Plus, it's a bit late in the day to worry about me not committing murder, don't you think? Ah, yes, I know where I was in my story. Mark's mum met and married the man who would be my dad and I was the rotten fruit of that unhappy union. Mark said our mum didn't drink or do drugs before she met my dad. I don't know if that's true, but all I can remember while growing up was her spaced out and ready to please whoever Dad brought home. He pimped her out. Can you imagine that, Lynda? My dad sold my mum for whatever he could get and however many times he could – quite a few judging by the number of men who came on a daily basis.'

Lynda looked around the office. What could she use against Cassie?

'Stop looking around and listen to me,' Cassie yelled. 'You might not like this bitch, but if you make one more move you'll be responsible for her death. Do you think you can live with that? Now, are you going to take an interest in my life story or not?'

Lynda forced herself to look at Cassie. 'Please go on. I'm listening.'

'The only problem, well, one of the problems with the men my father brought home was that some of them liked little girls. That would be me, just in case you're too stupid to catch on.'

'Oh God, Cassie, I'm so sorry.'

'So you should be. Mark was my protector. He was bigger and smarter than my father and he told him that if he or any of his friends came near me he'd wait until my father had passed out and then he'd kill him. He would have as well. Mark was the only one who could keep me safe. Our mother was too far gone to bother about either of us, and my father was evil through and through. He only cared about what he wanted. You know, he may have been a foul human being, but he wasn't stupid. He knew that Mark meant every word he said where I was concerned.'

Cassie shifted position and Lynda was relieved to see the point of the knife moved away from Sarah's neck, but the blood was still trickling out.

'Then Sarah decided to kill him. I didn't know it was her at the time. I thought it was you. Everyone said he'd jumped in front of that train, but I knew he'd been pushed. He would never have left me on my own. The police didn't believe me as I was just a kid, and ruled it a suicide. But I knew the truth.

And even if it wasn't you . . . it's still your fault he's dead. It doesn't matter that you didn't push him; it's still your fault. You led him on. You made him believe you were coming with us but you lied to him and then rejected him. You're the one who brought this bitch into his life. It's your fault she killed him. It's your fault he died.' Spit gathering at the corners of her mouth, she was panting, barely able to catch her breath as her voice rose towards a hysterical high-pitched scream.

Flushed with shame, Lynda felt tears running down her face. 'I am so sorry. So sorry.'

'Sorry isn't good enough, Lynda. Sorry isn't nearly good enough. The night Mark died, my father raped me. I was seven!'

Lynda crumpled down against the desk until she was on the floor.

Cassie smiled. It was harder for Lynda to see than her earlier angry expression.

'For eight years I couldn't escape, but when I turned fifteen, I ran. After that, I did the same stuff on the streets, but at least most of the time I got paid for it.'

Lynda couldn't bear the guilt that flooded through her. Mark's death had completely destroyed Cassie's life. If it hadn't been for her, Sarah wouldn't have killed him.

'I was on the streets for a couple of years and then a charity took me in. They gave me an education and helped me to find a place to live. They even put me through college so that I could learn computer skills. There are good people out there, Lynda. Truly good people who do charity work because they want to help others. Not like you, just trying to make up for what you'd done.'

Lynda wanted to argue, to say she'd volunteered at the

charity because she wanted to help others, but she knew deep down that Cassie was right. She had run her races and answered the phones purely as a way of wiping out her own guilt over not protecting Sarah and what she'd believed was Mark's suicide.

Cassie shrugged. 'I was happy in my new life. I'd even stopped wanting revenge, but then you appeared on the news acting like a fucking heroine instead of the cowardly bitch you really are.'

Cassie's hand shook as she pulled Sarah in closer.

'Did you like my nice touch in making sure Jason died in the same way that Mark had? By the way, the hoodie I wore was yours. It's the very distinctive one you wear for running when it's cold. I took it the night Amanda and I came over to your place. I chose it because I knew the design would stand out and you'd get the blame.'

Lynda looked up. 'The police know it wasn't me. I didn't leave the flat the morning you murdered Jason.'

Cassie laughed. 'Such an ugly word. It wasn't murder; it was justice. The fact that you didn't leave the flat, not even to go for one of your runs, means you have no alibi. While we're on the subject of death, poor Lucky took such a long time to die. The poison was very slow to act.'

Lynda felt as if she had been sucked into a whirlpool and was under water. She was struggling to breathe, but knew if she could just reach the surface everything would be OK.

'Sarah is going to die,' Cassie said, 'and you're going to get the blame for it.'

'That's crazy,' Lynda said. 'Your fingerprints will be on the knife.'

Cassie took the hand holding the knife away from Sarah's throat and waved it.

'As you can see, I have a latex glove on this hand. The knife is the one you used to cut the cake yesterday. The only finger-prints on it will be yours.'

Lynda struggled to her feet. She had to do something. 'I'll tell the police it was you. I'll tell them why. When they look into your background they'll know why you did it.'

Cassie laughed so hard Lynda hoped she'd choke.

'The police won't believe you. Did you tell them you thought Sarah was stalking you, and that you thought she'd killed your cat and pushed Jason off the platform?'

When Lynda didn't reply, Cassie continued, 'I thought you might have done. You've given them all the reason they need to lock you up for killing Sarah and throw away the key.'

'You won't get away with this,' Lynda said.

'That sounds like a line from a bad film. Believe me; I will get away with everything. You can tell the police whatever you like; I bet they've already decided you're a compulsive liar. They've known that since you tried to convince them someone drove your father off the road and refused to accept the coroner's verdict.'

'How do you know about that?' Lynda gasped.

She could see Sarah's breathing was getting slower and slower. The flow of blood was sluggish, but still dribbling down her neck. Thank God the blade was no longer pressing into Sarah's throat, but Lynda knew she had to do something or she would die.

'Can you really not remember what happened that night, Lynda? Or is that another of your acts?'

Lynda shook her head. As the knife wasn't touching Sarah, maybe she could throw herself at Cassie.

'Lynda!' Cassie yelled. 'You're not listening to me. Don't you want to know how I killed your precious family?'

Stunned, Lynda looked into Cassie's eyes. For the first time she could see the madness there.

'What?'

'Oh yes. I killed your family after seeing you'd got that award, but even that didn't destroy you as it should have done. It seems you don't have a soul. Don't you care about people you love? I went to East Midlands airport and hired a car the same make and colour as your dad's. It was a smaller model, but that was fine. I just needed to make sure the paint matched. I drove alongside and rammed his car just as he was approaching the bend. I only intended to run him off the road, but it worked so much better than I'd hoped.'

'You fucking cow,' Lynda said, taking a step forward. 'I'll kill you.'

Cassie put the knife back against Sarah's throat.

'You two sent me to hell. This is payback.'

As she said the words, Cassie plunged the knife deep into Sarah's neck and pushed her off the chair onto Lynda. Under the weight of Sarah's body, Lynda fell to the floor.

Cassie walked to Greg's desk and opened the drawer. She took the Dictaphone and put it in her pocket.

'You won't be needing this,' she said.

Horrified, Lynda watched as Cassie turned the blade on herself. She slashed at her arm and chest, then dropped the knife next to Lynda.

She winked, then turned and ran to the door, screaming: 'Help me! I've been stabbed. Help me!'

Chapter Fifty-Two

The custody sergeant's voice seemed to be coming from a long way off. Lynda heard it as if his words were muffled by a dense fog.

'I'll ask again,' he said. 'I need your full name, address and date of birth.'

This time she understood what he'd said, but not why he needed to know. What was she doing here? Why hadn't the police arrested Cassie?

'Is someone picking up Cassie? She killed Sarah. She's insane.'

'For the last time, what is your full name, your address and your date of birth?'

After she gave him her details, she looked around, trying to find the officer who'd brought her to the station. The paramedics had taken Sarah away in an ambulance, but when Lynda had tried to follow them she'd been stopped from leaving the office by two detectives.

'Are you taking any medication?'

'What? Sorry, no! Why are you asking me all these questions?'

'I need your phone and any other personal effects. These will be placed in a bag, which will be sealed and returned to you in the event you are free to leave.'

In a trance, Lynda checked her pockets. She had no personal items with her. She'd had to leave her bag and her phone at the charity office as it was now a crime scene.

'Do you want legal advice? We can arrange this for you, or you can call on your own solicitor if you have one.'

Lynda shook her head. 'I don't have a solicitor. Why would I need legal advice? I'm here as a witness. I watched as Cassie murdered Sarah.'

The sergeant looked at her with concern. 'Miss Blackthorn, you're not here as a witness; you've been arrested. Do you understand your rights? Is there anyone you wish to notify of your arrest?'

'This is crazy. Why have I been arrested? I didn't do anything.'

Lynda felt her legs give way and she crumpled to the ground. She'd been arrested! Who should she tell? The only person she could think of was Georgina, but maybe Greg would be better as he knew Cassie.

Strong arms helped her to her feet and she recognised the officer who'd been so dismissive of her earlier complaints. At least now he'd have to realise she hadn't made it all up, even if she'd accused the wrong person.

'Are you OK?' he said.

Lynda shook her head. 'No. I don't understand why I've been arrested. You need to bring in Cassie Grace. She killed Sarah.'

D.C. Fredericks looked beyond her. 'Shall I take her for her medical examination now, Sarge?'

'Let me just get the answer to my last question. Miss Black-thorn, do you want me to let someone know you're here?'

She nodded. 'Yes, Greg Makepeace. I'm afraid I don't remember his number . . .'

'Come with me, please, Miss Blackthorn,' D.C. Fredericks said.

Lynda followed the detective constable in a daze. She looked down at her clothes which were covered in blood.

'I wanted to get changed, but I wasn't allowed. When can I go home?'

'All in good time, Miss Blackthorn. Come with me now.'

As her DNA, nail clippings and fingerprints were taken, as she was examined by a doctor, her blood-stained clothing taken as evidence, and she was helped into a white sterile custody jumpsuit, Lynda tried to understand how Cassie had manipulated so many people. She had no one to speak the truth. As she entered her cell to await interview, she realised there was one person who might be able to help. Maybe Sarah had found out something about Cassie and had told Maria. She sat down on the cold, hard bench, relieved to think there was a chance she could be released if they spoke to Sarah's ex-girlfriend. Then it hit her: she only knew her first name was Maria. She hoped to god the police would be able to track her down.

Lynda sat in an interview room where the walls seemed to be closing in on her. Whenever she'd tried to talk to anyone about what had happened, she was told to wait for her legal representative. The female officer standing by the door hadn't spoken a word since she'd come in to relieve the earlier one who'd at least made sure Lynda had something to drink. It felt like an eternity before the door opened again and a woman came in. She looked harassed, as if being overworked was a standard aspect of her life.

'Lynda Blackthorn? Hello, I'm Erica Jones. I've been asked to come in as your legal representative. Are you OK with that?'

Lynda nodded and Erica turned to the female officer.

'I would like to speak to my client in private.'

The officer nodded and left.

Erica sat down opposite Lynda.

'I'll do my best to help you in every way possible, but the situation is —'

'You have to find Maria,' Lynda said, cutting across Erica's words.

Erica reached into her briefcase and put a legal pad on the table. 'Who is Maria?' she asked.

'She's Sarah's ex-girlfriend.'

'Would you mind if I called you Lynda?'

'No, that's fine.'

'I think we should start at the beginning, Lynda,' she said, picking up her pen.

Lynda began with the rosemary plant and covered every incident up to Cassie killing Sarah.

'You see, she planned it so that I would get the blame. She even killed her own ex-boyfriend because he tried to warn me.'

Erica's face was impassive as she carefully made notes on an A4 pad.

'I think we should allow the police to interview you now. If we can convince them there's some doubt about your guilt it's possible they'll allow your release on bail.'

Lynda realised her solicitor must have seen how relieved she was because Erica held up her hand.

'Don't get your expectations up too high though. It's very rare that bail is granted on a murder charge. However, as they haven't yet charged you we can still hope.'

She got up and walked over to the door. There must have been someone waiting outside because she nodded and then came back in.

'The two detectives who were at the scene of the crime will be coming in to conduct the interview. I would advise you to tell them exactly what you told me, but if at any point I don't feel you should answer a question I will say so. OK?'

Lynda nodded.

An hour later Lynda felt as if her brain had been pummelled. No matter how many times she told the truth, it was obvious that neither of the detectives believed her. Incredulity and scorn was clear on the face of Detective Inspector Warren. It was likely Detective Sergeant Morris felt the same, but so far he hadn't spoken.

'Once more for the tape, Miss Blackthorn, what happened in the charity?'

'I've already told you, again and again. Cassie killed Sarah as punishment for killing her half-brother. She wants me to take the blame for it.'

'A revenge that must have been several years in the planning. That's a bit too close to a super-villain plot, don't you think?' Warren said, disbelief obvious in his voice.

'Yes, no!' Lynda said. 'That's what happened, except she didn't know about Sarah until this year.'

She was about to say more when the door opened and a uniformed officer came in and put a file on the table in front of the inspector. He opened it and took out a piece of paper.

'Well, Miss Blackthorn. It's not looking too good for you . . .' he said. 'You were found at the scene, covered in blood, and now here's the fingerprint report.' The only fingerprints on the knife are yours – now, how do you explain that? Oh, yes, you've already told me. You say your charity colleague was wearing surgical gloves, but you didn't notice until she pointed it out to you. How do you think she was able to get hold of a knife with only your prints on it?'

Lynda felt tears come to her eyes. 'I told you already! She kept it after I'd cut the celebration cake yesterday.'

He picked up another piece of paper from the same file. 'Miss Grace was taken to hospital to have her wounds cared for. She has been interviewed. She says she came to the charity today because she was worried about you and felt you might need protection from Sarah.'

'That's not true!'

'Tell me, Miss Blackthorn, after all the complaints you made about Sarah, why did you set up a meeting in private?'

'As I've already said, I wanted to record Sarah's confession so that I could prove to the police she killed Jason.'

'But you don't have the recording, do you? Also, you now say it was Cassie who was responsible for Jason's death and all the threats that you reported. None of which you were able to corroborate with any evidence.'

'Cassie took the Dictaphone.'

317

'So you say. Your ex-boyfriend was pushed in front of a train by someone wearing a hoodie you admit was identical to yours. Where were you around six o'clock that morning?'

'I was at home. How many times do I have to tell you?'

'You didn't feel up to going out for one of your regular runs?'

She shook her head, thinking of the man in the blue car who had chased her a few times. 'Cassie's ex-boyfriend tried to warn me but she killed him in a hit and run.'

'Ah yes, the mysterious man who you say followed you on some of your runs . . . We have no record of any deaths as a result of a hit and run around the time you say this happened.'

The conversation went in circles until Lynda felt she was going insane.

'Detective Inspector Warren,' Erica said, 'if you are not going to charge my client I suggest you allow her to leave.'

He shook his head. 'I'm afraid your client isn't going anywhere. Lynda Blackthorn, I am charging you with the murder of Sarah Coulsdon. You will be held in the cells here on remand until tomorrow morning, when you will appear to answer the charge at Lincoln Crown Court.'

'I would like some time alone with my client, Inspector,' Erica said.

He nodded and ended the recording. Lynda watched as the two men got up and left the room.

'What did he mean about being remanded here until tomorrow? Does that mean I can go home after that?'

Erica shook her head. 'I'm afraid not. I'll organise some clothes and other essential items for your court appearance. It's highly likely that you will be held on remand in Peterborough Prison until the date of your trial.'

'I can't go to prison. I'm innocent. Can't you do something?'

'At this stage it's out of my hands. We have to let the procedure take its course.'

Lynda could feel the quicksand dragging her down. 'How long will I be locked up?'

'That I can't tell you as it will depend on the date set for trial.'

She started to shake and couldn't control the tremors. 'I don't understand. I didn't kill her. Please, please, can't you help me?'

'As I've said, I will do my utmost. Try not to worry too much. I realise that's easy for me to say and will be hard for you to do, but getting stressed is not going to help you through this ordeal. I'll come to visit you on remand so that we can plan your defence. You will need a barrister to represent you in court. That's something I can arrange for you.'

'Erica, please, can't you get them to let me go? I won't run away. I promise. Please, please, help me. I didn't do it. You do believe me, don't you?' Lynda begged.

Erica picked up her pad and slipped it into her case. She seemed to be avoiding Lynda's eyes.

'I'll do my best for you,' she said.

Lynda watched as she walked to the door, feeling as if her future was walking out with her.

Epilogue

Eight Months Later

Lynda sat back and looked carefully around Penelope's office. Everything was where it should be. Even the dried–flower arrangement she'd felt was out of place in the past looked glorious. She'd thought at one time that she'd never be back again. The ordeal of the last few months had been hard to cope with and she hadn't realised how much she'd valued her regular therapy sessions until they'd been denied to her.

'How have you been coping?'

'Not that well to start with, but I think I'm ready now to deal with everything that happened.'

'Shall we begin?' Penelope said.

Lynda inhaled deeply. 'Yes,' she said. 'I need to do this.'

'Do you want to talk about the time you were under arrest, or would you rather leave that to one side for now?' Penelope said, pen and pad at the ready.

That was another thing that used to irritate Lynda, but today she felt comforted by it. She was back where she belonged, free once more.

'I want to talk about everything. About being locked up,

320

about Cassie, Mark, Sarah, my family, all of it, but I don't know where to start.'

'Would you prefer it if I asked questions?'

Lynda nodded. It would be easier to answer questions than try to sort out the jumble of events which kept going round and round her head on a constant loop.

'After Cassie fatally stabbed Sarah, what did you do?'

'I screamed for help, but I think I knew it was already too late. There was so much blood. I was covered in it and there were pools of it on the floor. I couldn't stop the bleeding, no matter how hard I tried.'

Penelope nodded and wrote something down. 'What happened next?'

'The police arrived at the same time as the ambulance. I suppose that's standard response to the call Cassie made. I think I was close to hysteria. Actually, I know I was. Anyway, the police came and asked me what had happened, so I told them. After that, more police arrived. A detective inspector and a detective sergeant. I told them everything that I'd already told the uniformed police. The sergeant wrote down what I was saying and didn't ask any questions, but the inspector kept asking the same things over and over again. It turns out he knew about all the times I'd been to the station accusing Sarah of . . . accusing her of everything that I now know was down to Cassie.'

Lynda crossed her legs and leaned back in the chair. 'Cassie had said the police wouldn't believe me and she was right.' She sat forward and banged her clenched fists onto her legs. 'Because of what Sarah was doing in my apartment, I believed she was also behind the threats. I was so stupid; I fell for it all.'

Penelope sat forward. 'Are you OK? Do you want to stop for now?'

'No,' Lynda said. 'I need to do this. I have to talk about it or I'll never get the images out of my head. I can't remember too much of what happened after that. I was arrested and taken to the police station. I made a full statement, but even to me it sounded too far-fetched to be true. I could see no one believed me about Cassie. I found out that she had been interviewed, but managed to convince whoever it was that I was behaving irrationally and she'd come to the charity to protect me.'

'And then,' Penelope said, 'they believed the hoodie from the CCTV images was yours.'

Lynda nodded. 'So then I was on the hook for Jason's murder as well. The more I told them Cassie had done it, the more they believed it was me.' She shrugged. 'I could see why they believed that. I thought I would be going to prison and never allowed out again.' She sat forward. 'Georgina believed in me, but her evidence went against me rather than helping me.'

'In what way?'

'Because she corroborated the police's position that I blamed Sarah for everything. Which was true. I did.'

'But Cassie's ex-boyfriend saved you?' Penelope asked.

Lynda sighed. 'Not straight away. He was in a coma after Cassie knocked him down, but when he came round he told the police he had wanted to warn me she was unstable. But when it came to it, he couldn't bring himself to say anything as he thought I'd never believe him. Still, he was able to corroborate my story about Cassie running him down.'

She shivered as she recalled Cassie's matter-of-fact way of talking about the lives she'd taken.

'I don't know if he realised how far her madness had progressed, but he felt he had to warn me.' Lynda looked at Penelope through a haze of tears. 'Whether or not I'd have believed him, I have no idea.'

Penelope put down her pen. 'I would imagine that you would have done so once you'd been told that Cassie was Mark's much younger half-sister. I presume she must have told him how she felt or he wouldn't have known anything about you.'

Lynda nodded. 'You're right. He knew some of her past and that she believed I had driven her brother to suicide or, worse, pushed him, but he had no idea of how terrible her life had been after Mark's death.'

Penelope nodded. 'That makes sense.'

'Cassie's life from the age of seven was so horrible. Even as I was watching Sarah dying, I felt so sorry for Cassie. The things she had to endure only happened because of what Sarah did to Mark. And Sarah only killed him because of me! Cassie suffered years of abuse because Mark was dead.'

Penelope pushed the box of tissues closer to Lynda. 'That may or may not be true. You cannot know that. Cassie's father was an abusive man and her mother was a drug addict and alcoholic. In that environment, regardless of whether or not Mark was around to protect her, it is highly likely Cassie would still have been abused by her father.'

'We don't know that for sure,' Lynda said as she took a tissue from the box. 'I'll have to live the rest of my life knowing that because of me, lives were ruined and people died.'

She blew her nose.

'After Cassie's ex gave his statement, the police decided I might have been telling the truth after all. They called on

Cassie with a warrant and found she'd kept a journal on her laptop going back years. It was all there. Everything she'd done, right down to running my family off the road. I wasn't supposed to be in the car that evening. She told me her plan was for me to hear about my family's accident and suffer, and apparently that was enough for her until she watched me give that interview a year and a half later.'

Lynda swallowed. 'She hoped I'd been destroyed when I lost my family and was so angry because she thought I'd survived my loss. She came to volunteer as a way of finding out where I lived so she could target me.'

Penelope nodded. 'It seems that was always her intention,' she said.

'I was completely taken in by her friendly persona.'

'She was able to hide her true self,' Penelope said. 'That's something abuse survivors often do. During the periods of abuse they learn to disassociate from what is happening to them and create alternate personas. I would imagine the Cassie who outwardly befriended you was one of the personalities she'd created to cope with the horrors of what she'd gone through.'

'I know. I've been reading up on how to cope with trauma.' Lynda smiled. 'Don't worry, I'm not busy creating multiple personalities. At least, I don't think I am.'

'Are you back helping out at the charity?'

Lynda nodded. 'I am. Greg stood by me when I most needed a friend. He and Georgina both believed in me when it was clear that most people thought I'd killed Jason and Sarah. They're truly good people.'

'Has Greg accepted that you will never be more than a friend to him?'

'Better than that, he and my solicitor have become an item. They spent quite a lot of time together because of my case and got to know each other. He's happier than I've ever seen him.'

Penelope closed her pad. 'Our time is up for this session; I'd like to see you again next week. How do you feel about that?'

'I think it's a good idea. I know I've a long way to go, but for the first time since childhood, I believe I'm going to get to where I need to be.'

Have you read Lorraine Mace's dark and twisting D.I. Sterling thrillers?

'Crime fiction at its absolute finest'
MARION TODD

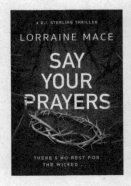

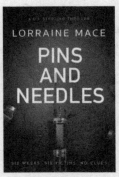